The Lolita File

Also by Bill Metzger

Microbrewed Murder
An Empty Desk
The Lolita File

The Lolita File

By

Bill Metzger

SILVER
LEAF
BOOKS

HOLLISTON, MASSACHUSETTS

THE LOLITA FILE
Copyright © 2016 by Bill Metzger

Cover Art by Hans Granheim.

First printing September 2016
10 9 8 7 6 5 4 3 2 1

ISBN # 1-60975-179-5
ISBN-13 # 978-1-60975-179-1
LCCN # 2016946751

Silver Leaf Books, LLC
P.O. Box 6460
Holliston, MA 01746
+1-888-823-6450

Visit our web site at www.SilverLeafBooks.com

The Lolita File

1

"Michael J. Brockton." The voice came over the speaker embedded in the thick glass reception window. Brockton pulled his eyes away from the file he was reviewing. "Thank you," he said, smiling briefly at the deputy behind the glass and wondering why they included his middle initial in the call. It wasn't like there were any other Brocktons practicing law in this city.

The deputy's reply was drowned out by the noise of a thick metal door opening next to him. Brockton stepped through the sally port and into the public safety building. He walked the few steps to an elevator, pushed the UP button and stepped back to wait.

No matter how often he had been in this building—"The Pub" they'd named it—Brockton was always impressed with the thickness of the walls. From the outside, the building promoted a sense of security from the criminals locked inside, some of the same ones he defended, he thought wryly. Once inside, the jail walls were even more reassuring. No one would get out of here without permission.

The elevator door opened. Several people were inside and he stepped back to allow them to exit. He looked fleetingly at an elderly couple, then a young girl. He caught the girl's eye, but she looked away quickly and walked by him as if he was a common city street gawker. Maybe it was the tie he wore.

Brockton stepped into the elevator. Once the door had closed, he glanced at the folder he carried. John Sienkewicz. Seeing the name reminded him of the newspaper story, where he had first learned of the case. They had spelled his client's name wrong, unforgivable given that the headline had been so big. The story had run on page one of the local news section because of the sexual abuse charge and the fact that Sienkewicz was a public school teacher.

Brockton leafed through the folder while the elevator ascended. There were some scattered notes he'd taken after speaking with his new client's wife and a police report that was as accurate an account of the crime as he was going to get. He closed the folder as the elevator slowed. He'd give his client the benefit of a first impression; his was usually accurate.

The doors opened and Brockton stepped onto the third floor of the building. To his left was a wire fence cage. Two sheriff's deputies lounged at a desk behind the cage.

"Good afternoon," Brockton said.

"Sienkewicz," one deputy, a woman, said. Brockton nodded.

The other deputy pulled his eyes away from the computer screen. "Three-oh-seven. He returned his face to the screen.

"We'll have the scum bag for you in a minute," the woman said. She left the caged office through a door that led into the cell area.

"Thanks." Brockton signed in, then stood quietly and waited. He had grown accustomed to the sheriff deputies' manner of treating prisoners. They dealt with too many criminals to be faulted for tough skin. He even understood their ill-concealed contempt for lawyers like him, although it irked him. They were out on the streets risking their lives to keep him safe by catching and incarcerating criminals so he could spend his time and energy freeing them. In court Brockton often portrayed law officers as inept and unlawful and that must irritate the shit out of them.

"Scum bag's in there." The deputy pointed to one of the consultation booths.

Brockton was reminded of why he did what he did. As difficult as the job might be, someone had to keep the law in check. There were rules to the game and cops tried to circumvent them when it served their purpose and they could get away with it.

"Thanks," Brockton repeated, mentally rebuking himself for being so friendly to the jailer. He turned and pulled open the door to meet his client.

Sienkewicz was good-looking, about six feet tall with blonde hair and grayish blue eyes. He was not what Brockton expected.

"Hello, Mr. Brockton." The man stuck his hand through the metal bars separating them. "You're here to help me, I gather."

"That's right," Brockton said, without extending his hand. He'd gotten into the habit of not shaking hands with his clients; they weren't the cleanest lot although this one appeared an exception. "Your wife called me not long after you were arrested."

Sienkewicz appeared to ignore the snub. "She said you were good. I don't know much about lawyers in this town, but I trust her judgment."

"I hope to prove her judgment sound," Brockton said, trying to sound modest. He was one of the best defense attorneys in the city and everyone knew it. Once the research was done, it was a question of focus and concentration, not letting your mind wander in the courtroom.

Sienkewicz leaned away from him, straightening up. "Have to stretch my back," he explained. "These cramped quarters make one ache."

"They don't give you a lot of room in here," Brockton agreed. He looked around at the familiar sight of cement walls. The room was no larger than three feet by five feet.

"Not a place I want to spend a lot of time. It makes you question your own innocence."

Brockton permitted himself a cynical smile. "Everyone in here is innocent until proven guilty."

"The food's pretty bad, too." Sienkewicz yawned.

"We'll be going to court tomorrow morning." Brockton was surprised to see his client so relaxed. "I don't think I'll have much problem getting a reasonable bail set since you have no priors." He looked up. "At least that's what your wife said, no record. She also said you could make bail."

"That's correct. Besides a few traffic tickets, I haven't had any run-ins with the law since my college days, when they caught me driving across the college president's front lawn. And we have enough money."

Brockton smiled, then laid the folder on the shelf in front of him. "First I need some background information. Are you ready to answer some questions?"

"Fire away."

"I'll go through them quickly. What's your complete name?"

"John Albert Sienkewicz."

"Age?"

"Forty."

"Address?"

"415 West Canfield Drive."

"Nice area," Brockton commented.

"Yeah, it was supposed to be 413 but they thought the 13 was bad luck."

Brockton checked off the box that said his client was married. "Any kids?"

"Two. A girl and a boy. Sarah and Leonard."

"Don't need their names. Employment?"

"Public School. Fourteen years."

Brockton remembered reading that in the paper. That was why it made the headlines, that someone who was around kids all day could assault and rape one. Worse, Sienkewicz had two of his own. Probably an absentee dad.

After another dozen questions, Brockton stopped writing and pulled a typed paper out of the file. "I have copies of the police and hospital reports, which I'll refer to now and then, but first, why don't you tell me what you know about the charges. Remember, tomorrow we're going in front of the judge and you need to appear like an honest, hardworking man, so tailor your story that way as you're telling it to me."

"O Carmen, my little Carmen," Sienkewicz said and Brockton looked up sharply. His client was looking straight at him, his eyes shining weirdly.

"What are you talking about?" Brockton asked, suddenly spooked.

"Lolita."

"What?"

"Vladimir Nabokov's classic novel. An older man falls in love with a girl of twelve. His main obstacle to consummating their relationship is her mother."

"What does that have to do with you?"

"Larisa is fourteen and I love her. There's a difference in age and it was a nurse not her mother who was the obstacle, but the rest of the story fits. The nurse reported me, I'm sure of it."

Brockton scribbled notes, hiding his distaste for what Sienkewicz was saying. He had a fourteen year old daughter himself. "How long have you known ... Lolita?"

"Larisa. A couple of months, but I fell in love with her the first time we met."

Brockton sat still, stunned. The guy showed no signs of remorse, was talking too logically. More shocking, he was coming right out with it, something Brockton wasn't used to. What the hell was the real story? He looked at the police report again. "She turned you in. She talked to the police."

"The nurse made her do it," Sienkewicz said. "Or her social worker. Do you know what happens to Lolita's mother?"

Brockton didn't reply, the eerie feeling returning. He let his gaze linger on his client's eyes, which still shone.

"She gets run over by a car," Sienkewicz continued. "That's how Vladimir manages to get to her daughter."

Brockton tried to regain his composure, but couldn't. He stood up. "I need some air." He pulled open the door and stepped into the hall.

2

When Brockton stepped out of the consultation booth, the deputy looked up. "Finished?" she asked.

He shook his head and held up his hand.

"He doesn't smell half as bad as most of 'em," the deputy commented, then returned her attention to the computer screen in front of her partner.

Brockton leaned against the wall and wiped the sweat off his brow with his shirt sleeve. Why had he left the room so suddenly? He had always been able to handle scum, prided himself in that. This was the first time he had ever been at a loss for words. No, spooked—he hadn't even run the charges past his client yet.

Sienkewicz had taken him off guard. Although Brockton was used to defending sleaze balls, this guy was different. That's what had shaken him. The guy was like him. Well groomed, especially for being in The Pub, had a family, and lived in a safe part of the city. Not that abuse didn't happen in middle class families, but they were usually more sophisticated about it. What if this guy had lived in his neighborhood? There was no excuse for this.

Brockton had been surprised when Sienkewicz admitted his guilt right away. Most clients lied so often he'd begun to expect it, but this guy had come right out with the truth. And there was this Lolita thing. That was real weird. The guy's eyes were glowing when he spoke.

"Mr. Brockton?" The voice came out of the room, reminding him where he was. He took a breath, smiled at the deputies and reentered the small, cement-walled room.

"Sorry," he said. "I haven't been feeling well." Even that much was hard to say. He was never sick.

"Are you having second thoughts about my case?" Sienkewicz asked.

"No problems," he replied. "Why do you say that?"

"I can understand if you are. Some lawyers would be hesitant to defend a sex abuser."

"You don't know much about lawyers," Brockton replied, glad to have the conversation center on something besides his behavior.

"I can pay you more if that's the problem," Sienkewicz said. "I know you will be able to win this case. In fact, I'm sure of it."

"Money's not the problem. Like I said, I don't feel well."

"You can come back another time," Sienkewicz said politely. He seemed genuinely concerned.

"No, your bail hearing's tomorrow and I need to get some information." Brockton returned his attention to the papers in front of him. "Do you know what the charges are?"

"No. What are they accusing me of?"

"They're serious. Rape in the third degree and assault."

"Assault?"

"Correct."

"I would never assault my little Carmen. We love each other."

"How did you meet her?" Brockton asked, stifling repellence.

"She came to me when she had no place to live. Her mother had kicked her out of her home."

"How long ago was this?"

"Several months. Did you know that she is an alcoholic?"

Brockton said nothing at first, surprised. "You're sure of that?" he asked after regaining his composure.

"Yes, I am sure. I met her in Millwood Treatment Center. She was an inpatient there and I was her tutor. She also used drugs frequently."

After going over the reports in more detail and asking his client several questions about his financial situation, Brockton gathered his papers. "I'll call you once I check out a few things you've told me."

"You are staying with the case then? If you're uncertain and it's a question of money, I will have my wife send you a check for another thousand dollars, for the retainer."

Brockton was about to decline the offer, but held back.

"I will not be offended if you don't accept," Sienkewicz continued. "I understand that you may not want to defend me for personal reasons."

"What you've said turns things around a little," Brockton replied. "I have to make a few telephone calls. I'll call you tonight."

After excusing himself, Brockton left The Pub and walked to his office. What a stroke of luck. He had momentarily panicked and the guy had thought he was backing out of the case. He'd take the extra money, could use it for the house renovation.

Brockton wasn't surprised that his client knew the victim. Most sex offenders were acquainted with their victims. Most of the ones he'd prosecuted while an assistant DA had been live-in boyfriends of the mothers, a standard for these cases.

At least Sienkewicz had given him some ammunition. If he was telling the truth about the alcoholism and drug use, the DA's office must know about it and would feel shaky about the case. They might offer an acceptable plea bargain despite the press coverage.

It was possible they had more evidence, a witness or something, but he doubted it. Since the election the police and DA's office had been bickering and consequently the ADAs had brought some pretty weak cases to trial. They might not even know the girl's background. If they didn't, he'd let them know and hint at what he was going to ask her on the stand. He could tear the girl to pieces in front of a jury. It was never hard to trip up the young ones and he'd already found several holes in the police report. If drugs were involved as Sienkewicz claimed, it would make a defense even easier. Drug abusers never sat well with judges.

He mentally reviewed his schedule for the next few months. He could handle a trial. And he could use the money. Taxes had jumped, and with the new home and three kids expenses were plenty. He hadn't talked to Stephanie about the case yet, but he planned to do that tonight. Even though he'd already decided to take a case, he'd always talk it over with his wife. It gave them a feeling of togetherness. If she felt uneasy about his representing a guy like Sienkewicz, he'd use the renovation angle. Just the other day she mentioned being impatient to begin. Hell, now he had the extra thousand to seal the argument.

Brockton briefly remembered bolting out of the room at the jail. His friends would laugh at that one. He had really jumped the gun. This was good money and every lawyer had a touch of the mercenary in him. That was how the system worked, assured that even the scum bags were defended. He'd use this case to keep his trial skills polished; it would be good for that. His feelings of distaste would disappear as soon as they were inundated with facts.

He reached the building that housed his office and took the outside steps two at a time. The DA's office had chosen another weak case to prosecute, to his gain. He wondered who they'd assign to prosecute. They were so disorganized lately that they hadn't even decided that yet. He'd mull the facts over a little more, then call Sienkewicz and his wife to say that he was in. He'd mention the extra mil, too. Then all he had to do was keep the guy from talking, acting freaky.

3

The city courtroom was old and poorly maintained. Strips of paint curled off the high ceilings, and brown, dense curtains were pulled back to display dirt-streaked windows through which light filtered. Tarnished brass lamps poked off the walls to provide as much light as possible given that less than half the bulbs worked—Brockton called them welfare bulbs. He glanced up at the large unpolished brass wall clock above the bailiff's entranceway. It read 7:45. The clock had been stuck on that time as long as he could remember.

The new DA, Gus White, had used the sad shape of the courtroom as a campaign issue, Brockton thought wryly. White had used the issue cleverly, saying that the courthouse was in the same shape as the city's drug problem, rampant neglect from the previous DA's reign. The new DA was a little off sometimes—the top spot in the prosecutor's office didn't necessarily lead to having the power to allocate money to fix courtrooms—but it had worked as a theme.

The late summer heat caused Brockton to refocus on the courtroom and without thinking, he almost pulled down his necktie, an act of legal heresy. A soft breeze wafted through the room, cooling him slightly. He could remember worse days, but wondered when they were going to get around to putting air conditioning in this building, another White campaign promise.

The judge's area was one part of the courtroom that was well kept. Anchored by a huge, intricately carved wooden framework, the area was impressive. Above the wood was carved *In God We Trust*. Below the motto the entrance to the judge's chambers was hidden by a brown, velvet curtain. The velvet looked like it was made from the same material as the window drapes, just cleaner. The large, comfortable seat in front of the curtain looked huge. Brockton had often said that if they got rid of the seats the older judges wouldn't fall asleep so often.

To the left of the curtain hung a frayed, aging United States flag, Old Glory on a pole. A small golden eagle perched atop the pole.

To the right of the curtain, on top of the judge's huge wooden desk, a carved female figurine stood upright, holding the scales of justice. Once, as an assistant DA, Brockton had pulled a coin out of his pocket and placed it on one of the scales, causing them to tilt. It was obvious, he'd told a packed courtroom, that the number of lawyers the defendant had hired had given him a lop-sided advantage like the situation he'd just created. Brockton had lost the case, but the move had raised a few heads and got him some good press.

They'd called him B Money in the ensuing press reports. As the lobby door opened, Brockton glanced back to see the bright lights of a camera unit. The TV stations were waiting for him. He wondered how they had found out that the bail sentencing was being done so quickly. It was probably Channel Five; they had an insider.

A side door opened and a sheriff's deputy appeared, leading the prisoners who were to face Judge Jacquelyn Holmes that morning. Five prisoners followed the deputy to one side of the bench. Behind them came a second deputy, both looking bored. The prisoners sat, handcuffed. Sienkewicz's pale face contrasted with the other prisoners, all of whom were black. He appeared scruffier than Brockton remembered. Maybe he was feeling some stress after a second night in The Pub. Brockton glanced quickly at the audience and spotted Sienkewicz's wife. Her face remained emotionless.

From behind the curtain came the sound of a toilet flushing. Like clockwork, Brockton thought. Within minutes Holmes would appear. She always used the toilet just before coming into the courtroom and like an old house, the courtroom's plumbing informed everyone of her habitualness. A door closed and the curtains behind the judge's seat rippled, then parted. Brockton stood automatically, along with the rest of the court's officers.

"All rise."

The deputies, who had been leaning against the railing separating them from the spectators, also stood, pulling the prisoners to their feet.

Judge Holmes nodded and sat. Everyone followed suit, including the deputies, who returned to their lounging positions, bored and seemingly inattentive. Brockton looked at Holmes and wondered if she would be harder on his client because he was the only white man and she was black. He dismissed the thought. Holmes was hard on everyone.

The door opened in the back of the courtroom and lights flooded in as someone entered. Normally, talking to the press was part of his strategy, but not this time. He wondered how he was going to avoid the cameras when he left. He took it as a personal challenge to play—or dodge—cameras and this was one time in particular that he wanted to dodge them. One of the older, more inert judges might let him slip out through the back, but he doubted Holmes would let him get away with that maneuver.

"The case of The People versus John Albert Sienkewicz," the bailiff said loudly. Brockton stepped forward, glancing at Sienkewicz. His client was watching him and he winked to reassure him.

One of the deputies unlocked Sienkewicz from the chain of prisoners and led him to where Brockton stood at one of the two tables facing the judge. The assistant DA prosecuting the case, Milton Ritter, stood at the other table, avoiding Brockton's glance.

"Watch me and don't say a thing," Brockton whispered to his client. Sienkewicz nodded.

"Let the record reflect that John Albert Sienkewicz has been charged with rape in the third degree and aggravated assault," Homes said, taking over from the bailiff. "This hearing is to determine whether bail will be set and if so, how much it will be." The judge looked at Ritter.

"Your honor, in view of the heinous nature of the crime committed, and the possibility that this man may flee, the people recommend bail be set at no less than fifty thousand dollars," Milton Ritter said.

Brockton wanted to let out his legendary whistle of disbelief, but remembered who was on the bench. Instead, he put his emphasis in his response. "Your honor, it's obvious that my client is going no place. He's got a wife, two kids and a home here. And he's determined to prove his innocence." That last sentence was for the newspaper reporters, a couple of whom he'd spotted in the audience. It was about time they heard his client's side of the story.

"Your honor, the nature of this crime is particularly heinous and given that fact, I recommend a high bail be set," Ritter repeated. Brockton noted that the assistant DA mispronounced heinous again.

"Again, your honor, there is no danger of this man fleeing," Brockton said. "He's been living in this community for fifteen years and has a home of considerable equity that I'm sure he's not about to give up."

"Then let him post bail," Ritter retorted.

"And as I said before, he is determined to prove his innocence."

Judge Holmes looked at both lawyers impatiently and Brockton shut up. She didn't appreciate hearing the same arguments more than once.

Suddenly Sienkewicz cleared his throat. Brockton threw a warning glance at him, but his client ignored him. "I thought I was innocent, at least until proven guilty." He finished the sentence with a broad, white-toothed smile.

Holmes looked sternly at Sienkewicz, then at Brockton. "This is not a humorous matter," she said.

"I'm sorry, your honor," Brockton replied. "Mr. Sienkewicz realizes that. I think he's just so sure of his innocence that he's not taking this as seriously as he should."

"He should well be advised to take this seriously, Mr. Brockton," Holmes said. "And as his representation, it is your job to make sure that he does."

"I have informed him of that," Brockton said. "Unfortunately, I was only able to see him for a short time last night. This all happened rather quickly."

"I'd prefer not to hear excuses, Mr. Brockton," Holmes replied.

"I did inform him of the seriousness of the proceedings, your honor. Please don't think he is making fun of this court."

"The moment I think he's making fun of this court, I'll slap him with a contempt charge."

"Understood, and—" Brockton began, but Holmes held up her hand, cutting him off. She started to leaf through the papers on her desk.

Brockton looked at Sienkewicz. The son of a bitch wasn't exactly starting off on the best note. He needed to see what was happening and paste a serious look on his face.

In the silence following the exchange, the sound of the toilet flushing could be heard. Brockton started counting to himself. As he approached thirty seconds he heard the toilet flush again. He knew what was coming and kept his eye on the bailiff. As soon as the man wrinkled his nose, Brockton took a gulp of air and held his breath.

The smell of shit wafted through the room, causing several people to turn their faces down. Holmes, as soon as she smelled it, nodded to the bailiff, who disappeared behind the curtain next to her. A door closed and the bailiff returned.

"Would you two gentlemen please approach the bench," Holmes said to the lawyers.

Brockton strode forward. "Good morning, your honor," he said. The judge nodded. "Morning, Milt."

"Good morning," the assistant DA replied evenly.

"By the way, Milt, it's heinous with an a, not an i."

Ritter ignored the comment.

"Have you two gotten together to work out a plea for this case?" Holmes asked.

"I tried to get the DA's office to talk about it," Brockton replied. "Milt said to meet him in court."

Holmes swung her gaze to Ritter.

"We're still preparing some key elements of the case, your honor," Ritter explained. "We plan to take this to trial."

"Very well. Bail will be ten thousand dollars. I hope that satisfies both of you."

Brockton heard a door close and suddenly had an idea. "It's awfully smelly in here, your honor," he said.

She looked at him hard, then said, "I'll worry about the courtroom smell. You worry about your defendant."

"Maybe you should station the bailiff back there some day," Brockton suggested. "Where is it coming from?"

"The window in the bathroom carries the breeze in here," she said. "If someone forgets to close the bathroom door, the smell follows."

Brockton shook his head. "We need that breeze, your honor. This place gets too stuffy without it."

"Your honor, could we please discuss the matter at hand?" Ritter interrupted. "With all due respect, we shouldn't be wasting the court's time talking about odors."

"What's the matter Milt, yours doesn't stink?" Holmes let the comment pass and Brockton continued. "We've got a problem here. Your honor, I have an idea you may be interested in. Would you permit me?"

"Please do, Mr. Brockton," Holmes replied, leaning forward.

Brockton whispered something in her ear and after listening, she nodded. Then, before he had time to pull his head away, she picked up the gavel and slammed it down. He cursed silently, his ears ringing. She always got that gavel down before he could move, beat him every time.

4

Brockton waited until the waitress delivered their sandwiches and left, then continued his story. "So I told her that I just read in this health manual how extremity temperatures drop after people shit—defecate, I said—and she agreed to let me go out the back door to investigate. I left Channel Five standing stupid."

"I can see why you didn't want them to catch you leaving," Leach replied. "I wouldn't want to be seen defending that pervert."

"There they are with all their cameras and lights and no lawyer to film," Brockton said.

"They should castrate him for what he's done."

Brockton looked at his friend and shook his head. Chuckie would never appreciate his best moves. He was too caught up in the right and wrong of everything. That was part of being a "good" cop. "You want to use the camp this weekend? Stephanie and I are staying in town to finish painting the house."

"No one's gonna be up there?"

"It's all yours. Swing by the house and get the key. If I'm not home, it'll be under the plant on the porch."

"I don't work this weekend and Brenda and I could use the time out of the city," Leach said. "I think I'll take you up on the offer."

"Don't mention it," Brockton said. He considered Chuckie a close friend. They had known each other since college and had maintained their friendship when they ended up in the same city. Chuckie didn't have the cowboy mentality many cops had, but he kept Brockton in touch with what they were thinking. That was the previous DA's main problem. He didn't pay enough attention to what the cops felt so they weren't as likely to go through the extra effort needed to present him with good evidence to prosecute cases. Maybe White would be different.

After several moments of silence, Brockton asked, "So why did you want to meet me, just to say hello?"

The policeman set down his sandwich, picked up his napkin and wiped his lips,. "Did I tell you a buddy of mine knows your slime ball?"

"Who, Sienkewicz?"

"Yeah. Says he's sure it's him. He was involved in some slimy deals there, too."

"Who is he?"

"Sergeant O'Connell."

"*The* Sergeant O'Connell? The crazy one?"

"He's not that crazy. And he's a good cop."

"So?"

"Says he wants to talk to you."

"Why?"

"I don't know. The only thing I know is that he was in on the arrest. He wrote up the police report. He told me he wants to talk to you."

Brockton didn't reply, but now that Chuckie mentioned it he did remember seeing the cop's name on the police report. And thinking that wasn't good, because O'Connell could lie better than most and seem as sincere as snow.

"He says there's something wrong with the report," Leach said, lowering his voice.

"What the hell does that mean?"

"I don't know. I told you I don't know anything, just passing the information along."

Brockton hesitated a moment. He wouldn't get any more out of his friend. "That'll help me," he finally said.

"Don't think this means I approve of you defending that scum bag. He's guilty as far as I'm concerned and I'd like to see him get his dick cut off."

"He hasn't been tried yet," Brockton said, smiling at Chuckie. He loved to get him going.

"Yeah, how would you like him to get near your daughter?"

"You know what he reminds me of?" Brockton replied. "I finally figured it out. He's that college professor that every student runs into. The one that everyone says is screwing his students." He saw Leach getting heated, so he continued. "He fits the description to a t."

"Except he's a high school teacher and he beat the girl up. Bad."

"You know an awful lot about this case, Chuckie."

"So do a lot of cops. Anyway, I did what I promised. I told the sergeant I'd get in touch with you."

"Thanks."

"Is he out of jail yet?"

"Yeah. I got him out for ten mil. With Holmes, no less." Leach didn't say anything and Brockton added, "You're supposed to be impressed. Holmes is tough."

"You're proud 'a that?" Leach said. "You put another perv back on the streets and you're proud?"

"Come on, Chuckie boy, give the guy a break. You don't even know him." Like most cops, Leach believed that anyone they arrested was guilty. "Remember, he's gotta be proven guilty."

Leach snorted in disgust. "Don't even start. I told you what I had to and that's all I'm gonna do. I hope they fry the son of a bitch."

"How can I get in touch with this sergeant?"

"O'Connell?"

"Yeah."

"Call the station. He's easy enough to find."

"Thanks, Chuckie, you're a dream." Leach didn't respond and Brockton watched him eat his sandwich silently. As reasonable as he was, Chuckie had that potential to get violent quickly. Brockton had seen him go off once, when they had been outside a bar downtown and a couple of drunks were hassling a working prostitute. She screamed and one of the drunks took a swing at her. Chuckie had exploded into action, tackling the man, then throwing him against the building. He'd accidentally smashed the guy's nose, which was bleeding all over the place, but instead of seeking first aid he'd summoned a cop car to take them all to the station.

In the excitement, Chuckie forgot Brockton was even there. Not that that bothered him. He was just as bloodthirsty in a courtroom. But as sensible as Chuckie was, his actions that night were overkill. They convinced Brockton that no matter how reasonable cops appeared, they were always ready to act.

They finished eating and Leach said, "You know, I take a lot of shit just talking to you."

"That bothering you again?"

"It always bothers me. You put too many guilty people back on the streets."

"You put them on the streets," Brockton countered. "Do a better job collecting evidence and I wouldn't have to shoot you down."

Leach was about to reply, but didn't, instead waved the waitress over. The issue was so familiar that Brockton wondered why he had even brought it up again.

5

"Look Milt, I think you're going a little too far with this," Brockton said as politely as he could. He switched the phone to his other ear. "I can convince him to plea bargain if you offer probation time, but three to five? Sure he took advantage of the girl, but it's not like he's got a record of it. And the girl wasn't hurt. No broken bones or scars. Nothing that doesn't happen on a nightly basis in this city."

"My hands are tied, Mr. Brockton," Ritter responded. Brockton grimaced at the use of his last name. The assistant DA still hadn't gotten over the past and this was one time Brockton regretted not being on better terms with him.

"Don't think I don't know why all this is happening so quickly," Brockton said. "Post election, you need a win, the whole thing stinks of politics."

"Is that it?"

"Come on, it's obvious. You got the grand jury together in less than a week and after leading them around by their

noses you're gonna try to turn this case around in a month?
When is the last time that happened?"

Ritter didn't respond.

"The election is over," Brockton continued. "You can
drop the tough guy shit. I'm not trying to twist your arm or
anything, but I have to think seriously about requesting
more time, maybe even a postponement. After all the media
attention, it'll be hard to find an unbiased twelve."

"A postponement won't bother us."

"You could use a plea bargain. It's as good as a win."

"We could survive a postponement," Ritter replied
frankly and Brockton silently agreed. After all the bad press
the previous DA's office had gotten for losing a couple of
open and shut cases, taking a chance on this one was risky.

"Is someone going to make a lot of noise? Is that the reason you don't want a plea?" Brockton asked. Ritter didn't
respond and for a moment Brockton felt sorry for the dilemma the DA's office was in. The election behind them,
losing this case would be quite embarrassing for White given
his focus on taking the gloves off with criminals. On the
other hand, they could get what they needed out of this if
they played it right. They could settle quickly, almost as
good as a win.

All Brockton wanted was a reasonable plea bargain offer
to present to his client. Now was the time to use his ammunition. "Whoever's pushing for an early trial should know
that my client's got an alibi," he said. "A solid one." There
was silence on the other end of the line. That was good. He
needed to knock Ritter off balance. "And your alleged victim's reputation is nothing to brag about."

"That information is impermissible."

"Milt, let's knock off the bullshit. If you think you can prevent me from bringing up that girl's background when I get her on the stand, you're crazy. Prostituting, drug use, Christ the girl was in an alcohol rehab program when she met my client. A jury is bound to go my way. Can you really risk the loss?"

"Maybe you ought to speak with your client," Ritter said, a little too calmly Brockton thought. "He told the officer questioning him that he'd never allow the girl to be put on the witness stand. Seems like he's in love with her."

"I know, he told me the same thing. But you don't think the press is going to have a field day with that?" Maybe he'd better talk to Sienkewicz before he said anything else. "So what's the best you can offer?"

"The same."

"Nothing better? I can't believe you're not going to offer me anything." As he was talking, Brockton noted the blinking light on his telephone system. Sienkewicz must be here. "It couldn't be that you've got something else on him..." he said, letting the question hang. Ritter didn't respond, as he expected, but it was worth a try. "Listen, Milt, I'll be around all day. I still think five year's probation is an acceptable deal. The guy lost his job."

"I'll see you in court," Ritter responded, a little too emotionally this time. He said good-bye to the assistant DA, then pushed the button for the blinking line. "Just a minute." He put Candy on hold and turned his chair around to look out the window, feeling invigorated. He always felt this way when he was dealing. It was a part of the job he loved.

Brockton's office overlooked the city's vital organs—the courthouse, city hall, police headquarters, and the DA's office. He had conquered it all. He tried to imagine Ritter down there, scurrying around to organize the evidence for this case. The assistant DA reminded Brockton of a mouse. No matter that he had been there for almost four years, the guy was just another peach fuzz lawyer who hadn't learned how to win cases yet. His friend, Bart McCormick, had hit the nail on the head when he said that the previous DA had filled his office with loyal people who were no match for the city's trial lawyers, and White hadn't even tried to recruit any of those veterans.

Brockton had enjoyed his time as an assistant DA and the give and take it involved. It had been a great education and given him a clear view of how the justice system worked here. But unlike this group, he had worked with a couple of battle-scarred veterans. He had learned a lot from them. Meanwhile, White was unwilling to ask some of those veterans to return. He'd claimed he was unable, but he hadn't even tried.

He pushed the blinking button on his telephone. It was time to find out what the hell Sienkewicz had told the cops. "Yes, Candy?"

"A Mr. John Sienkewicz to see you."

"Send him in."

Moments later the door opened and Brockton turned to greet his client.

"Good morning," Sienkewicz said, stepping into Brockton's office. His client stopped inside the door, below the carved wooden sign that hung over it. The sign read: *No poet ever interpreted as freely as a lawyer interprets the truth. - Jean Giraudoux.*

Brockton waved toward a row of seats. "Do you know a guy named O'Connell? He's a city cop, says he knows you from the military."

Sienkewicz's face clouded. "There are a lot of guys in the military."

"You don't remember him?"

"I can't say," Sienkewicz said. "I don't remember the name, but I might recognize his face. Why?"

"No reason. Listen, what's this you told the cops about not wanting to put this girl on the witness stand?"

"That's right. I won't permit it."

"Well that may be irrelevant if I can get the DA's office to give us a good plea bargain, but as a piece of advice for your future, don't say things like that to cops. It can only hurt you. As far as the plea bargain is concerned, they're stalling for time, but once they get organized I think they'll make a good offer."

"I don't want a plea bargain."

"We'll get a good deal, probation time."

"I don't want a deal. I want to go to trial. And I'm not going to lie. That's important to me."

"A plea bargain isn't going to force you to lie," Brockton explained. "In fact, it will allow you to tell the truth, with the minimum amount of punishment. If we go to trial, you'll be forced to lie, according to what you've told me."

"I want a trial," Sienkewicz repeated. "I want a chance to show people how innocent I am, a chance to prove that I have lived a morally acceptable life."

"What are you talking about?" Brockton asked.

"Here is someone who came to me for help. A young girl who was confused and needed help, whose mother didn't care for her, keep her safe. And I helped her. I..."

"...assaulted and sexually abused her," Brockton interrupted. "You left her with two black ones and a huge bruise on her face. That's why you're here, remember?"

"I didn't assault anyone," Sienkewicz said. "That's a lie. I'll tell the jury the truth, that I would never have hurt my Carmen. They will understand. Fyodor said the more decent a man, the greater the accumulation of things he is afraid to admit. I am willing to admit those things."

"Who said what?"

"Fyodor Dostoyevsky. A Russian author. Didn't your English professors have you read him?"

"Forget Dostoy-whoever, a jury isn't going to want to hear anything he said even if I was crazy enough to let you tell them that. And if that's what you're planning to say, I'm not even going to let you near the witness stand. Judge Holmes won't care about that, either. She's gonna see an adult white male exploiting a young black female. Holmes is black, if you haven't noticed, and she'll bury you if you admit to this without a plea bargain agreement." Brockton stretched the truth on that one, to scare his client.

"Larisa's not black," Sienkewicz said and Brockton said nothing, surprised. "You looked at her address, saw where she lived and immediately thought she was black, right?"

"The police report said she was black."

"The police see things the same way you do. The truth is that her mother is white and her mother, God roast her soul, is the one who raised her."

"Even if she's half black, Holmes is going to see her as black."

"Her mother is the one they really should be prosecuting," Sienkewicz said. "I want a chance to show people how wrong they are to prosecute me when she threw her daughter out. Don't you think there's a little hypocrisy there?"

"Parents are allowed to be hypocritical," Brockton replied.

"I saved her from an abusive situation."

"We're going to need a postponement," Brockton said, more to himself than to his client. The memory of Sienkewicz's outburst in the court returned. The man was going to need coaching.

"I've been made out to be a villain," Sienkewicz continued, "when in reality I am a loving, caring human being. I am as innocent as anyone in this town."

Brockton held his hand up. "First of all, you're not even going to get a chance to explain yourself, not on my time. Second, you need to listen to their plea bargain offer, which will come soon, I'm sure."

"You don't understand."

"No, you don't understand. I'm the lawyer and I know how to approach this case. You hired me to defend you and that's what I'm going to do."

"Not by perverting the justice system."

Brockton raised his eyebrows at his client's use of terms. "This isn't a movie, Mr. Sienkewicz."

"Call me John."

"Mr. Sienkewicz. This isn't some made for TV movie where you can get up in front of a judge and tell some story and free yourself. This is reality. You know, I don't think you realize you could be spending the next five years behind bars. Five years is a long time."

"Doesn't it bother you that what you're suggesting has nothing to do with finding out what really happened?" Sienkewicz asked. "Doesn't it bother you that we aren't searching for the truth?"

"When I was younger, it might have. But right now I'm trying to keep you out of jail, the truth be damned. That's what you're paying me for."

"Did you receive the check for the extra one thousand dollars?" Brockton nodded and his client continued. "Good. Now I mean to have a say in what happens. I refuse to plea bargain. By law I may be guilty of a sexual offense, but Larisa was a willing partner. I love her and would never have hurt her."

Brockton held himself in check. This guy was going to be a real pain in the ass, not one he wanted to even bring into the courtroom not to mention put in front of a jury. He was stubborn to the point of stupidity, which meant it would take some time to break through his resistance. "Let's go over the police report," he said, deciding to take care of business until he could figure out what strategy he was going to take with Judge Holmes.

6

Brockton turned the key to unlock the car door, then cursed. The lock was still stuck. He'd have to get in from the other side and slide across the seat. He loosened his tie and opened the top button on his shirt. He had gotten too used to the Beamer, and everything working. He'd started driving Stephanie's beat up Ford to work ever since they had broken into his car and stolen the stereo system. That was one thing crack had done, made it unsafe to park an expensive car downtown without installing an alarm. Even then you'd often end up with a broken window.

Once in the car, he turned on the radio and pulled out of the parking lot and into traffic. He searched his memory. Did he need to pick up anything at the store? Milk. Stephanie had asked him to pick up milk. Three teens meant constantly running out of it. He pulled into the line of traffic and headed toward the freeway ramp. He'd stop at a store nearer home.

Once on the freeway, his thoughts returned to Sien-kewicz. The son of a bitch had a screw lose. He wanted Brockton to go into the courtroom armed only with the truth. He wanted him to get massacred.

Frankly, he could care less what happened to his client. Sienkewicz would get what he deserved. But Brockton wasn't about to lose a case to Milton Ritter. The guy would love to beat him after the whipping he'd given the assistant DA two years ago. He'd gone up against him when the city attempted to close down a smut shop and Brockton had turned Ritter's sorry prosecution into a rout.

It was one of Bart McCormick's favorite stories; each time his former partner related what had happened at the trial, he embellished on it. He called it Brockton's signpost case, the beginning of his reputation as the greatest trial lawyer the city ever knew. Since then, he ate assistant DAs alive, according to Bart.

A picture of Ritter standing in front of Judge Bachmann popped into Brockton's head. Why they had let a rookie go up against him on that one was unfathomable. An experienced prosecutor might have been able to win the case—they'd had decent evidence—but Ritter messed it up and they had let him go on and on, digging himself deeper into a hole of unsubstantiated muck. By the end of the trial Brockton was objecting to just about every one of Ritter's sentences, and Bachmann was sustaining the objections.

To make matters worse, Ritter had grown emotional. At one point Bachmann had to stop the proceedings to let the assistant DA compose himself. Brockton had never discovered why Ritter had taken that case so personally. Maybe it was just that he knew he should have won it.

Before handing down his decision, Bachmann spent a quarter of an hour complimenting Ritter on his "spirited prosecution", which made it even more obvious the assistant DA was going under. The judge probably felt his ego needed to be stroked. The last thing Brockton would ever do was listen to some inert judge like Bachmann build him up because he'd lost a case.

He remembered feeling sorry for Ritter at the time. The guy just didn't know how to use the courtroom yet. They had sent a peach fuzz lawyer into the courtroom to get a drubbing and that kind of defeat didn't leave you quickly. It would give Brockton an edge over him in this case.

What they had against Sienkewicz seemed weak even without this cop who Chuckie had mentioned. The girl would be a shaky witness with her background and although that information was difficult to bring up in court, he would manage to introduce it under some pretext. He could claim that the addition was relevant to the inconsistencies in her story after he tripped her up several times. Then he'd create a character ravaged by drugs and alcohol. He was the best at creating characters on the witness stand. He'd compare her to Sienkewicz, a teacher and family man. He'd have the jury eating out of his hands. Ritter was going to regret bringing this to trial, even if Brockton didn't want to let on to his client that a plea bargain was preferable.

Getting the drug and alcohol stuff past Holmes would be the difficult part. Or Sienkewicz, for that matter. His client wanted to tell the truth. It was a good thing the guy had offered to pay him more money, to make up for the extra time he'd have to spend convincing him how to keep his ass out of jail.

Brockton spotted a convenience store and remembered the milk. He swerved into the parking lot. He was going to win this case with or without his client's cooperation.

Twenty minutes later Brockton pulled into the driveway of his home, a large, new building surrounded by trees. His oldest son, Michael, was sitting on the sidewalk steps in a tee shirt, baseball pants and cleats.

"Hey Babe, did you win today?" Brockton asked. His son nodded but didn't look up, just stared at the sidewalk. Brockton tousled his hair and stepped past him and into the house. "Atta way, Babe!" he yelled as the door closed behind him.

Stephanie was in the kitchen preparing dinner. She was the perfect match for him. Attractive but not flirtatious or loud like some of his friends' wives. Her parents lived far enough away for comfort and she wasn't obsessive about seeing them too often. He really was lucky.

"Hi," he said, kissing the back of her neck and grabbing her ass.

"Did your son tell you what happened today?" she replied.

"What happened?" he asked, ignoring the barb. She called Michael "your son" when he'd done something she didn't like.

"He quit the team."

"What?"

"Harry called a little while ago and said when he took Michael out of the game, he tore off his shirt and stormed out of the dugout. He said he quit."

"Why?"

"Why don't you go ask him? He won't talk to me."

"How did he get home?"

"He walked."

"From the baseball diamonds?" Brockton asked.

"Michael, it's less than a mile! And this isn't the city!"

"Why did Harry take him out of the game?"

"He swore. Harry said he won't tolerate that on the field, so he took him out."

"What did he say?"

"I don't know, but does it matter?"

"Sure it does. He's the cleanup hitter."

Stephanie brushed his hand off her ass. "Just make sure you talk to Harry before you take Michael's side again," she said. "Remember what happened the last time you did that."

"I'll talk to him all right," Brockton said. "You know he doesn't like Michael. I've said that all along."

"You know that's not true," Stephanie responded. "Harry loves Michael. And he also knows our son needs to control his mouth."

"So you're taking the coach's side?"

"No, I'm just saying talk to him before you fly off the handle."

Brockton snorted and turned to the refrigerator, taking out a beer and opening it. He pulled a mug out of the freezer, poured the beer and watched it frost up. "You're right, of course," he said. He needed to sit down for a minute.

"Daddy, look at the insect I found." Roger, his youngest, entered the kitchen holding a large bug in his hand. "It's a Cleopatra."

"Roger, get that out of the house," Brockton said. "You know the rules about bugs in the house."

"It's Coleoptera, honey," Stephanie added. "And you're the smartest little kid on the block."

As Roger obediently trudged out the front door, Brockton watched him. How he had ever given birth to a child like Roger, he'd never know. At the age of six the kid was so into the world of bugs that he spent half his life hunting them down.

Brockton humored his son's interest even though he had hoped for another ball player. He spent countless hours with his kids at the nearby park, hitting fly balls, but inevitably Roger would lose interest and start looking around for a bug. At least he had Babe. Babe would make a name for himself on the diamond.

Brockton left the kitchen, then yelled back, "Where's Michele?"

"At the pool," Stephanie yelled in reply. "I told her you'd pick her up before dinner."

Brockton nodded to himself. He loved his daughter like he loved his entire family. He had grown to admire her as much as the boys, something he never thought possible. Funny, he'd always thought of girls as weak until Michele had come along and cured that. She was probably the best athlete in the family. And with two males, no one was going to say that he wasn't virile.

The idea of family was important to Brockton. Here were three persons he had created. They had his features and personality. They were him. He was proud of them.

As soon as he entered the living room, he spotted the newspaper on the chair and saw the bold print headline. He cursed. In the uproar over a little league game, he had forgotten to mention the case to Stephanie and there was a front page article on the trial. He opened the paper, wondering if she'd seen it yet. Inside were two pictures, one of Sienkewicz and one of himself, side by side. He swore again. He had snuck around the media so they had pulled a stock photo out to use in their article. Newspaper people were vindictive little bastards.

The doorbell rang and someone raced to get it. "Daddy, it's for you!" Roger yelled. 'It's the police!"

Brockton smiled. Roger loved Leach ever since he'd given him a ride in a squad car. Maybe he'd be a cop some day, once he got over his bug stage.

"Hey Chuckie!" Brockton greeted his friend as he stepped into the living room.

Leach smiled and reached out to shake his hand. He always shook people's hands, even if he knew them well or had already seen them that day. He was real formal that way.

"When are we going for another ride?" Roger asked, hanging on to Leach's hand.

"Soon, Rog," Brockton said. "But for now you gotta leave us alone."

After his son left the room, he turned to Chuckie. "Got time for a beer?"

"No, I really gotta get going," Leach replied. "Supper is ready and you don't keep Brenda waiting."

"Hi, Chuck!" Stephanie called from the kitchen. Brockton thought he saw his friend wince before calling back a greeting.

"You tell her about the case yet?" Leach asked.

"No, but she probably knows," Brockton replied. "Check this out."

Leach looked at the headlines of the paper Brockton held out, then shook his head. "If I was her, I'd divorce you."

"She can't, I got her hooked on the lifestyle."

"Poor girl."

"Until the check arrives. Then she's a happy shopper."

"Aren't they all," Leach agreed.

"Did you get the key?"

"Yeah, it was in the plant. How about electricity?"

"It's the same deal. Switch is behind the front door. You gotta plug in and prime the pump. There's beer in the fridge, mustard, ketchup, so on. Feel free to use them."

"Hey, thanks Mike," Leach said. "Sorry I gotta run so quickly. I'll get back to you later."

"Enjoy yourselves."

"Hey this O'Connell guy stopped me again. He's going to call you. He's from the old school, but he's all right. He's okay."

"I thought I'd call him in the morning," Brockton said.

"Yeah, good idea. If you don't hear from him, give him a call. I told him you would." Leach thanked him again and left.

7

Brockton looked across the kitchen table at Stephanie. His wife had borne their three children gracefully. Her face, only slightly aged, was still attractive. And she hadn't lost her figure. She was a woman any man would envy having. Not that he was thinking of leaving, even screwing around on her. That was for other guys. He was intensely loyal and having three kids made him even more so. He wouldn't do anything to disrupt the successful course of his family life. Besides, divorce was a financial nightmare. He remembered the joke: *Why is divorce so expensive? Because it's worth it.* That was not for him.

"What did Chuck want?" Stephanie asked.

"I thought I'd let him use the cottage this weekend, since we'll be painting."

"That's nice. I spoke to Brenda today and she didn't mention it."

"I didn't offer it to him until this morning," Brockton explained.

"Oh." She looked at him, then glanced meaningfully at their eldest son.

"So what's new, Mike?" Brockton asked.

"Nothin'," Michael mumbled.

"How was your game today?"

His son didn't respond.

"Your mother says you had a problem with the coach," Brockton said.

Still no response.

"What happened?"

"Tell him, Michael," Stephanie said.

"He took me out of the game," Michael finally said.

"Why?" Brockton asked.

"I don't know." His son's eyes remained on the plate of food in front of him.

"He swore, Daddy," Roger said and Michael directed a murderous glance at his brother.

"I'll take care of this, Roger," Brockton said, more to placate Michael than to rebuke his youngest son. "Did you swear?"

His son didn't respond.

"What did you say?" Brockton asked.

"He took me out of the game with runners on second and third and nobody out!" Michael finally replied. "I would have creamed the ball!"

"What did you say?" Brockton repeated, but his son just hung his head, saying nothing. "Well, I'm going to talk to the coach. I'll straighten this out one way or another."

"I'm not going to play for him anymore!" his son said.

"Pff," his daughter said. "Michael, don't be such a ba—"

"—I'll handle this, Michele," Brockton interrupted. "Mike, I don't want to hear that. I'm going to talk to the coach. You be ready for practice tomorrow." He looked at Stephanie, who was looking at him with an almost pleading expression. He turned back to his son. "You got that?"

His son mumbled a yes.

"What?" Brockton asked sharply.

"Yes," his son said, a decibel louder.

"And be ready to apologize. You have to understand that sometimes you're not going to like everything a coach does. But he's the coach and you have to do what he says. Without swearing."

After a decent interval, Brockton turned to his daughter. "How did your day go?" He was careful to give Michele an equal amount of his attention.

"Good," she said, then continued to shovel food into her mouth. "Someone almost drowned in the pool today."

"What happened?" Stephanie asked.

"A kid got pushed in and almost drowned. The life guard had to jump in after him. Then they made everyone leave the pool for a half hour while they gave us a lecture on no pushing."

"Sounds like you needed one," Brockton said.

"It wasn't me," Michele responded. "They didn't have to lecture everybody."

"At least no one swore," Roger said, adding levity to the discussion.

"Daddy, are you a Communist?" Michele suddenly asked.

"A what?" Brockton asked, surprised.

"A Communist. Someone at the pool said you were one. His father said you were, because you were defending some guy in your court."

Brockton smiled. "I don't think you have to worry about your father being a Communist. They don't make any good cars."

"Oh I don't really care but I hit him anyway," his daughter said, shrugging her shoulders. She returned her attention to her food.

Brockton waited until they had finished supper and the kids had left before he brought up the case. "I took Sienkewicz as a client," he said casually.

"The pervert," Stephanie said. He looked up in surprise and she continued. "I've already heard about it from Sheila, next door. She didn't call you a Communist, though."

Brockton smiled. Their next door neighbor was a busy body, but he was happy that Stephanie wasn't making a big deal about the case.

"You shouldn't have told Michael that you'd talk to his coach," Stephanie said. "You should make him do that."

Brockton looked at his wife, then at the ceiling. He always looked at the ceiling when he was irritated, as if he was asking God for help. "She's telling me how to raise our son again," he said. Then, to her, he added, "I thought I did a good job with him."

"I just think this is a perfect opportunity to teach him good sportsmanship," she replied. "You know as well as I do that he takes sports too seriously."

"He does not," Brockton countered. "How can you expect him to be competitive if he doesn't care about winning?"

"Michael, this isn't about winning. He acted like a baby today. He tore off his uniform and threw it on the ground because the coach took him out of the game."

"I would have done the same thing," Brockton replied.

Stephanie laughed. "The court officers would love to see that!" Brockton smiled ruefully and Stephanie continued. "You probably did tear off your uniform when you were young, and that worries me."

"How could Harry have taken his long ball hitter out of the game with two men on?" Brockton mused. "I would have had him swing away, even if there wasn't a runner on first."

"You, fortunately, are not the coach. If you were, your son would probably be playing all three bases at the same time. I don't know that much about baseball, but I watched you play several seasons and I suspect that it's still a team game."

"You don't understand. Michael has a lot of potential and it's important to keep his confidence up. I was the same way when I was young, but no one gave me the support I needed."

"I don't want to argue about this again. You are horrible when it comes to sports. You can't even watch TV without cursing, I wonder where Michael gets that behavior. If you want to raise the same type of monster as yourself, go ahead but you're going to have to deal with all the coaches and teachers he fights, not me. I'm not going to support that behavior. Michael should be able to apologize to the coach himself and you should stay out of it."

His wife stood up and started clearing the dishes off the table, signaling an end to the discussion. Brockton didn't reply, knew better than to waste his time. She'd never understand anyway; women just didn't get it when it came to raising a sports hero.

At one time he could have been a ball player. He had dreamed of playing professionally at some level, but his father had been too busy to encourage and support him. Not that he blamed the man; his dad had a life, too. But Brockton wasn't going to make the same mistake with Michael. He was going to give him the time and encouragement.

Brockton stood up and started to gather dishes, glad to have Stephanie there.

8

"You know what the problem is?" Sergeant O'Connell began.

"What's that?" Brockton asked.

"Civil rights," O'Connell said.

Brockton didn't reply. They were driving down a section of the New York State Thruway, which is where O'Connell suggested they meet. The weekend had passed before he'd managed to meet the police officer and Brockton hadn't had much time yet to develop a case for Sienkewicz.

"That's why this fuckin' country has gone down the tubes," the sergeant continued. "It's all this civil rights shit. My old man was a cop and he retired because of it. When he was a cop, they were respected. You walked into a place and a guy gave you shit, you took him out back and settled it. Now you can't take him out back. Now they got civil rights."

"You've got a tough job," Brockton said.

"You bet your ass it's tough." The car went under a bridge. As it emerged several small stones fell from above, hitting the pavement near the car.

"You see what I mean?" O'Connell said. "Damn niggers stand on the road up there and throw rocks at the cars going by. And you can't do nothin' about it 'cause they didn't do anything." He glanced quickly at Brockton to gauge his reaction.

Brockton looked back, unwilling to believe that black kids would be found this far north of the city.

"Fuckin' niggers. I saw 'em coming."

Brockton considered correcting the sergeant but kept silent. He didn't want to alienate someone he might need. Yet.

"The other thing is the paperwork," O'Connell continued. "They buried my old man in it. Being a cop ain't what it used to be. It's a damn shame."

A few minutes later, O'Connell pulled into a Thruway service area. "We can get some coffee here."

As they were getting out of the car, a young girl walked past. O'Connell pointed to her. "Look at those titties! Not bad!"

"It's one thing I like about summer," Brockton replied, wanting to develop a sense of comradeship with the policeman. "Girls don't wear bras." He was glad O'Connell wasn't dressed in his uniform, if only for Leach's sake.

"Ooo-oo!" O'Connell said, staring blatantly at the girl. "How'd you like to be spearin' that." He grabbed his crotch.

"Hey, honey!" he yelled and the girl glanced at him. She started walking faster, disappearing behind a van. "All my kids got blue eyes, I can tell you that. My wife ain't been fuckin' no wop. You gotta watch them 'cause they'll fuck anything that moves. And when it ain't movin', they'll fuck it anyway!" O'Connell laughed loudly at his joke, then said, "You ain't Italian are you?"

Brockton shook his head.

"I don't want to offend you is what I mean."

Once they were seated inside the rest stop, O'Connell started talking about Sienkewicz. "You know, I'm glad you decided to take this case."

Brockton said nothing. Being a good lawyer, he was used to compliments on his work, even from people he didn't know.

"I really respect the guy," O'Connell continued. "I mean, he's a man with some principles. I know he got a little careless, but Christ a man's entitled to a piece of ass now and then, ain't he?"

"Leach says you knew him in the army," Brockton said.

"Palmerola. He taught GIs how to speak spick."

"With a name like Sienkewicz?"

"He speaks better than any spick I know."

"He was involved in a scandal?"

"He took a couple of GIs to the whorehouses in town. He told them to pick out a honey to live with for a couple months. Then he'd leave. He said they'd learn to speak better that way."

"How did you find out about it?"

"It was all on account 'a some disease that a GI brought from 'Nam, called Flor de Vietnam. That means Vietnam flower. It was a new type 'a VD. The papers got hold 'a that and told us they were gonna do a story. That's when the bosses decided they had a PR problem.

"A buddie 'a mine ran into a couple of guys who said they were only there 'cause they were followin' orders. They told him the story.

"You know, you gotta admire the guy for his balls, pullin' a stunt like that." The sergeant looked down at his coffee cup. "Will he get off?"

"He might," Brockton replied. "But the stuff that's been coming out in the newspaper worries me."

"Shit, that ain't nothin'," O'Connell replied. "Don't think there ain't nobody downtown who ain't ripped off a piece of ass themselves, newspaper people included. And that little slut, I've seen her at the jailhouse more than once. She sells her skinny little ass for crack. That's what bothers me, you know. These sluts go out and sell themselves for drugs, then the chance to cash in on someone comes along and suddenly they're little Miss No Pussy. They act like they're too proud for that shit all of a sudden. You remember that scandal a bunch 'a years ago, when we swept all those whores outta the convention area?"

Brockton sure did. He was part of the team assigned to prosecute the case. It was right before a convention of politicians and most of the representatives were staying downtown, in a hotel near the city's red zone. A week before the convention the police decided to clean up the streets so they arrested all the girls. To make sure they didn't return during the convention, they kept the girls locked up for the entire week.

The story hit the headlines the day after the convention was over. Several prostitutes alleged that while in jail they had turned tricks for their jailers. It had been real messy until the newspapers stopped covering it.

"It was the same thing," O'Connell continued. "One 'a the girls told me she was willin' to earn some money and that was all it took. We set them up with some big money, too, even had a couple preachers doin' 'em." The sergeant smiled widely. "This one honey, she dressed up like Mary Magdalene. The preacher boys loved her."

"I didn't hear about that," Brockton said.

"That's 'cause we fed what we wanted to your man, Dixon, then gave the papers just enough 'a the story to get 'em off our backs. You don't know the half of it. Tell me I don't know the right people!" the cop finished proudly.

Brockton shook his head, unsure whether to believe O'Connell. As a member of the DA's office, he was hearing this for the first time and with something that big, he heard at least the rumors. He set down his coffee. "So...what did you want to talk about?"

"Not much," O'Connell replied. The policeman's eyes shifted from one side of the cafeteria to the other, then back to his coffee. "I just always respected the guy and hate to see him get a raw deal for this."

"How do you know it was a raw deal?"

"Well..." O'Connell said, looking around again. He lowered his voice. "I suspected the damn slut was lying even while she told me her story. Then, after I had written the whole report, she changed her mind, said it wasn't him that beat her. Also refused to take the rape test."

Brockton hesitated a moment, taken aback by O'Connell's admission. This was more than 'not much'. Either the cop had been inexcusably careless, or he was not willing to commit perjury. "She told you he didn't rape or assault her?"

"Yeah."

"But—"

"—I know, why did I file the report," O'Connell interrupted. "That happened by mistake. I had it with my other reports and it got handed in. Next thing I know the DA's office is contactin' me about it. I didn't want to look stupid, see. And he was fuckin' the bitch, and she's too young for that. I feel bad about it now, though. At first I didn't know it was the same guy I knew in the army 'cause the girl gave me the wrong name. She couldn't spell it right."

That checked out, Brockton thought. The name had been misspelled in the police report, then in the newspaper. "What about the information the emergency room has?" he asked.

"She never told 'em who beat her. Assaults like that happen every day. It was no big deal to them and 'cause she refused to give 'em any names or get a verified rape exam, they didn't call us back."

O'Connell was right about the hospital report not mentioning names, although Brockton didn't know how he knew. "How did you find out this happened?" he asked. "Didn't they call you in to take a report?"

"That's the funny part. It was pure chance. I was off duty and happened to be drivin' by the hospital when I saw her outside. She wasn't strugglin' or nothin', but I knew somethin' was up. That comes from bein' a cop. I spun around the lot and saw her face was beaten up, so I stopped."

"At two in the morning?" Brockton asked, almost to himself.

"Hey, I'm a cop twenty-four hours a day," O'Connell said, bridling.

"Of course," Brockton replied. He should have remembered he was dealing with a cowboy.

"I wasn't going to file that report, like I said. Shit, I was glad I did at the time, though. The bitch should'a told the truth and stuck to it instead of makin' me go through all that paperwork. She can't get away with changin' her story that easy. Poor guy, I had him in cuffs already 'fore she tole me he didn't do it."

"Sienkewicz?"

"Yeah."

"He was there?"

O'Connell nodded. "He came after I finished the report and started talkin' to her. If I'd 'a recognized the son of a bitch I'd 'a congratulated him. Shit, I guess I was kinda rough on him, didn't give him much of a chance to talk, but it was dark out. Once I did and she said he hadn't beat her, I let him go."

"Does the DA's office know about all this?"

"Nope."

"Do they plan to call you to the stand?"

"Yeah. That little dink's doing the case."

"Milton Ritter."

"Right."

"You're willing to admit this in court?"

"Like I said, I don't want to see him get nailed for something he didn't do."

"Neither do I, but I don't want to put you in a bind either," Brockton said, thinking quickly. "Why didn't any of this come up during the grand jury investigation?"

"Nobody asked," O'Connell replied, smiling. "I didn't think the guy was gonna have ta do time. Hell, if it was only probation, I say he deserves it for fuckin' with a minor. But them DA boys want blood. Jail's too hard."

"That's political," Brockton said, surprised to hear this from a cop, especially O'Connell. "That's why this trial's being rushed through."

O'Connell grunted and Brockton tried to think out what he should do next. The cop's admission would get the case thrown out, but how could he do it without embarrassing him and the department?

He looked around, then up at the ceiling, his mind racing with the new information. Suddenly he had an idea, a daring one, but if he could pull it off it would be a coup. "If you're willing to admit that you weren't on duty when you took the police report, we may be able to get this case thrown out without even getting into the other stuff. Holmes is real strict about proper procedure and that'll make her throw the case out. I've already decided to go for a bench trial because the guy's not presentable. That'll mean less press.

"When we go to trial, you play it cool. Answer Ritter's questions and stick to what's in the report—it doesn't mention that my client was there. If he asks how you got involved, just say you responded to the call. Don't volunteer any information. When I cross examine you, I'll hit on that, then get you to admit you weren't on duty. Admit it reluctantly, like you know you're wrong. That should do it. If I need to, I'll get into the rest of it, how he was there and you didn't arrest him, etcetera, but I don't think we'll even need that. And don't worry about looking bad. I'll only mention what I have to."

O'Connell didn't respond, just looked around and waited.

"We should get together and practice what you're going to say."

"I don't need no practice. I been in front 'a judges plenty 'a times."

"But this needs to look realistic, for your sake. And I'm gonna have to get pretty sarcastic. Can you handle that?"

"You're askin' the questions."

"It'll get tricky if I have to get into the fact that my client was there and you didn't arrest him. We need to practice that one. Did anyone witness this? Did other policemen see him?"

"Her mother was with her."

"She's no problem." Brockton started to picture what the papers were going to say when this came out. The police were going to take some heat.

"Shit, the old lady's the one that beat her, I'm sure of it. She's been on welfare since before she was born."

"She told you that?"

"Tole me what?"

"That she beat her daughter."

"No, but I seen it a million times. Mother finds out her daughter's sluttin' and beats her. Daughter keeps it to herself or blames it on someone else. Most times the mother's a slut, too."

"This is turning out better than I had hoped," Brockton said, almost to himself. O'Connell grunted, then started to finish his coffee. "For a while I was worried," Brockton continued. "My client wanted to get in front of a jury and admit to the charges, the sex part."

"He *what*?" O'Connell put down his coffee.

Brockton shrugged his shoulders. "He says he was having an affair with the girl, that he was in love with her. What's more, he tells me he wants to admit it in court, tell the whole story. He says there's more to it. I didn't even ask him what. The guy's a screw ball."

"That no good son of a bitch!" O'Connell snapped, his face darkening.

"Don't worry, he won't testify," Brockton said quickly, surprised at O'Connell's reaction.

"Shit, I outta let him stew. That'd fuck him good." O'Connell stood up abruptly and disappeared into the rest stop foyer.

9

As he entered the city the next morning, Brockton's thoughts were on his meeting with Sergeant O'Connell. After waiting ten minutes for the policeman to return to the rest area table, Brockton had left and found him sitting in his car. O'Connell had acted as if nothing had happened and that he was more interested in looking at girls in the parking lot.

But something in the relationship between his client and the cop was missing. Brockton had gotten careless, hadn't meant to open up to the cop but his mistake revealed something—he was unsure what—about that relationship. Why had O'Connell grown so angry?

He needed to speak with Sienkewicz. The two of them were connected somehow. Maybe that was why his client acted so unconcerned about being sent to prison; he knew he'd get off this charge from the start. But why had they arrested him in the first place? As often as Brockton had defended someone without knowing the real story, it shouldn't bother him. But this case did.

The press was going to have a field day if what O'Connell said was true. They would write this up as another example of a poorly run DA's office, something they had accused the previous DA for. It could be the beginning of a rocky relationship. Was that what O'Connell wanted?

As he neared the city's main intersection, Brockton closed on a traffic light that was turning red. He noticed a car closing in his rear, as if the driver was going to run the light, so he accelerated and went through it himself. The driver behind him followed, then passed him. Seconds later the flashing lights of a police car were in his rear view mirror. He swore and pulled over. Why hadn't the son of a bitch gone after the other driver!

"License and registration you no good son of a bitchin' lawyer," the cop said.

"Fuck you, officer," Brockton replied. It was Leach.

They shook hands. "You want to get a cup of coffee somewhere?" Leach asked.

"Sure," Brockton replied. Maybe Leach could answer some of his questions.

Once they were seated, the cop handed Brockton the key to his cottage. "Hey listen," he said. "Don't mention anything to Brenda about this weekend. I didn't take her after all."

"No problem," Brockton said, concealing his surprise. "You got a broad on the side?"

"And tell Stephanie I didn't go, if she asks you," Leach said, ignoring Brockton's question.

"Brenda's a nice woman."

"Who are those neighbors on your left? They're wild."

"I know. They're Arabs. Lots of money."

"I thought they were Josés," Leach said. "I heard them speaking a foreign language and thought it was Spanish."

"No they're from Jordan. Must be oil money. They bought the place outright, then added that second floor and the wraparound porch. They even winterized the place."

"I noticed the money, but figured it was drug money."

"Everything's drug money to you."

"You can't let that shit go on if it is," Leach said.

Brockton shrugged. Leach was touchy when it came to drugs. He did some undercover buying and had to deal with the scum.

"Somebody should shake them up," Leach pushed the issue.

"They're not Josés, so they don't fit the profile." Brockton smiled. "I met O'Connell. He's something."

"One of the veterans."

"He lets you know who he does and doesn't like."

"The sergeant is retiring soon, so he's getting crusty. Most of us ignore him."

"No one's ever talked to him about control?"

"You know us cops. We stick together."

"Yeah, but a guy like that could create a scandal any minute. I can't believe he's lasted this long."

"He hasn't always been that bad," Leach said. "Just the last couple of years. He says he wants to retire with a bang, make a difference."

"He's crazy. He was telling me about—"

"—We need guys like him," Leach interrupted. "With all the drug money in the street, we need a few cops who aren't afraid to shoot."

"What?" Brockton wasn't sure he'd heard his friend.

"Believe me, if you knew what was coming down, you'd be glad to have him on your side. You live out in the burbs now, so you don't know."

Brockton shook his head. "I just can't figure him out. Do you think he and Sienkewicz are connected in any way?"

"What do you mean?"

"I mean since their time in the army."

"All right, maybe this girl isn't as innocent as I thought," Leach replied, "but the guy's still slimy. She was too young."

"That's not what I asked," Brockton replied, confused by his friend's answer but searching for some meaning in it. Leach was usually simple and direct. "Do you remember when I defended that smut shop they wanted to close?"

"Yeah."

"One of the whores there was also involved in the scandal involving the police department."

"So?"

"She told me O'Connell was involved in the convention scandal, even though his name was never mentioned," Brockton lied.

"You gonna believe some whore?"

"I'm just wondering if he has any connection with this girl. He says she's a prostitute and..." Brockton let the sentence hang, but Leach didn't respond. "What's going on? I don't like taking this to court without knowing the full story."

"I told you I don't know nothin'," Leach replied. "I just told the sergeant I'd put him in touch with you."

"A lot of good that did me." Disappointed that his ruse hadn't worked, Brockton finished his coffee silently, then called the waitress over, paid the bill and left.

As soon as he entered his office, Candy waved to him. "Mr. John Sienkewicz is on the line."

"Ring him in," Brockton said, continuing to his office.

"Hello, Mr. Brockton?"

"Mr. Sienkewicz, I need to talk to you."

"Yes. Listen, I want you to defend Larisa."

"Who?"

"Larisa. She's been picked up for cocaine use and I want you to defend her. I'll pay your fee."

"Wait a minute. What are you talking about?"

"I just told you. Larisa's been arrested."

"When did this happen?"

"They picked her up this morning. She's in the city jail."

"Oh." Brockton wondered where Sienkewicz got his information.

"Will you go see her today? I think she needs some comforting and her mother's refusing to visit her."

"I can't take that case. It's a conflict of interest."

"Then I'll have to hire someone else. I want to get her out as soon as possible. Can you recommend anyone good? I need to see her as soon as possible."

Brockton detected a note of panic in his client's voice. "You can't see her. Where they have her you can't go. Listen, I need to talk to you about your situation."

"Can you recommend someone to represent Larisa?"

Brockton looked quickly at his appointment book, then his watch. The guy was more disturbed about this girl than about himself. "I'll do what I can. Can you get down here now? I've got a court appointment at ten."

"I'll be there in fifteen minutes."

Once Sienkewicz had hung up, Brockton swiveled in his chair to face the window. He had to try to get something out of his client. At this point in a case, he had usually unraveled most of the real motivations behind the players' actions, but with so much conflicting information he wasn't sure what was going on. It was frustrating, as if he was at the beginning of the case. He had been on it for almost a week.

He thought about the relationship between O'Connell and Sienkewicz again. It was obviously deeper than either would admit, but in what sense? Why had the police busted the girl? Was it coincidental? One thing he did know, there would be a lot more tension between the DA's office and the police because of it. He was tempted to ask Leach about this latest news, but after this morning's conversation, he didn't think his friend would help him much.

And where the hell was Sienkewicz getting money to hire a lawyer for someone who had gotten him thrown in jail? Teachers didn't earn much, as far as he knew.

When Sienkeiwicz entered Brockton's office, his eyes were shining like the first time they had met. Brockton felt uneasy.

"Do you know how it feels to go through life just waiting for something meaningful to happen?" his client began. "That's how I've felt for a long time now. It's as if I haven't accomplished anything of consequence. Henry David Thoreau said the mass of men live their lives in quiet desperation. Do you know that feeling?"

"We need to talk about you."

"Me? For the first time in years I feel like I'm alive! I'm doing something I've been yearning to do, taking a stand! I can help Larisa and at the same time make a statement to the entire city!"

Brockton shook his head, shocked by how far removed Sienkewicz was from reality, and further confused by his attitude. He was glad this guy was out of the classroom. For a moment he let himself consider what would happen if he let his client loose on the witness stand. He would love to see how the court dealt with him. What a scene that would make.

"Don't you realize how hypocritical this drug bust is! I mean, if they really cared about her, would they be harassing the girl? This is just the case for me to do something! They are the real criminals, the people who make and enforce these laws!"

"It may be those same laws that get you off the hook," Brockton replied. "Now you can continue to live in your make believe world, but I've got reality to deal with."

"I would just like the chance to stand up in front of a jury and explain to them what really happened."

"That's not going to happen. In fact, from the way it looks we may get this case thrown out of court before you get near the witness stand. Yesterday I talked with Sergeant O'Connell. What else do you know about him?"

"I told you I don't know him. He was involved in an investigation the army did on me, but I only met him once or twice."

"What about the fact that right after he finished the police report, you showed up at the hospital?"

Sienkewicz shrugged. "I never said anything to him. He didn't even recognize me."

"Even when he cuffed you?"

"No."

Brockton decided to approach this from another angle, hoping to reveal something. "He's an admirer of yours."

"He's the kind of cop who admires anyone who's white."

"So you do know him."

"I know that much about him. What does it matter?"

"Because the police report he wrote is an essential part of the case against you. And there are irregularities in it."

"I know there are irregularities."

"You may know that, but it's surprising for a cop to admit it."

"The truth? Why is it so hard for everyone to admit the truth? You know, that's the issue here. Everybody is lying. No one can tell the truth."

"Let's not start on the moral issues again. You aren't going to win that way. This is a court of law." Sienkewicz didn't reply, as if satisfied that he had made his point. "But while you're talking about the truth," Brockton continued, "maybe you should tell me the truth about you and O'Connell. He's helping me more than you are and he's one of the DA's witnesses."

"What do you want to know?"

"Everything."

"Have you decided who you can recommend to defend Larisa?"

Brockton said nothing at first, taken off guard by the change in the conversation. "What about you," he finally said sarcastically. "Why don't you defend her. You'd do just fine now that you know so much about the law."

"I didn't mean to give you that impression," Sienkewicz replied. "I'm sorry if I've offended you."

"I told you I'd think about it," Brockton said. "I'll call you when I get back from court this afternoon. For now, you need to dig a little deeper into your memory and tell me what you know about this cop who's willing to rescue you."

"Good because I'm willing to pay whatever they ask."

Brockton shook his head at his client's continued non-responses, then dismissed him with a wave. He wasn't going to get anywhere.

Once Sienkewicz had left, Brockton put away his folder. He really wasn't looking forward to being with him in court.

This was going to make a great story at O'Malley's tonight. It was his night to meet Bart and the boys for a drink. When they heard this, their eyes would pop. He'd tell Bart about the girl getting busted, too. Maybe his friend would take the job. It was no conflict of interest and he could keep tabs on what was going on with her.

10

O'Malley's had a dimly lit interior. Recently redesigned to imitate an Irish pub, its newness lent the bar a church-like opulence. A polished wooden bar began at the right side of the room and extended around the corner and back to the wall, a horseshoe shape that allowed for more bar seating. The walls were decorated with antique lamps and ornaments. A large clock hung over the bar. Glasses hung upside down above the bartender. U2 was playing on the juke box.

O'Malley's was a favorite drinking spot for city lawyers and Brockton saw several of them gathered at the far end of the bar. Bart McCormick was there, as much a fixture as the lamps and ornaments. Several younger lawyers stood around him, their attention wavering between him and a television hanging in a corner, near the ceiling.

"Hey, it's the Rooster!" McCormick yelled as soon as he saw Brockton. He waved as Brockton made his way toward his friend. "It's the Red House Rooster!" McCormick continued loudly. "He is bad! He is the Rooster!"

Brockton did his patented strut, snapping his head and neck forward while holding his shoulders immobile. Bart had nicknamed him the Red House Rooster after he had won the smut house case.

"You ever see a rooster do it?" Bart continued. "He picks out his hen, races over and hops on. Holding her loving head to the ground, the rooster gives her the quick one-two. Then he's off to another. This man in front of you, gentlemen, is a courtroom Rooster."

Brockton repeated his strut, exaggerating it until everyone was laughing. He reached the group of lawyers, who all gathered around him, jostling each other to shake his hand.

"Yes, he is the Rooster!" McCormick yelled loudly again. "He defended the hen house and the owner was so grateful he gave him free run of the hens. Don't think he wasn't there every night taking care of business. Show us the card, Rooster!"

Brockton pulled a red, partially frayed card out of his wallet. After he'd won the smut house case, McCormick and his friends had fabricated a free admission card, signed by the owner, Howard Gutenberg. He'd even gotten Gutenberg to put an official Bavarian seal on it.

"The Red House Rooster could please ten hens an evening in his prime!" McCormick yelled. "How did you ever juggle so many, Rooster?"

"Say good-bye before they fall in love," Brockton replied.

"Oh yeah! Let me borrow the card," Bart said.

"What's the matter? Married life isn't good?"

"Agony. Cheryl and I have reached the penny arcade stage. She only gives it up when I make a payment, like a slot machine. You want me to take off my clothes? Get the lawn mowed. You want sex? Take the screens out and put the winter windows in. You got to feed the machine to make it work." Several people laughed and McCormick continued. "I swear it's that bad. Listen well all you single males, enjoy it while you can!"

Brockton shook his head. "This is from the same man who married an insatiable woman."

"Insatiable! I couldn't keep up, had to pretend I was asleep. And look at me now."

"Then it was your fault," Brockton said. "You went to sleep and she found another."

"Not true, Rooster. It's a biological difference. Women want to breed. And once we marry and agree to participate in the breeding, we become products of whim. We dream about what once was."

"Jesus, Bart, that was almost philosophical," Brockton said.

McCormick shrugged and motioned Brockton away from the group. "What are you drinking?"

Brockton order a pint of draught beer. "Where are the DA boys?"

"Preparing cases. They've got reputations to destroy."

"Like mine?"

McCormick laughed and nodded. He had a good rapport with the DA's office, which helped keep the defense lawyers apprised, if not exactly in the loop.

"Why did they choose Ritter for this case?" Brockton asked.

McCormick shrugged. "He's learned a lot."

"I'm not gonna let him beat me and they must know that. He's still peach fuzz."

"What's your angle on the case?"

"I wanted to push for postponement," Brockton said. "The papers heated it up too much."

"The papers?"

Brockton nodded. "And they've got some evidence, apparently."

"Wonder what they know," said Bart.

"They're going with Class E felony. And assault. They're crazy to take this one to trial, especially in front of Holmes."

"I'm not acquainted with the details."

"Three to five isn't happening. Unless they've got something else up their sleeve."

"Maybe they'll go for a plea," McCormick said.

"I tried already. Ritter refused, insisted on a bench trial," Brockton said. "He's doomed, but let's talk about something more exciting, the plans for your victory party." Bart had won a seat on the city council in the same election that saw a new DA take over. And used some of the same law and order jargon.

"Everything all set?"

"I got it covered."

"Hey, thanks for handling that last fund raiser," McCormick said. "It put us over the top and into the win column."

Brockton nodded. "What about invites to the victory party? You gonna keep postponing that, like a trial lawyer?"

McCormick laughed. "No, just trying to get loose ends tied up. Trying to figure out who to invite and who not to invite."

"Not a problem," Brockton said. "Just make sure I get my choice of tickets to the basketball games. Stephanie's in love with the new center."

"Done."

Brockton lifted his glass. "What kind of beer is this?"

"What kind did you ask for?"

"I don't know but it's making me want to piss." He set the glass on the polished wood bar and headed for the Men's room.

McCormick followed. "What's up?" he asked, once they were along at the urinals.

"The guy I'm defending wants to pay for his accuser's defense against a crack charge."

"What's her name?"

"Larisa something."

"This just happen?"

"Last night, I think. You want the job?"

"Of course," McCormick said. "And thanks."

"No problem, glad to help."

"So your witness is a coke freak, too? Shit, what are they thinking?"

"That's what I'm trying to tell you. Ritter is doomed."

"And no postponement?"

"No, he said he'll be ready and Holmes put it on the schedule. She warned us that there better be no delays."

McCormick whistled. "Shit, she might have just as well told you you'd won."

"I think it's a slam dunk. But something's bothering me, not sure why. It just seems odd the way things all went down."

"Shit, this is worse than I imagined. They'll take a load of shit from the papers about being disorganized again."

Brockton finished pissing and made for the sink. "New DA needs to make some changes over there."

"I told him that," McCormick said, "but White don't listen. He's a stubborn mother fucker."

"Stupid, not stubborn." Brockton shook his head. "He sealed stupid when he chose Ritter to prosecute this case. He's got a bug up his ass about me and I think it's about to grow bigger."

"Damn," McCormick said.

"My client is no fun, either. He's crazy about the girl and wants to get her up on the witness stand."

"What a shit show that would be," McCormick said.

The two left the Men's room together, rejoining the group at the bar.

11

"The people call Sergeant O'Connell to the stand," Milton Ritter said, once the courtroom preliminaries were over and everyone was seated. As the sergeant strode to the stand, Brockton closed his eyes and squeezed the bridge of his nose. He had drunk too much last night and his head ached. Why did they have to start this trial on a Friday, going against all the rules of logic?

The assistant DA started with a long series of questions establishing O'Connell's involvement in the case, but Brockton only half listened. Ritter was saving him from having to do that boring but necessary task.

"Sergeant O'Connell, when did you first meet the defendant, Mr. John Sienkewicz?" Ritter's question caught Brockton's ear because it was unexpected.

"About seven years ago," O'Connell replied.

"Is he present in the courtroom today?"

"Yes."

"Could you please point out Mr. John Sienkewicz?" O'Connell pointed to Sienkewicz sitting at the table next to Brockton. "Thank you," Ritter continued. "Can you tell me where you met Mr. Sienkewicz?"

"In the United Sates Army," O'Connell replied.

Brockton shifted in his seat. Where was Ritter headed, the little mole?

"Would you briefly explain the circumstances under which you met Mr. Sienkewicz?" the assistant DA continued.

"Objection!" Brockton said, half rising. "Your honor, this is immaterial to the case Mr. Ritter is attempting to create."

"Your honor," Ritter replied, "it is relevant—indeed essential—to the people's case to show that Sergeant O'Connell had previously known the defendant. It will become clear why, if I am allowed, to delve briefly into his background."

"Very well, but proceed quickly," Holmes said. She turned toward Brockton. "Overruled."

"I was investigating an incident he was involved in," O'Connell said, without waiting for the question to be repeated. Wouldn't Holmes be surprised to hear the real O'Connell, Brockton thought, instead of the polite, rational man he had become on the stand. The courtroom certainly changed some people.

"In what capacity was Mr. Sienkewicz serving when you met him in the U.S. Army?" Ritter asked.

"He was a United States soldier and a language teacher at Palmerola Air Base, in Honduras, Central America," O'Connell replied with the same measured care that Brockton and he had practiced.

"What did he teach?"

"He taught our soldiers how to speak Spanish."

Brockton was about to object, but Holmes interrupted. "Mr. Ritter, please get to the point. You promised me this would be brief. And relevant."

"Yes, your honor," the assistant DA said. He turned back to the sergeant. "What was the nature of your investigation of Mr. Sienkewicz?" he asked.

"He was running a prostitution ring," O'Connell replied.

"Objection!" Brockton yelled, quelling an urge to hide under the table. "Your honor, what the hell does this have to do with the charges my client is being accused of?" The curse slipped out and Holmes looked at him in surprise. "I apologize, your honor."

"Your honor, may I finish my line of questioning so that my objective will become clear?" Ritter asked.

"What exactly is your objective, Mr. Ritter?"

"I would like the witness to elaborate on the nature of his activities at Palmerola Air Base."

"For what purpose?"

"To establish the defendant's tendencies toward sexual abuse."

"Your honor," Brockton said, "this whole line of questioning is illegal and impermissible. It should be thrown out."

Judge Homes looked at Brockton with an irritated expression, then swung her gaze back to the assistant DA. "Is that the relevance you promised me, Mr. Ritter?"

"Your honor, it is essential for the people to establish that this is not, as Mr. Brockton has claimed, a man without a past record of convictions, but one who has systematically abused children and should be locked up!"

The vehemence with which Ritter's last statement was said surprised even Holmes and her eyes widened. "Mr. Ritter, you know as well as I do that prior evidence of wrongdoing is impermissible in a court of law. We are not in courtroom kindergarten anymore."

"Is, therefore, evidence of a clean record impermissible also?" Ritter queried, failing to keep the emotion out of his voice. He pointed toward Brockton, then said, "He has managed to enter that into the record."

Brockton sat quietly, amazed at the ridiculousness of the assistant DA's point. He was going to smash the little mole to pieces.

Holmes shook her head. "Mr. Ritter, your point isn't relevant. And please don't even begin to assume that I will decide the merits of this case on anything but the evidence relating to it."

"Yes, your honor," Ritter replied, shuffling the papers in front of him. He was obviously flustered. "I just wanted the sergeant to elaborate on the nature of the operation Mr. Sienkewicz was involved in, as it is a perfect example of his exploitation of minors."

"That much you have established," Holmes responded, "despite its irrelevance." She turned to the court reporter.

"Strike the previous line of questions from the record, starting with Mr. Ritter's inquiry into Sergeant O'Connell about his past relationship with Mr. Sienkewicz." While the reporter did as she was ordered, Holmes turned back to the assistant DA. "Please be advised, Mr. Ritter, that I will be considerably less tolerant of this behavior from now on and keep the remainder of your questions directed toward proving your case."

Ritter didn't say anything, still flustered.

"Do you have any more relevant questions for the witness?" Holmes pressed.

"I do, your honor."

"Then please proceed."

Brockton should have been enjoying this latest exchange because it meant that the assistant DA was still a weak opponent. Instead, he had momentarily panicked, reminded of the hidden connections between his client and O'Connell. He scribbled some notes quickly, his mind turning over the pieces of his client's background that he was aware of. What was the connection between Sienkewicz and O'Connell that neither of them wanted him to know about?

Ritter was still sifting through the papers in front of him, deciding on his next question when a man entered the courtroom from a side door. The man walked up to the judge and whispered in her ear.

"Mr. Ritter, I don't mean to prevent you from having the full time you need with this officer and other witnesses," Holmes said suddenly, "but can you finish quickly or should we recess until after lunch, say one o'clock?"

"I'll need more time."

Holmes looked at Brockton. "A recess would be fine," Brockton said. He wanted more information from his client before he cross examined O'Connell.

"Good," the judge said, picking up the gavel and rapping it against its holder. She disappeared behind the curtain after repeating the time they would resume.

"A prostitution ring!" Brockton snapped once they were in the hallway outside the courtroom. "Why didn't you tell me about that?!"

"I didn't think it was important," Sienkewicz replied calmly.

Brockton pushed his client into a corner. "Don't think!" he said in a lower, meaner tone. "When I ask about your connection with someone, tell me! A fucking whorehouse! Don't you realize how something like this can screw you?!"

"As Judge Holmes said, prior evidence of wrongdoing cannot be used against someone in a court of law," Sienkewicz replied, still calm.

"What the fuck else haven't you told me?" Brockton snapped, ignoring his client's response.

"I sent all my classes to the whorehouses," Sienkewicz said. "It was a better way for them to learn Spanish and I proved it when they called me in to explain. In that short time, my students had learned more Spanish than any other classes."

"Was O'Connell in on that deal? Is that where he comes from?"

"It's interesting that you should mention Mr. O'Connell, a man who was as guilty as any other as far as visiting prostitutes. He was known for that at Palmerola. A true pillar of the community."

"I couldn't give a shit what O'Connell did when he was younger. What about now? What haven't you told me about now?"

"But it's really who gets caught and who doesn't, isn't it?" Sienkewicz replied, as if holding a conversation with himself.

"Listen," Brockton said, "you can be as uncooperative as you want and get your three to five. Or you can tell me the truth and find yourself free. I don't care which any more. I just hope you're not hiding anything about your buddy that's gonna screw you."

Sienkewicz looked at Brockton, his eyes shining. "Give me one more chance, kind people, to live," he said. Brockton looked at his client in disbelief. "Fyodor Dostoyevsky, Notes from Underground," Sienkewicz said. "I need to make a telephone call." He left.

Brockton turned to look out a nearby window. The son of a bitch was playing him again. If there was anything he hated, it was someone playing him.

He looked around for O'Connell, who had agreed to talk to him. The sergeant was sitting on a bench just outside the courtroom.

"He's a son of a bitch, ain't he," O'Connell said, as if he'd just heard their conversation.

"Who?"

"Your buddy there, Senky."

Brockton nodded.

"That's what we all called him around the base. He had a good thing going there and would never have got caught if it wasn't for bad luck."

"What about the report?" Brockton asked, trying not to show the tension he felt. "Are you ready?"

"I got it down," O'Connell replied. "I've been practicing with that dink of a lawyer. How'm I doin' so far?"

Brockton managed a smile. "Okay. No, good, you sounded good."

"Thanks."

"Remember, things may come up in Ritter's questions, so you have to be consistent throughout." Brockton resisted the temptation to call the assistant DA a dink himself.

"Gotcha."

"And we want it to seem on the up and up, so I'm going to come at you hard. That's the only way it'll work."

O'Connell winked. "We got this one wrapped up."

"I'll see you inside." Brockton left the sergeant. At least he was ready to help. He looked around for his client. If his own reputation wasn't on the line, he'd skin Sienkewicz's ass for being such a prick.

12

Judge Holmes looked at the clock in frustration. It read 7:45, as it had for years. "Mr Ritter, please try not to be repetitive," she said. "As I informed you at the break, I'd like to get through this witness's testimony before the weekend."

Brockton silently applauded her. He wished the mole would go more quickly himself, so he could get to O'Connell today and put an end to this. Holmes sudden schedule change, although not unusual, didn't give him much time to get the cop to admit to the bogus report. The rest would be moot. The DA's office could pick up the pieces over the weekend, if they even wanted to continue.

"Yes, your honor, I'm just trying to make a point with the sergeant," Ritter responded.

"I have no problem with you making a point, Mr. Ritter, but you have now asked the sergeant where he first met the alleged victim three times. And he has told you where he met her three times. That is repetitive."

"Yes, your honor." Ritter returned to the police officer. As the assistant DA continued his line of questioning, Brockton wondered if Holmes might take it over herself. He'd heard that she had been known to, on occasion. She was probably refraining because of the reporters, who had returned and were sitting in the courtroom.

"Sergeant O'Connell, when you first met the victim, was she bruised in any way?" Ritter asked.

"Objection," Brockton said, playing the part of a vigilant defense attorney by rote. "He's leading the witness."

"Sustained," Holmes said.

"Sergeant O'Connell, when you first met the victim, did you notice anything unusual about her facial features?"

"Objection. Your honor, he's still leading the witness."

Holmes turned to the sergeant. "Sergeant O'Connell, would you please describe, as best as you can remember, the victim's appearance when you first met her?"

Brockton glanced briefly at the reporters in the back of the courtroom. They were busy scribbling notes. He wondered how they were going to write this one. They'd have to make it especially interesting for weekend reading.

"Yes sir," O'Connell replied. "She was a young black female, approximately fourteen years of age."

"Objection," Brockton said. "Hearsay. He didn't know how old—nor could he surmise—from simply looking at her. She could have been a young eighteen for all he knew."

"Sustained," Holmes said, glancing irritatedly at Brockton. Everyone knew how old she was.

O'Connell also looked at Brockton and smiled coyly. He shrugged.

"Continue, please, Sergeant O'Connell," Ritter said, taking over the questioning.

"She was slightly built, about five and a half feet tall," the sergeant said defiantly.

Brockton let that one go. It was irrelevant.

"Her face and arms were covered with bruises and welts," the sergeant continued.

"Large bruises and welts?"

"Very large bruises and welts," the sergeant replied, being careful to use all the necessary words of violence.

"How large?"

"Several were over an inch in diameter."

"Objection," Brockton said. "Unless Sergeant O'Connell used a tape measure, how could he know how large they were?"

"Overruled," Holmes said. "I think Sergeant O'Connell can accurately determine how large an inch is."

Brockton shook his head and O'Connell smiled. He certainly seemed to be enjoying giving testimony that would be shot down with one simple confession.

"Did you ask her about those large bruises and welts?" Ritter asked.

"Yes, I did."

"What did you ask her about those large bruises and welts?" Ritter continued to use the words of violence, which were really more effective in front of a jury, not a judge.

"I asked her how she got them."

"And how did she respond?"

"She told me she had been beaten."

"By whom had she been beaten?"

"Objection!" Brockton said.

"By whom did she say she had been beaten?" Ritter asked, correcting himself before Holmes could sustain.

"By a man."

"Did she happen to mention the man's name?"

"Yes."

Brockton had a sudden sense of foreboding. What if he asked, in his thoroughness, whether anyone had been with the girl that night? What would O'Connell say? He jumped up. "Your honor, this is all repetitive. It's written in the report, which counsel has accepted into the record."

"Are you objecting, Mr. Brockton?" Holmes asked.

"Yes, objection."

"Overruled." Holmes turned to the assistant DA. "However, Mr. Ritter, what counsel has said is true. Please proceed to the essential part of your questioning. I have read the record."

"Yes, your honor," Ritter replied.

"She said Mr. Sienkewicz," the sergeant said again, not waiting for the question to be repeated.

"Mr. John Sienkewicz?"

"Yes."

"Would you be so kind as to tell me if Mr. John Sienkewicz, the man you earlier testified to having arrested, is in this courtroom?"

"He is."

"Would you point him out to me?"

O'Connell pointed to the defendant, who sat next to Brockton.

"I have no further questions, your honor," Ritter said, with a finishing flourish that almost caused Brockton to laugh. He couldn't wait to demolish this peach fuzz punk.

"Mr. Brockton?" Holmes looked toward the defense attorney. "Would the defense like to cross examine the witness?"

"Yes, your honor." Brockton stood and walked quickly to the pedestal. He'd start on the bruises—something for the press—then go for the throat. He was going to enjoy this.

"Sergeant O'Connell, is it usual for a policeman to question the victim of an assault at the hospital?"

"Yes."

"And that's what you did?"

"Yes."

"Is it usual even if the victim is in serious need of medical attention?"

"We question them only if they are able to talk."

"So these inch long bruises you testified to seeing on the victim were not that serious?"

"Objection," Ritter said. "Sergeant O'Connell is a policeman, not a doctor."

"Sustained," Holmes said.

"So you determined—as a police officer—that she was not so seriously injured that you couldn't talk to her," Brockton said, rephrasing the question.

"She seemed okay with the questions," O'Connell replied.

"So she wasn't seriously injured," Brockton repeated.

"Objection," Ritter said. "Your honor, you have already determined that Sergeant O'Connell cannot make that judgment, given his profession."

"Sustained," Holmes said. "Mr. Brockton, keep your questions in line with the exact extent of the injuries, not generalities such as whether the victim was seriously injured or not."

"Alleged victim, your honor," Brockton replied.

"Alleged victim, Mr. Brockton," Holmes said, bottling up her intolerance.

"Sergeant O'Connell, how many of those marks on the alleged body were an inch in diameter?" Brockton asked, suddenly changing his tack.

The police sergeant shrugged, then looked around him. "Several," he finally said.

"You don't know exactly how many?"

O'Connell shook his head. "Why don't you look at the hospital report."

"And this is the first time you had ever met the alleged victim," Brockton said. Ritter shifted impatiently in his chair. "Are you aware, sir, that the alleged victim has several large birth marks?" Brockton asked.

"Your honor this is ridiculous!" Ritter burst out. "Sergeant O'Connell knows the difference between a birth mark and a bruise!"

Holmes looked at the assistant DA and frowned. "Mr. Ritter, you're out of order. If you'd like to object to something, there is a procedure."

"Sorry, your honor. Objection. Sergeant O'Connell has been a police officer long enough to determine the difference between a birth mark and a bruise. The question is ridiculous."

"Ah, but the sergeant is not a doctor," Brockton shot back.

Holmes shook her head. "Overruled. Sergeant O'Connell, answer the question, as ridiculous as you may find it."

"They were bruises," O'Connell replied. "I also saw several birth marks that were not bruises."

"But they looked like bruises," Brockton pushed. Ritter threw up his hands.

"They were different than bruises," O'Connell countered.

"But you are not a doctor, is that correct?"

"I know the difference between—"

"—Please answer the question, Sergeant," Brockton interrupted.

"No," O'Connell admitted, glaring at Brockton, who shrugged it off. He had warned O'Connell that he wasn't going to be nice. It was time to get this over with. He took his time formulating his next question.

"Sergeant O'Connell, exactly how did you come to be at the hospital emergency room at two o'clock in the morning on the date of..." Brockton looked at the police report in from of him. "...August the fourth of the current year?"

"Objection," Ritter said. "Your honor, this hearing is about whether Mr. Brockton's client committed this criminal act, not about how the police acted."

"Your honor," Brockton replied, "I will attempt to show that my client was unfairly and unjustly set up. If the police acted incorrectly, then the sergeant's report should be thrown out of the record."

"Continue," Holmes said, "but keep relevance in mind, Mr. Brockton. This court is not so lenient that it will extend you free rein in setting up a scene of your fancy."

"Thank you, your honor," Brockton said. He turned to O'Connell. "Shall I repeat the question?"

The policeman said nothing.

"Please do," Holmes said.

"Sergeant O'Connell, exactly how did you come to be at the hospital emergency room at two o'clock in the morning on the date of August the fourth of the current year?"

"I don't recall," O'Connell said.

Brockton smiled. He was playing this up perfectly. "Were you sent there by a dispatch?"

"Objection!" Ritter said. "Your honor, counsel is being repetitive himself. This is all spelled out in the report in front of him."

Brockton looked at the assistant DA in mock surprise. "Perhaps Mr. Ritter would like to defend my client as well as prosecute him," he said sarcastically. "He seems to be doing quite a good job at both." He turned to the judge. "Your honor," he continued, "although it may not yet be clear to the prosecution, I am still attempting to show that this arrest was a set up and in no way legal, beginning from the first call made to the police."

Holmes nodded. "Overruled. Repeat the question, Mr. Brockton."

"Sergeant O'Connell, were you sent to the hospital by a dispatch?" Brockton asked again.

"I don't recall exactly," O'Connell replied.

"Your report indicates that a police dispatcher sent you to the hospital. Is that what actually happened?"

"I don't recall."

"Isn't that what usually happens?" Brockton said, starting to panic. When the fuck was O'Connell going to spill it? They'd agreed that "dispatch" would be the key word! His mind went into high gear.

"Yes," O'Connell replied, after a moment.

"Does it ever happen any other way?" He'd given O'Connell enough leads. Was the policeman pissed off at the way Brockton had questioned him?

"When you see a crime being committed," O'Connell replied.

"Did you see a crime being committed at the hospital?" Brockton asked, improvising.

"I don't recall."

Brockton shook his head. "Are many crimes committed outside hospital emergency rooms?"

"Objection," Ritter said. "How is the Sergeant to know that?"

"Sustained."

"Sergeant O'Connell, have you ever been in a situation where you see a crime committed outside a hospital emergency room?"

"I don't recall," O'Connell replied, still uncooperative.

Brockton looked at the judge and lifted his arms. Maybe the idiot had forgotten what they had worked on. He was going to have to lead him right to it. "Sergeant O'Connell, the police report says that you happened to be in the medical center emergency room on the day of August fourth, at two o'clock in the morning. Weren't you, in fact, off duty at that time?"

"No sir," the sergeant replied. "I started work at midnight. I've been working the graveyard shift for seven straight years."

Brockton stared at O'Connell, shocked. He looked at Judge Holmes, who looked back at him questioningly.

"Are you going to continue, Mr. Brockton?" Holmes finally asked.

"No further questions, your honor," Brockton said, "but I'd like to reserve the right to recall Sergeant O'Connell."

As O'Connell left the witness stand he stared at Brockton, a smirk on his face. Brockton ignored him, realizing the magnitude of what had happened. Why hadn't he checked up on O'Connell's story! The son of a bitch had been lying and he'd believed him! They'd set him up!

13

"He's lying," Sienkewicz said, once the two of them were out of the courtroom. "He was the one who beat her."

"Fine," Brockton said. "Whether he's lying or not, you may spend time in jail because you neglected to tell me about your relationship with the son of a bitch. Not to mention that you made a fool of me."

"I didn't want to get you involved in this," Sienkewicz said.

"Get me involved!" Brockton snapped. "How the fuck was I supposed to defend you without getting involved!"

A court attendant walked by them in the hallway and Brockton turned away from the squeak of his shoes, not wanting to show the emotion he felt.

"Personally, I mean," Sienkewicz explained as the noise of the shoes receded. "This is a personal struggle between him and me. Have you ever read Friedrich Durrenmatt's The Judge and his Hangman?"

"Look, do me a favor and skip the English lessons. This isn't a story. It's real life."

"Ah, but good literature is an imitation of real life," Sienkewicz replied. "Your law books can help you with what goes on in the courtroom, but if you knew more about literature, you could have deciphered the truth more quickly. You would have known—"

"—the truth about what happened at the hospital that night would have helped me more than any literature I could have read," Brockton interrupted.

Sienkewicz looked at Brockton silently for nearly a minute and the lawyer began to feel that now familiar sense of uneasiness. He glanced around. The walls of the court hallways seemed closer than he remembered. "Very well," Sienkewicz finally said. "Larisa told me that he had beaten her up. Later, I spoke to the sergeant and he admitted it."

"He knows the girl?"

"You haven't been listening. I told you before he is the one who beat her. When I spoke to him, he threatened to kill her. He put my name in the report."

"And you said 'Okay officer, I'll take the blame for assaulting this girl.' Sure."

"Not at that point. You see, you know so little. I must tell my story. I must speak to everyone."

"You aren't speaking to anyone until I know what's going on," Brockton snapped. "Either that or find another lawyer." Sienkewicz didn't respond. "When did all this happen?" Brockton asked.

"What?"

"What the hell do you think?" Brockton said, disgusted. He should have trusted his instincts, that there was something more to this one. "That night!"

"He took her to the hospital emergency room. I found out later and approached him. He had this all worked out, you see."

"Why didn't you go to someone for help?"

"I was afraid. He had been seeing her for several weeks by then. He threatened her." Sienkewicz sighed. "You see, I know this man. I had hoped to avoid a confrontation with him. Now I'm afraid that is inevitable. This has gotten much too complicated."

"Why blame you?" Brockton asked. "Why not just say she had gotten in a fight?"

"That is what he wanted. He said he would kill my little Carmen. You don't understand how much I love her."

The tone of Sienkewicz's voice changed and Brockton turned away from him, just let him speak.

"You see, no matter how many cases you have tried, Michael, you don't know what is going on in a man's heart. The despair, the hardship, make you do things you wouldn't normally consider. I have tried to explain this to you but you are concerned with legality and courtroom strategy. Perhaps it cannot be explained. Love doesn't fit into a courtroom. You see an age difference and immediately think of immorality while I was trying to help this girl.

"At first all I wanted to do was give her a chance to experience her childhood. I wanted to get her away from this evil man so she wouldn't wake up ten years later beaten and ragged and wishing for relief that only death would bring. Young people without guidance don't see where they're headed until it's too late. I wanted to help her. Then I fell in love with her. That man is evil I tell you. He..." Sienkewicz stopped talking, his eyes tearing.

While observing the emotional outpouring, Brockton tried to figure out what the real truth was. He remembered O'Connell's explosion when he'd told him Sienkewicz admitted to having an affair with the girl, if affair was even the right word. Had he gotten angry because he had been caught in a lie, or was it jealousy? Maybe Sienkewicz and O'Connell were fighting over this girl in some debased manner.

"She's still in jail, in the clutches of that man," Sienkewicz said. "Why haven't you gotten her out?"

"She's not in jail, she's in The House."

"The House?" Sienkewicz asked.

"The juvenile detention center. She's safe there."

"But I cannot see her! I need to see her!"

"You need to forget her."

"I can't! I love her!" The man started choking up, then sobbing.

Brockton gazed out the courtroom window.

"Have you found a lawyer to represent her?" Sienkewicz asked. "I told you I'd pay you."

"She's got a lawyer."

"What's his name?"

"What's the difference?"

"Is he good?"

"He's good," Brockton lied. McCormick wasn't great, mostly went through the motions but he knew a lot of people.

"Can he get her out of jail?"

"Listen, whether he does or not is immaterial. You have to stay away from her or you'll be facing more charges. Then you'll never see her."

"She wants to see me."

"She's not old enough to want anything. She's a child, you said that yourself."

"You're right," Sienkewicz said, wiping his face with his sleeve. "I'll have to wait until everything has blown over. You see, it will."

Brockton didn't reply at first, just noted Sienkewicz's quick recovery. "Look, I have several things I need to do this afternoon. I haven't figured out how to attack this, but I'll call you once I do and I expect you to be ready to see me. Don't go anywhere far."

Once Sienkewicz left, Brockton headed toward his office. No one was making this easy for him. Christ, his own friend Leach had set him up! Brockton knew Chuckie was going to say that he didn't know anything about this, but he must have known O'Connell's reputation. He should have steered him clear of the son of a bitch. Or at least warned him. A friend would do that much.

If he was going to win he'd have to bring O'Connell back to the stand and hammer him. He'd love to do that, but he'd have to be careful about shattering too many egos downtown. And he wouldn't be able to depend on Sienkewicz for anything. His client was still trying to manipulate him. Sure the man had broken down, but he turned his emotions on and off too easily.

How could he have gotten caught in this! The warning signs had been there! He had ignored them in his haste to beat the DA's office again and gotten burned.

This whole thing stressed him out. He needed to get it out of his mind for a while. There were too many contradictory messages to sort out. He told himself to calm down, get control of his thoughts. He needed to relax.

"Hey Rooster! What are you doing here?" McCormick greeted Brockton from his habitual seat at O'Malley's. It was three in the afternoon and his friend was alone.

"Court let out early," Brockton replied. "Problems with scheduling again."

"Let me guess, Holmes."

Brockton nodded.

"She's always over-scheduling. Very ambitious. But good."

Brockton nodded again.

"Let me get you a drink."

Once McCormick returned and put the bottle of beer in front of Brockton, he asked, "What happened at the trial? Ritter was in here at lunch bragging about what he was going to do to you."

"So you heard."

"Only what Ritter said earlier today."

"The fuckin' back stabber."

"I heard him say he was going to waste you. Finally. A legal haymaker, he said. Not a bad description from a peach fuzz."

"The son of a bitch didn't have anything to do with it. He just sat there and watched."

"What happened?"

Brockton drank half of his beer. "My own fuckin' setup turned on me," he finally said. "I've had it with cops. I should have known better than to trust them. They'd protect their asses if it meant turning in their own mothers."

"What else is new?" McCormick responded.

"Not that I give a shit about this client. He knew I was being set up and didn't say a thing. I ought to let him rot in jail."

"He knew?"

Brockton nodded again, then finished his beer. He signaled for another one. "I don't know who I want to put it to more, my own client, the cop, or Ritter. They're all scum."

"Spoken from one who has arisen from the swamp," McCormick said and Brockton grimaced. "Try to appreciate the irony of the situation," McCormick continued. "I mean, you've stuck it to ... how many lawyers when you were an assistant DA? Now it's coming back at you."

"I stuck it to them fairly. This was a cheap shot. And from a cop who doesn't have the cleanest record in the world."

"What'd he do?"

Brockton looked at his friend. "Can I trust you?"

"Shit, I'm offended," McCormick replied, a pained expression forming on his alcohol-reddened face.

Brockton lowered his voice, anger overriding his sense of caution. "This guy is dirty and I'm gonna stick it to him." Immediately he knew he'd said too much. "To all of them, I mean," he added, then decided to change the subject. "What's this Lolita girl like?"

"Who?"

"Lolita, the girl my client raped."

"You mean Larisa?"

"You must have spoken to her already."

McCormick said nothing. Then smiled. "Of course I did, just busting your balls. Despite having more work than an ox, I did the research and looked over the file. I even went to visit her at The House."

Brockton was surprised. "So what do you think?"

McCormick whistled. "She reminds me of what I've always said about women. You have two kinds, one kind to breed and another to screw. And she's not the breeder. Even at fourteen she's a fox. The first thing to pop into my mind was sexual intercourse. She's—"

"—What's going to happen to the drug charge?" Brockton interrupted.

"Hard to say. From what she says, it was a setup, but she's probably lying."

"What does the police report say?"

"I haven't gotten to see it yet. Too much else going on."

"Can you move it forward?"

"I don't know, maybe. If Bachmann wakes up long enough to schedule a hearing, I could. He gets slower every day. The son of a bitch didn't even get to court till after ten yesterday and I could've sworn I heard him snoring a couple of times. He's got that slit-eyed look so you can't be sure whether he's eyeballin' you or sleeping.

"But get this. I'm asking the kid for the basic information and she doesn't even mention her family name, says she lives with a Mrs. Washington. At first I thought it was just one of those cases where the kid takes on the father's name even though he's nonexistent. But she tells me no, that she lives with this Mrs. Washington and hasn't lived with her biological family in years."

"What about the night she was beaten up? Her mother didn't go to the hospital?"

"No idea, I'm working on the drug charge, remember?"

Brockton thought about what McCormick had told him. "Where does this Mrs. Washington live?"

"South side. Why?"

"I want to visit her. I'm gonna find out what really happened that night."

"I don't know if she'll want to talk to you."

"I want to talk to her," Brockton said emotionally.

"Hey, easy buddy. You're getting too involved with this. Remember rule number one, keep your distance. You don't want to lose perspective."

"I just want to even a score." Brockton drank again. "What's her address?"

"I don't know offhand. I got it in the car."

"Let's go get it."

"Easy, Rooster, let me finish my beer. And we gotta talk about the party."

"I need that address," Brockton pressed.

"Jesus, you're crazy."

"You're right, I can wait," Brockton said, trying harder to hide his anxiousness. He was going to need a break and someone who had seen what happened might help. He drank again. If this woman could shed any light on what had happened and O'Connell was lying, he was dead. If he could get Mrs. Washington to talk.

"Hey, listen to this!" McCormick said. "I been doing my research on my new council position. You know how you can get your sidewalk repaired in front of your house for free?"

Brockton nodded absentmindedly. McCormick still lived in the city, but he was thinking of meeting Mrs. Washington, not city politics.

"It's easy, a lot of people do it," McCormick continued. "You file a complaint in the spring, saying that while plowing, the DPW damaged your sidewalk. You put your common councilor's name on it and when Torrelli sees it, he pushes it through. Torrelli's the guy in charge of sending out work crews. If anyone looks into it you've covered your ass with the complaint form. The city comes out smelling like roses, too, cuz they're responding to their citizens."

Brockton needed to talk to this woman. He had just been beaten badly and to think that O'Connell had planned this burned him. He had a sudden urge to nail the cop to the wall. He wished he was certain enough about what Sienkewicz had told him to go to the press and blow this thing wide open. If anyone deserved it, O'Connell did.

"Where do you live?"

"What?"

"Where do you live? I'll tell you who your councilor is."

"I live in the burbs now, remember? You helped me move."

"Right, you don't live in the city. What am I telling you all this for? I can't help you with your sidewalk."

"Listen, can I get that address?" Brockton asked.

"Which?"

"The woman."

"Christ, when the Rooster wants something, he wants it now. You're really gonna hook your claws into this and rough someone up."

"Damn right."

"I'll go get the address if you promise to have another couple beers with me and talk about the party."

"Sure."

Brockton followed McCormick to the car and got the name and address he wanted. After thanking him, he headed for his car.

"Hey, where you going?" McCormick yelled. "You promised to have another beer with me!"

"I'll call you." Brockton got in his car. "I gotta get home to Stephanie."

14

Brockton pulled onto Delacorte Street and parked. Delacorte was one of the blackest sections of the city. Most lawyers made clients who lived here come to their offices downtown because it was such a high risk area for cars being broken into, especially luxury cars. Although he drove through often, using certain streets as short cuts through the city, Brockton had never parked the Beamer down here. He had no choice today since that was the car he was driving.

He put the plastic radio front onto his tape player, then changed his mind and returned it to the glove compartment. Better to take the entire player out. Looking around him, he decided to take his tie and jacket off, too, so he would look less a target. Suits and ties weren't worn here unless you were black and a follower of the Nation of Islam. Or it was Sunday.

The sun was out and a group of black youths were hanging out up the street from where he'd parked. He loosened his tie, slipped it over his head and put it in the pocket of his suit jacket. Covering the stereo cassette player inside a towel, he got out of the car carrying the bundle and his jacket to the trunk. No sense tempting anyone by leaving something valuable within sight. He opened the trunk and lay his jacket across several cases of beer and soda he'd bought for McCormick's celebration. The beer reminded him of the story Bart had told when they had broken into his car down here. The thieves snapped open the trunk, stole two cases of beer and left four three hundred dollar suits untouched.

The house was several doors up from where he parked and while he walked toward it, Brockton was unusually aware of the slap his shoes made against the sidewalk. He tried to keep his pace even and his manner calm, but he could feel the sweat begin to trickle under his arm pits. Why the hell should he feel uneasy! He'd probably played basketball with some of these guys. They were okay. But they would sense his uneasiness.

A police car drove by, its blue and white colors standing out more starkly than usual. Brockton suddenly felt secure. He rechecked the address in his hand, then spotted the same numbers on a large blue two family house to his right. Popping another mint into his mouth to hide the smell of alcohol, he walked casually up the driveway.

A young girl answered the door and Brockton introduced himself. "Mommy, it some white man!" the girl yelled into the interior of the house.

"Tell him to come in!" a woman's voice yelled back.

Brockton followed the girl through the kitchen and into a living room. A small framed woman sat in an easy chair, holding a baby in her arms. The room was dimly lit, but Brockton immediately noticed several children playing in the room. Two men were sitting on a sofa to his left.

"Mrs. Washington?" he said, trying to hide his uneasiness behind a smile. She nodded and he introduced himself, then reached to shake her hand, stepping carefully to avoid the children sitting on the floor. The woman shifted the baby to her left arm and shook his hand. He looked around again, nodding at the men. They nodded in return. Instinctively, he backed up against a wall.

"Can we talk?" he asked.

"Sure," she replied and nodded at the men. One took the baby from her arms and the two left the room.

Brockton nodded at the men again, the fear that they might break into his car flitting through his mind. He moved through the children and sat on the sofa. He put his briefcase on his knees, snapped it open and took out a writing pad.

"Mr. McCormick said I could get in touch with you," he said. "He said you know Larisa."

Mrs. Washington nodded. One of the children on the floor, a girl, crawled to Brockton and grabbed hold of his pant leg. She pulled herself up using her grasp on his leg. Brockton smiled. "You have quite a group here."

"I run a day care," Mrs. Washington replied.

"Must be quite a job trying to keep up with them all," he said, visions of lawsuits flashing through his mind. "Do you have any help?"

"My son and daughter help. 'Toya, come here." The little girl that was holding Brockton's leg turned and let herself drop to the floor. He reached for her, wanting to avoid an accident, but she crawled away.

"Well," he said, "I'm here because Mr. McCormick told me you were at the hospital the night Larisa was assaulted. My client is Mr. Sienkewicz and I'm having trouble finding out what happened that night."

"He okay," Mrs. Washington replied. "He treat Larisa okay, buy her things."

"Was he there that night?"

"I didn't see him. I only seen police."

"How many policemen did you see?"

"Just one."

"Did you recognize him?" Mrs. Washington shook her head and Brockton continued. "Could you identify him if you saw him again?"

"I could."

"Did you see him do anything to Larisa?"

"What you mean?"

"Did you see him hit her?"

She shrugged. "Coulda' been that he beat her. I don' know that."

"You didn't see the officer hit Larisa then," Brockton said, noting her response without changing his expression.

Mrs. Washington shook her head.

"Did he see you?"

"Can't say. He was concentratin' on one thing, that was Larisa."

"What was he saying to her?"

"I didn' catch none a' that. He kept her apart."

"Would you be willing to get on a witness stand to testify that you were there with Larisa?"

"What good would that do?"

"It's not mentioned in the police report. I'm hoping to show that there are too many discrepancies in the report. That means they left out a lot."

"I know what that mean," Mrs. Washington replied. Then, overlooking Brockton's slight, she said, "Look Mr...."

"...Brockton."

"Mr. Brockton, I got no reason to go down to the courtroom. I could tell you the whole story, that this man been botherin' Larisa for a while an' that he and Mr. Sienkewicz been fightin' over her, but it ain't gonna do no good. An' I don't want no trouble. Not to mention I got these kids to take care of."

"Do you want Larisa freed?"

"My talkin' ain't gonna get her freed. Lord, that girl ain't touched cocaine in her life and look what they done to her. She in jail for it. You think she gonna have any luck fightin' that?"

"Have you had a chance to talk with her?"

"She in the detention home and they don't let no one but relatives visit her there. Her lawyer say she gonna be out soon and I figure she gonna come back here, where there always a place to lay her head."

"Was she living here before?"

"On and off. The girl gettin' herself into some trouble. She in a rehab program for drinkin', that's where she met this Mr. Sienkewicz. Larisa not disrespectful, mind you, but she can be a hard-headed girl. She jes' gonna have to learn the hard way."

Brockton weighed the reaction he was going to get, then decided to take the risk. "I could subpoena you to testify on my client's behalf. I wouldn't ask you to talk about the beating, of course, just the fact that you were at the hospital with Larisa.

"You see, I think they're trying to blame Mr. Sienkewicz for something he didn't do. I believe he's innocent and if we can prove that the police report doesn't mention that you were there, we can get this case thrown out of court."

"Mr. Sienkewicz said you might come by and ask me to testify," Mrs. Washington replied. surprising Brockton.

"He came here?"

"He come by now and then. Not no more now that Larisa gone."

Brockton talked with Mrs. Washington several more minutes, then excused himself. O'Connell was involved in this. He felt great. Mrs. Washington might not want to testify right now, but he could change her mind. Or find someone else who knew about this. O'Connell would be dead meat after he finished with him.

Pulling into the street in the Beamer, he passed the group of men on the corner. He had been so engrossed in thought, he had forgotten to check out his car for damage. He'd have to remember to look as soon as he got to a safer place.

Brockton sped west, toward Summit Ave. The street led to one of the nicer areas in the city, where the most expensive homes were. The light at West Belvin stopped him. There was one car in front of him. Brockton saw the green change to yellow for the intersecting street and slipped into the inside lane, then jumped ahead as the light turned green. He was good at getting a jump at traffic lights, had just about everyone in the city timed.

He accelerated through the intersection and veered left without using his blinker, scurrying onto Summit. He liked that turn. It always gave him a thrill, as if he was scooting into a safety zone, across the border where rich and poor were separated.

He gunned the Beamer and once he had gained enough speed, shifted to third. The left wasn't too sharp for him to gain speed and he gunned the motor again. He wasn't going to make it to fourth gear this time. On a good day he could get to fourth on this curve, before he reached the hill, but he had to be concentrating. He had to build up more speed before he took the turn.

Brockton took a sharp right at the top of Summit and sped along the north side of the park. It was the nicest park in the city, with a huge pond, a swimming pool and basketball and tennis courts.

As he sped along, Brockton spotted several Blacks sitting in a car on the side of the street and wondered what they were doing there. They didn't live around here and he wondered if he should double back to check up on them. He was on his own turf now, an area of the city that had succeeded in staying wealthy and neat by keeping poor families out. They had even managed to get the basketball courts built lower than the main section of the park, closer to the Black section. Years before, the courts had been located close to the upper section of the park, but they had been replaced by the tennis courts. Residents in the upper area had requested that they be moved to cut down the noise, but it wasn't coincidental that the Blacks were now farther away and at a strategic disadvantage. It was a good move from the standpoint of property values.

Reaching the west entrance to the park, he pulled into it. He drove about a quarter mile into the circle and pulled over. Opening the trunk, he grabbed his gym bag and pulled out his jogging gear. Changing quickly, he slipped the car key into the small pocket on his sneaker and closed the Velcro flap. He put his feet, one at a time, on the bumper and stretched. Today wouldn't be such a loss after all. He would get in his jog and keep his record going. He'd get to run some things through his head while jogging. He got a lot of things sorted out each time he ran and he needed to digest all this new information.

15

"The People would like to call Ms. Joan Winston," Ritter said.

While Ms. Winston was sworn in, Brockton looked her over. He'd heard about her from Sidney Greene, a fellow attorney. She was a stereotypical social worker, not bad looking, but up and down on her weight gain and loss. Many of the social workers were like that according to Sid, from pushing paper. But more to the point she was a lesbian, Sidney said, something unusual. Sidney said she just couldn't keep a man interested in her for long. And she worked too hard, got too involved personally with her clients.

Sid knew about the social worker because she testified in a case he'd worked on. His friend had a lot more to say about her and much of it would help Brockton out. He looked down at the notes he'd jotted down.

"Mrs. Winston," Ritter began, "are you currently employed?"

"Yes."

"Where are you employed?"

"At the County Department of Social Services."

"What is your job there?"

"I am a foster care worker."

"Would you briefly describe the duties of that job?"

"I work with children who have been removed from their homes due to the negligence or abuse of their parents. I also work with the parents."

"Do you know Larisa Moran?"

"I do."

"How do you happen to know Larisa Moran?"

"She was referred to the Department when I was working in a placement unit there."

"How long ago was that?"

"About three years."

"Why was she referred, Ms. Winston?"

"There was an allegation of sexual abuse. It was found to be of enough substance to remove her from the home. I was involved in that procedure."

"Ms. Winston, how long did you work with Larisa Moran?"

"About two and half years, officially."

"Why do you say officially?"

"Because I have maintained our relationship since I first met her."

"And how would you characterize that relationship?"

"I would characterize it as going beyond a mere case worker. Larisa and I have become good friends."

"Why is that, Ms. Winston?"

"Larisa often calls me for help when she is having problems at school or home. I help her out. I also take her places."

"Ms. Winston, aside from the initial allegations, did Larisa ever talk to you about problems she might have had with someone approaching her for sex?"

"Yes, we talked about that."

"Do you remember any of these conversations enough to relate them to this court?"

"I remember several of them quite well."

"When and under what circumstances did these conversations occur?"

"The first time she revealed to me that she was engaging in sexual activity was on May fifteenth," the social worker said. "I remember the exact date because that was when I left my previous job to become a foster care worker. I was taking Larisa out to lunch to celebrate."

"Please continue."

"We were driving past the Planned Parenthood offices in my car and Larisa pointed to the building and told me she had just gone there the day before. I asked her who she had gone with and she said with her teacher."

"Did she tell you why her teacher had taken her there?"

"Objection," Brockton said. "Miss Winston never said that her teacher had taken her there. She said that they had gone there."

"Sustained."

"Did she say why they had gone there, Ms. Winston?"

"She said that he had taken her—excuse me, that they had gone there—so she could get on the pill."

"You mean the birth control pill?"

"Yes."

"Your honor, I—the people—would like to refer to Exhibit number three, a copy of the appointment slip from Planned Parenthood on the day in question."

"Ms. Winston," Ritter continued, "did Larisa Moran tell you why she decided to go on the pill?"

"Yes. She told me she was having sex with someone and that she didn't want to get pregnant."

"Did she tell you who she was having sex with?"

"No."

"Did she tell you anything that might have revealed who this someone was?"

"I asked her who she was having sex with and she said she couldn't tell me his name, that it was a secret. She did admit that the man was older than her. She said a lot older, as I recall. She later told me that her teacher recommended that she go on the pill."

"Ms. Winston, do you know Mr. John Sienkewicz?"

"Yes."

"How long have you known him?"

"Several months."

"Where did you meet him?"

"I met him outside Millwood Treatment Center."

"The treatment center that Larisa Moran was in earlier this year?"

"Yes. She was in there at the time."

"Would you describe that meeting as best as you can re-call?"

"Mr. Sienkewicz introduced himself to me there. I had already talked to him a couple of times over the phone, of course, so I did recognize him by his voice."

"Do you recollect what he wanted?"

"Yes, he said he wanted to talk about Larisa. In occa-sional phone conversations, he had kept me updated on how she was doing at the Center. When I met him, however, he immediately started saying that she needed to get out of the Center, that it was bad for her and would drive her crazy. He seemed to know an awful lot about her for only being her teacher."

"Objection, your Honor. Conjecture."

"Sustained."

"Ms. Winston, approximately when did this meeting oc-cur?"

"It was some time in April."

"Would you have any trouble identifying Mr. John Sien-kewicz?"

"Not at all."

"Is he in this courtroom?"

"Yes, he is."

"Would you please point him out for the court."

Joan Winston pointed at Brockton's client. Brockton glanced quickly at Sienkewicz, who sat expressionless.

"Let the court note that the defendant, Mr. John Sien-kewicz, is occupying the seat at which Ms. Joan Winston is pointing."

"So noted," Holmes said.

Brockton stood up. "Let the court also note that my client is the only blonde-haired, blue-eyed person in this courtroom."

Holmes looked at Brockton in disbelief. He had used that line with Hispanics he'd defended, when there were only Hispanics in the courtroom, but he'd never used it in reverse, with a white person. "So noted, Mr. Brockton," the judge finally said, trying to keep the cynicism out of her voice.

"Ms. Winston, do you feel capable of identifying one blonde-haired, blue-eyed male from another?" Ritter retorted.

"Yes, I do."

Ritter looked at Brockton, a half smile on his face. He continued. "Ms. Winston, do you remember where you were on the night of August the fourth, at two o'clock in the morning?"

"Yes, I was at home."

"And did anything unusual happen that night?"

"I received a call from Larisa that night and she was crying."

"Objection," Brockton said. "How could Miss Winston know Larisa was crying if she was talking to her over the telephone?"

"Your honor, Ms. Winston has testified that she knew Larisa Moran well. I should think she could tell if she was crying," Ritter said.

"Your honor, Miss Winston's and the court's definition of knowing her well may differ greatly. The defense hasn't yet established that definition."

"Sustained," Holmes said, giving this one to Brockton.

"What kind of state was she in when she called you?" Ritter asked.

"She was upset," Ms. Winston replied.

"Objection, your honor. That's still conjecture." Winston looked at him questioningly but Brockton kept his facial expression emotionless.

"Rephrase the question, Mr. Ritter," the judge said.

"Ms. Winston, why did Larisa Moran call you that evening?" Ritter asked.

"She said she had been raped and beaten. She was crying."

Brockton let her get away with the small victory. He was more interested in getting her worked up.

"Did she say who had raped and beaten her?"

"She said, 'That older man'."

"Meaning Mr. Sienkewicz."

"Objection. Leading the witness."

"Sustained."

"Did she mention a name, Ms. Winston?"

"No, but I knew she meant Mr. Sienkewicz."

"How did you know that?"

"First, it was the only older man I had spoken with her about at that time. Second, since Mr. Sienkewicz's name was hard to pronounce, when she talked about him she often called him 'that older man'."

As Ritter continued, Brockton added some notes to his brief outline of how he was going to cross examine the social worker. She had said a few things he wanted to touch on, but there were other, serious skeletons in her closet that he planned to rattle.

Sienkewicz hadn't had a lot to say about this woman, he could only guess why, but he had provided Brockton with the information needed to destroy her testimony. Brockton wondered why Ritter had put her on the stand. She was too soft, a perfect target. He would shake her up until she didn't know which end was which.

"Mr. Brockton, your cross examination," Holmes said after Ritter had finished questioning Winston.

"Miss Winston, you seemed confused about several things," Brockton began. ""Let me see if I can clarify them in my own mind, at least. You said that sometime in April you met Mr. Sienkewicz outside Millwood Treatment Center."

"Yes."

"Do you remember if it was the earlier half or the latter half of April?"

"I believe—yes it was the latter half."

"Was that the first time you had seen Larisa Moran since she had been admitted to the treatment center?"

"Yes, I believe it was."

"Did you know that she had been in the treatment center for over a month?"

"Yes."

"Yet being a good friend, as you phrased it, this was the first time you went to see her." Winston didn't reply. "When was the last time you had seen Larisa Moran before that, do you remember?" Brockton continued.

"I honestly don't recall."

"Try."

"Objection," Ritter said. "Your honor, she said she couldn't recall."

"Sustained."

"It had to be at least a month, though, since she'd been in the treatment center that long, am I correct?" Brockton pressed.

"That was why I hadn't seen her," Winston replied. "She was no longer living at home and it took me a while to find her."

"Despite being a good friend of hers, you didn't know she'd been placed in a treatment center. Did you know she had a drug dependency?"

"No."

"I'm sorry to bring up this inconsistency, Miss Winston. I just needed to clarify it in my own head. Were you or weren't you her good friend?"

"Yes, I was—I am!"

"Not enough of a good friend for you to know she had a drug dependency and had been placed in treatment, but enough to know that on the night of August the fourth, at two o'clock in the morning when most of us are groggy, that she called you and was crying."

"I tried to testify that she was crying," the social worker replied.

"Miss Winston, Larisa Moran told you she had been raped and beaten the previous evening, correct?"

"Yes."

"But she never said—that morning—who had raped and beaten her."

"She did."

"You testified that she told you an older man did it. Isn't that correct?"

"Yes, but—"

"—So she never told you she was assaulted and raped by my client, just some older man."

"Naturally I—"

"—She didn't even say her teacher. She said, I quote, 'that older man'."

"I put two and two together. As I said, she told me that it was 'that older man' and the only older man we had spoken about was Mr. John Sienkewicz. She called him that."

"Miss Winston, if this friendship of yours was so strong, then how is it the only older man you ever talked to her about was my client? Didn't you ever tell her about any other older men, perhaps a boyfriend of yours or someone like that?" Brockton watched for a reaction to this subtle dig at her sexual preference.

After a momentary silence, Winston said, "Perhaps I misspoke when I said it was the only older man we had talked about. What I meant was that we had talked about her teacher several times. And as I said, she often referred to him as 'that older man' because she couldn't pronounce his name."

"Why didn't she say Mr. S, or her teacher?"

"I really don't know why."

"Did she ever call my client Mr. S, or mention him as her teacher?"

"Sometimes."

"But when she called you that evening, she didn't say her teacher had raped her. She said some older man."

"She said 'that older man'."

After a silence, Brockton continued. "Miss Winston, did you ever approach my client with any of the suspicions you have testified about today?"

"No."

"Did you ever file a report on him?"

"No."

"Why not?"

"Why not what?"

"Why didn't you file a report on him?"

"Because I didn't suspect him until after Larisa had been assaulted. By then the police were involved."

"You see that's what confuses me most of all. What you're saying now is that when Larisa first mentioned she was having sex with an older man, and mentioned that Mr. Sienkewicz had taken her to the Planned Parenthood offices, you didn't suspect him of sexual abuse. You never filed a report either, which the law requires you to do if you suspect abuse of any kind. Why, Miss Winston, did you just spend all this time testifying about these suspicions toward my client when at the time the events occurred, your suspicions never existed?"

"They certainly did exist. I just wasn't rash enough to pin them on anyone without hearing it from Larisa herself. She refused to talk about it at the time."

"But those suspicions weren't strong enough to cause you to do anything about them until now, were they?"

"No, but that's easy to say given the privilege of hindsight. In actuality, the reason I didn't report what Larisa told me was that I assumed she had a boyfriend."

"But you testified that she admitted the man was, I quote, 'a lot older than' than her. Did you feel that it was okay for her to have sex with a boyfriend, possibly a twenty-five year old, but that if it had been Mr. Sienkewicz that wouldn't be okay?"

"It wouldn't be okay in either case."

"But you did nothing about it, which is the point. Even after she told you she had gone to a clinic to get birth control to have sex with a man who was a lot older than her."

"When she told me the man was a lot older, I did not immediately think it illegal. I thought more in terms of her safety, which she assured me was not an issue."

"Miss Winston, sex between a male over twenty-one and a fourteen year old is illegal no matter if the male is a boyfriend or not."

"Perhaps you should speak to those persons who permit girls under seventeen years of age to obtain birth control, Mr. Brockton. Myself, given the realities, would rather have seen her sexually active and not pregnant that sexually active and pregnant."

"As long as it wasn't Mr. Sienkewicz."

"Your honor, what's the point?" Ritter asked.

Holmes looked at Brockton, who shook his head and returned to the defense table momentarily. Before continuing, he turned so he was facing Judge Holmes as much as the witness. "Do you know what hearsay is, Miss Winston?"

"Objection!" Ritter jumped to his feet.

Holmes looked at Brockton. "Your honor," he said, "I just want to clarify a technical definition as it is extremely relevant to what I intend to point out. And I want to make sure the witness understands this."

"Continue," Holmes said, a look of suspicion on her face.

"Hearsay," Brockton repeated. "Do you know the technical definition?"

"I have an idea," Winston replied.

"Because hearsay is what you have done throughout your testimony. Larisa told you this, she told you that. Did you ever see my client actually touch Larisa Moran?"

"No."

"Did you ever hear him say anything of a sexual nature to her?"

"Of course not. Sexual abusers don't work that way."

"Whatever way they work, Miss Winston, most of what you have said is hearsay."

"I am only answering the questions I am asked, Mr. Brockton," the social worker shot back.

Brockton shuffled through the notes in front of him. It was time to send Winston's testimony to the graveyard. "Miss Winston, you testified that you initially met Larisa Moran as the result of a referral to your job at the Department of Social Services."

"That is correct."

"And it was approximately three years ago that you were assigned to her case, as a placement worker."

"Yes."

"What, exactly, does a placement worker do, Miss Winston?"

"They no longer exist, Mr. Brockton."

"What did they do?"

"A placement worker takes cases through their initial stages, arranging for placement of victims outside their homes, getting clothes and things together, entering them into a new school where appropriate."

"And then, from what I understand, the case is passed on to someone else."

"Yes. If the placement is long term, the case is then passed to a foster care worker."

"As a placement worker, is there a specific time you are given to move a case to a foster care worker?"

"There are no definite requirements for a worker to move each case."

"But there are guidelines," Brockton said.

"Yes."

"And how long do the guidelines recommend?"

"Ninety days."

"How long did you have Larisa Moran's case open?"

"I'm not exactly sure how long."

"About how long? A year, two, three..."

"About two and a half years."

"Thank you for being so honest, Miss Winston."

"I am under oath, Mr. Brockton."

"That's correct, you are under oath. Miss Winston, during the time you worked to place Larisa Moran, how many cases did you have?"

"Objection," said Ritter. "Irrelevant, your honor."

"Your honor, this is indeed relevant," Brockton responded. "I aim to establish this witness's incompetence so that anything she says can be seen in that light by the court."

"Overruled," said Holmes.

"How many cases did you have, Miss Winston?"

"I'm not sure."

"Approximately."

"I'm not sure. It varied greatly."

"One, ten, one hundred?"

"Between ten and twenty."

"And on an average, how long had they been open?"

"Objection!"

"Overruled."

The social worker said nothing.

"Would you like me to repeat the question, Miss Winston?" Brockton asked.

"You can, but I'm not going to be able to answer it," the social worker said, barely able to hold in her anger.

"On average, how long had your cases been open and on your desk?"

"I don't recall."

"More than ninety days?"

"Some."

Brockton gave her a look of disbelief, then said, "How could you not know, Miss Winston?"

"I really couldn't tell you. I don't see them as cases, or clients. I see them as people."

"Let me refresh your memory," Brockton said, making an obvious flourish about picking up a document from in front of him. "Every case you had on your desk when your job as a placement worker ended had been there for over a year. Most of them had been there for over two years."

"You're giving the court the wrong impression," the social worker responded. "The reason I kept cases open was because it gave me a chance to help the children involved. Unlike many of my colleagues, I try to make a difference with the people I work with."

"But as long as those open files sat on your desk gathering dust, a foster care worker would not be assigned. In fact, nothing further could be done with them."

"I did plenty of things."

"Including Larisa Moran's file, which sat on your desk while her needs went unmet."

"I did plenty to address Larisa's needs!" the social worker replied heatedly. "I did what I could to make a difference!"

"You made a hell of a difference there, Miss Winston," Brockton retorted with as much sarcasm as he could summon. After a short silence, he turned to Holmes. "That is all, your honor."

16

Brockton felt better after taking apart the social worker, as if the momentum had shifted a little his way. If this was the best Ritter could do, all he had to concentrate on was finding some way to neutralize O'Connell. He would love to shake the cop up, but none of his attempts to find anything contradicting him had succeeded. If Mrs. Washington would testify just to reveal the cop's relationship with the girl, he'd be set. Earlier this week he'd called and asked her to sign an affidavit, but she refused, repeating her reluctance to get involved. He doubted she would say anything even if served with a subpoena.

The telephone interrupted his thoughts. It was Bart McCormick asking if he would go to lunch with him. Brockton agreed to go after making him promise not to say another word about preparations for the victory party.

By the time Brockton had put a few things in order and left the office Bart was outside waiting. He was standing next to an old white VW bus. "Hey Rooster! Hop in!" he yelled.

The VW resembled an old hippie van like the one he'd owned in college. Instead of flowers on the side, it bore the words "City Data Collection."

He walked over to the bus, hoping it wasn't as dingy looking inside as it would mess up his suit. Bart slid the door open and Brockton entered. He sat in the small couch in the middle of the bus, the cleanest seat. "Where'd you get this antique?" In front of him, a periscope-like tube rose out of the top of the bus. "What's this?"

"That's for the camera mounted on the roof," McCormick said. The smell of alcohol filled the back of the van when he started talking. "It's so the city can take pictures on the run. Rooster, this is Freddie. He's the driver. Freddie, this is a good buddy of mine, Rooster!"

Brockton shook hands with the driver, an unshaven guy who, when he smiled, showed a missing tooth. "How'd you get hold of this? " he asked.

"I borrowed it from the city. Perk of the job. Torrelli took care of it for me. Come on, let's go have some fun!"

"Where are we going?"

"The Wild Wild West, where else? Can you imagine what fun we would have had if we'd had this ride when we were working for the DA's office! Take it away, Freddie!"

When they had worked for the DA, Bart used to drive through the city's west side on their way to lunch so he could look at the people hanging out in the streets. He called the area the Wild Wild West, because there was always something going on, from shootings to drug deals to just plain fun. Many of the people they prosecuted lived there and the thought that at any moment they might run into someone they'd put in jail thrilled McCormick. Brockton had always been uneasy about that. As an assistant DA he had been tough, especially on drug offenders.

"Is everything ready for the party?" McCormick asked.

"You said you wouldn't ask."

"I lied. You're my manager. You know I lie."

"Stephanie went up to the camp with Cheryl to make sure everything's ready. The tent's set up and the food and drink are all there."

"Great! You're a *gallo*, Rooster."

"A what?"

"A *gallo*, that's rooster in Spanish. When a friend calls you a *gallo*, it's the ultimate compliment. A Dominican told me that."

The bus turned onto a wide street crowded with outdoor tables and people. Cars were parked on both sides of the street. Three young kids walked slowly in front of the bus and Freddie beeped the horn. They moved to the curb. Bart jumped into the couch next to Brockton and took hold of the periscope device. Brockton continued to look out the rear window since the side windows were painted over. It was a familiar scene, a wild mixture of people.

"Fox alert!" Bart yelled. "On your left, Freddie's side! Hey, is she a fox or what!"

Brockton waited until the bus had traveled far enough so he could see the alert from the rear window. A woman was walking her baby, her hips swaying above a nicely shaped ass. "She looks nice from behind," he said.

"You missed the African goddess side," Bart said, still excited. "She was wearing a low cut and had a pair of knockers that could stun on sight!"

"She looks Dominican," Brockton said. "Dominicans are dark, too."

"Dominican, African, Caribbean, it's all the same when you get to the important parts," Bart replied. "Slow down, Freddie, I got another possible sighting. Imagine if we had this thing when we were in the DA's office, Rooster. We coulda' told the boss we were doing surveillance, then done some real ogling!"

McCormick played with the periscope a while longer, then passed it to Brockton to take a turn.

"How's the trial going?" McCormick asked.

"I put it to one of Ritter's witnesses."

"What'd you do?"

"He sends this social worker to the stand who claimed the girl told her my client had sex with her, without mentioning his name. He probably did, but her testimony was weak and I tore it—and her—to pieces. I mean, come on, she never even filed a sex abuse report. Can you imagine? Ritter hurt himself using her."

"You gonna get the perv off?"

"I don't know. Still gotta find something on O'Connell."

"The cop."

"Yeah, you know him?"

"A little. What have you got on him?"

"Nothing yet. I'm hoping that woman you told me about will come across."

"I was talking to Ritter at the beginning of the week," McCormick said. "They want this guy bad. I don't know why, but they do."

"Don't know why?" Brockton asked. "And you call yourself a lawyer? They need this to appear tough after the election. They ran on it."

"I know that, but this is worse. I mean they really want to get your guy. Can you believe Ritter asked me to talk to you and try to get a guilty plea? Now, after the trial has started!"

"They're worried. I'm not gonna take this shit and I told them so. I've been fishing around, letting them know I'm gonna bring up the police report again. It's a fake."

"He did sound a little worried."

"Fuck him. I'm gonna bury him and all the other assholes who built this case."

"I told him that would be your reaction. He said he'd be willing to talk some reduced time."

"Fuck him," Brockton repeated. "I'll go to the press and break this open if I have to." After a few moments of silence, he asked, "How's your defense of the girl going?"

"Moran?"

"Yeah."

"She's out."

"That's good considering what she has in her background. How much was the bail?"

"Two. She ain't goin' nowhere. We had the pretrial yesterday and she showed up well dressed, on time and serious."

"What's the case look like? Can you get her off?"

McCormick shook his head. "I'm gonna try. I hope to get her off on technicalities. The cops who carried out the search warrant weren't even the ones who found the coke. Guess who found it?"

For a minute Brockton was tempted to name O'Connell. "Who?"

"Who else? Tulley. The cowboy. He wasn't even supposed to be in on the bust, was driving by he said. He sees the bust go down and decides to help. He goes into the house to look for his boys and finds the cocaine. The cops with the warrant had already searched the house and Tulley comes in and finds the shit stored in a baby's shoe of all places. My client's in the room so he arrests her, along with everyone else in the place."

"Think it was a plant?"

"Tulley? Anything can happen with him on a bust. He's crazy. He was at O'Malley's last night talking about how much he likes busting people. Better than shootin' your wad, he claims. Drug busts are his only true love."

"You don't think they set her up?"

"I don't think so. They were probably transporting the shit up from the city and storin' it there. She just got caught in the wrong house."

"What was she doing there?"

"Says she was staying with a friend of hers, some girl who wasn't even there."

"You believe her?"

"Fifty fifty. Her friend's name was on the mailbox, at least the girl she claimed was her friend. But she was the only one who spoke English in the house. She's probably just hangin' with a drug crowd. Check it out!"

Brockton looked to where McCormick was pointing. Two raggedly dressed black men were sitting on a curb, passing a brown paper bag between them. "Now there's a couple of brothers that tried to buck the system. You know 'em?"

"No."

"That reminds me. I'm thirsty. You wanna get somethin' to eat at O'Malley's so I can get a beer?"

"Sure, O'Malley's is as good as any place."

"Okay," Bart said. "One more swing, Freddie, then it's O'Malley's for lunch."

The information Bart had given him made Brockton wonder if the bust had been set up. Maybe it was just a coincidence. It would be irrelevant anyway, if he could find what he was looking for, a witness to the night the girl had filed her report.

As they were on their last sweep of the neighborhood, they saw a crowd of people gathered on one corner where a man was waving his arms and yelling. Before the crowd had disappeared from their view two police cars had arrived.

"Shit could've been a fight," Bart said. "You gotta see that every once in a while to remind you why we need so many cops. Like I always said, someone's gotta do the dirty work and keep anarchy from takin' over the streets."

"And lawyers," Brockton added. "You need enough lawyers to process the scum, get them back out there so we can keep the cycle going."

"Yeah. Let's go drink to the lawyers," Bart said. "Freddie, to O'Malley's Pub for a drink to lawyers. First one's on me."

17

Brockton put the straw to his nose, then held it over one of the lines and sniffed hard. He felt the powder hit his nose and the sudden numbness. The rush came slowly. He tilted his head back. This was good coke. He sniffed hard a few more times, laying the straw onto the small mirror and passing it to the right to one of the Extrajudicials.

The Extrajudicials was a secret group of attorneys who held meetings impromptu, at parties. They all used cocaine but unlike their clients, they used it only recreationally. They didn't let the drug interfere in their professional lives.

"I was down on Delacorte Street this week," Brockton said. Several heads turned toward him.

"The lower part?" one the EJs said.

He nodded.

"Alone?"

He nodded again, then sniffed.

"You're crazy going there alone," someone else said, but Brockton detected the note of admiration in the voice.

"I was definitely in the minority," he said. "I bet I'm the only white guy in about...how many blocks would you say, Bart?"

"Fifteen, twenty," his friend said.

"Right. Only white guy in twenty blocks. There I am getting out of the Beamer and I look up. Less than half a block away is a group of bros, standing, eyeing me. Things don't look good."

"What'd you do?"

"First I try to convince myself that it's just a cultural experience. That doesn't work. They're eyeing me as if they want to hurt me right there. Just when I think they're making their move, a cop car drives by. I use the time to scoot to where I'm going."

"The last time I had to stop on Delacorte I called a cop and asked him to drive past where I was going," McCormick said. "He refused, said I was crazy to be there in the first place."

"So I find myself near this house," Brockton continued, "which is set too far back. I say no way, this is too dangerous. By now I got the gang on the corner closing on me."

"Where on Delacorte?"

"The four hundred block." There was another moment of silent admiration. "You want to defend a client, you gotta go to the wire." He felt the cocaine start to kick in.

"I would've run for the car," one Extrajudicial said.

"What were you doing there?" asked another.

"Like I said, working on a client's behalf," Brockton replied. "No running."

"A drug dealer?"

"Yeah, the same one who's responsible for what just went up your nose," Brockton replied. Everyone laughed.

"No one recognized you?"

"I don't know, but I recognized one of them."

"All you gotta do is know one of them," Bart said. "Then they won't bother you."

"Unfortunately, this is someone I put away." Another respectful silence followed this revelation and Brockton continued. "But it was a while back since I got him sentenced and I figure he wouldn't remember me. I'm wearing my ghetto suit, not as expensive.

"So I ease past the gang while the cop car diverts their attention and go straight to this house. I'm walking fast, hoping I can get inside where I'll be safe and I end up walking down this long driveway."

"From the frying pan into the fire."

"But I make it. I get inside and there are several bros sitting on the couch. Big ones, staring me down. I back up against a wall, thinking uh oh, what's next? It was anyone's call for a minute. There are babies all over the place, a regular day care.

"The woman I need to talk to is sitting in the middle of all these babies. She nods and the bros file out without saying a word. I'm standing there wondering how long before they trash my car, or perhaps this woman is the neighborhood drug boss, so I'm cool."

A whistle sounded from downstairs and Brockton excused himself, slipping out the door. "What's up?" It was Sid.

"That cop is looking for you," Sid said. "He's pissed. I think he knows what's going on."

"Chuckie?"

"Yeah."

Brockton composed himself. He had never told Leach about the Extrajudicials. He'd never understand.

He found his friend out by the lake and seeing the look on his face, led him away from the crowd of people, where they could talk privately.

"You know what's going on upstairs?" Leach said angrily.

"What?"

"They're snorting the white shit!"

"You sure?"

"Fuck I'm sure!"

"I told them not to. I'll tell them to put it away."

"That's against the fuckin' law! Why don't you tell them that! You know, it's guys like them that are the problem! It's rich asshole lawyers that keep drugs coming into this country!" Brockton didn't reply and his friend continued. "Are you doin' it, too?"

"Fuck no."

"I'll bet Greene is up there. That son of a bitch was caught selling coke red-handed and got off with probation. When are you lawyers going to police your own?!"

Brockton thought of O'Connell and was tempted to tell Leach to practice what he preached, but held back, not wanting to further the argument.

"I'll bet there are a couple a' lawyers up there who are making money defending drug dealers," Leach continued. "How do they justify doin' coke?"

"They don't try to."

"Yeah, well fuck them and all the other drug users out there!"

"I'll tell them to put an end to it," Brockton repeated, but Leach had stormed off toward his boat, which lay anchored offshore.

When Brockton rejoined the party the Extrajudicials had already broken up and were mixing with the rest of the people at the party. Sid Greene and Bart McCormick caught up to him. "What's wrong with him?" Sid asked.

"He thinks people are using drugs and he's pissed."

Sid snorted. "Hey, fuck him. This is a free country."

"He's a cop and deals with a lot of scum," Brockton replied. "I guess it pisses him off when he sees people he knows doin' the same thing." He looked at Leach, who stood by the lake staring out toward his boat.

"He looks pretty pissed," Bart said.

"I'd better go talk to him again." Brockton walked over to Leach. "Hey Chuckie, relax. There are always a few assholes who are going to push the limits."

"I know all about assholes," Leach replied. "That's my job. Look at your fuckin' neighbors. They're over there snortin', too. Your friends are snortin', those assholes are snortin', that's what makes my job so dangerous."

Brockton shrugged his shoulders.

"Do you do that shit?"

"Not any more. But I just don't think I have a right to forbid anyone else from doing what they want. It's a party fer chrissake."

"Fuck have a right. It's your house. You could get in trouble."

"Hey, if they want to destroy their lives, that's up to them."

"What are you doin' foolin' around with that shit! It's against the law let me remind you. What happens to your family when one of those assholes falls dead from an overdose in your house?"

"That won't happen."

"You don't think so?" Leach continued. "And what are you going to do when your daughter starts suckin' that shit up her nose?"

"That ain't gonna happen either."

"That's just it. You don't know."

"Listen, you sound awfully self-righteous for a guy who can invite another woman other than his wife away for a weekend," Brockton replied, growing irritated.

"I told you Brenda and me are going through some tough times right now."

"So that's how you handle it? Is that any less of an escape than cocaine?"

"Cocaine is illegal. It's a felony and carries jail time."

"I told you I don't use it."

"Who do you buy it from, your neighbors?"

"I don't have anything to do with my neighbors."

Leach didn't reply, redirecting his gaze to the cottage next door.

"I told them to put the shit away," Brockton said. "They said they hid it well, so I wouldn't worry about anyone having seen you near it."

"I ain't worried about that," Leach replied.

"You want a beer?"

"In a while. Just leave me alone for now."

"Sure," Brockton said. He left his friend by the shore and returned to the party.

18

Brockton looked around. Many of the guests had left. The music was still playing loudly and ten or fifteen people were dancing. Bart was standing under the tent holding the main pole for balance.

"I want to thank all of you for making this victory celebration a party to remember!" He was yelling to be heard over the music. "I want you to know, I will remember all of you!" When the time comes to hand out the plums, I will remember you all!"

The music continued and most people only half-listened to the speech. He looked around, then grabbed the back of a chair and pulled it to him. He stepped up on the chair and raised his arms. "I look around me and see that everyone's having fun!" he began, yelling louder. "That's good! That's why we're here! We have fun and then we got work to do!" He pointed to a couple sitting in a corner talking. "Now there's a happy couple! Aren't you going to get up and dance? Get up and dance 'cause the music won't last forever!

"Now you all know that I'm a nice guy! And you all supported me, helped me plan strategies to win. We all will divide up the spoils and all that!" He pointed to Sidney Greene. "My campaign manager!" Sidney stood up and bowed.

"But I think we're here for another reason, too, aren't we? I mean, if we only came to support Councilor McCormick, you would have gone home by now!

"So why are we still here? Let me tell you why and let me tell it to you straight! You all know that I'm not the kind of guy who talks indirectly, so I'm gonna talk about the thing that's on everyone's mind. I'm gonna tell it like I see it!

"It's simple! We're here because we're lonely! We're lonely and we want to share that loneliness with someone else! Tonight!

"What do I mean by that? Well, do I have to spell it out, folks? I don't want to bore you with the biological details that they never taught us in school. As adults, what is our primary function? Come on now, admit it!

"You know that us men want to do it! And so do you women! You've just developed more defenses so to speak. Hey I'm not saying anything that I know about more than you, I'm just preparing you! That's all I'm saying!

"Don't get pissed off! Think for a minute. Why is it that our parents kept us so busy with extracurricular activities? And what led us to enter into marriage, where we use those same strategies on our kids? Let's not get fooled by all this socializing! Let's be honest! We're old enough! Everyone wants to be with someone tonight, and by that I mean men with ladies!

"Now I'm willing to set things in motion, take the first step! If any of you ladies want to come over here and join me, I'm sure that's all I need to get over my shyness! Come on, come on over here!"

Everyone kept dancing, some waving their arms at Bart and yelling, others intent on their dance steps. A pained expression filled McCormick's face. "Okay, so we're still a little shy tonight!" he yelled. "What I'd like you all to do is think about what I said for a while! You'll be able to find me here the rest of the evening, and if you feel like taking me up on my generous offer, please come and speak to me!" Getting no reaction, he stepped down from the chair. "This is hard work," he said to Brockton. "How about a couple of lines?"

Brockton didn't make it back upstairs for nearly an hour because the party was winding down and he had to say his good-byes. The Extrajudicials had been there a while. Bart and Sidney were dominating the conversation, talking about the campaign.

"I will hand out plums, as many as they allow me," McCormick was saying. Brockton smiled. His friend had just won a seat on the council for the Summit Hill neighborhood, yet he was talking as if he was in charge of the entire city.

"I want to be on the Board of Estimate!" Sidney said.

"The Board of Estimate is gone," Bart said. "Where have you been?" He looked at Brockton. "Rooster! Look what I have to put up with! My own campaign manager doesn't know the first thing about our city!"

"All I really want is a job with the privilege to hire any secretary I want!" Sid continued.

"If you want a secretary you need to go through me and I'll talk to the mayor to hook you up," McCormick continued. "And let me tell you, I plan to stay in this position for a while. If I ever start losing voters, a little reapportioning will take care of that! Nothing major, just a few line changes to maintain my percentages." He winked.

Brockton took the mirror as it was passed to him.

McCormick continued. "That's what I love about the political system. It's like when you were a kid playing Monopoly. You could make the rules if you owned the game. If anyone objected, you threatened to take the game home."

"I can hire any secretary I want?" Sid asked, fixated.

"Any one," McCormick replied.

"Good. I'm gonna hire that girl I was talking to earlier."

"Sid, you were pressuring her big time. What was her name?"

Sidney shrugged. "I don't know. But she said she wasn't in a generous mood tonight."

"I thought you were still married," Brockton said. He squeezed the bridge of his nose, hoping he didn't have a headache tomorrow after all this cocaine. Stephanie had left early, gone back to the city to let the babysitter go home.

"My wife cut me off," Sid replied. "Maybe for good this time. I told her she looked like she'd aged and she hasn't talked to me since."

"Jesus, I can see why not."

"Hey, I apologized, told her what I meant was she was like a wine, that the aging made her more attractive. But no deal. This is one even a dozen roses can't rectify."

"You earned that freeze," Bart said.

Sid continued. "My marriage is so bad that when I get out of the car and my wife's at the wheel, I walk behind a curb so she don't run me over. She actually tried once, claimed it was a mistake."

"You only have yourself to blame," Brockton said, yawning.

"Oh listen to the Rooster," Sid said. "I suppose he gets it five times a week."

"Not counting the weekends, when I lose count," Brockton replied.

"Bullshit."

"Okay, last lines," Sid said, holding up the mirror. "Time to prepare for the twenty minute drive home." His friend turned to him. "This place is in a perfect location, Rooster. Just one line from the city."

The mirror was passed around, each one of the remaining Extrajudicials snorting up two lines. "Here, Rooster," Sid said, holding the last two out to him. He took the straw and snorted up one.

"Do 'em both, Rooster," McCormick urged. Brockton shook his head but McCormick held the mirror up. He bent his head over the second line and snorted.

"Where's that cop?" someone asked. "He sure was pissed."

"I just hope he never gets the police chief's position or he'll bust us all."

"Where is he anyway?"

No one answered at first and an uneasy silence grew.

"Probably out cleaning his boat," Brockton said. "He's pretty fanatical about it."

"He wasn't too happy to find out about the sniff," McCormick said.

"He'll get over it," Brockton replied, downplaying the incident for Chuckie's sake.

"Would he turn us in?" Sid asked.

"Not Chuckie," Brockton replied. "He's serious about the stuff, but he wouldn't go that far."

The reality was that Brockton wasn't even sure of that. Ever since the pretrial hearing he had lost the ease with which he talked to Leach. The courtroom cheap shot had been inexcusable, so much so that he was still too mad to talk about it. Brockton refused to raise the issue, acting as if nothing had happened, but Leach must sense something. Even his thick-headed cop brain must know that something was amiss.

"Hey listen!" McCormick yelled. The music below cut off suddenly, replaced by the sounds of car doors slamming.

Brockton stood up and looked out the window facing the road. The red lights of police cars flashed outside. "Everybody out the front!" he yelled.

19

Once outside, Brockton ran toward the lights while most of the partiers hid down near the shore.

"Hey Michael!" Leach yelled. The policeman was still in his bathing suit and sandals. Two cars with their flashing lights were pulled up to the cottage next door and several sheriffs were swarming around it.

"What the fuck..." was all Brockton could manage.

"Here's another job for you or one of your lawyer friends," Leach said. "I've been working on this one ever since the other weekend. I didn't tell you that I snuck up to their window that time and saw them weighing and measuring, stacking up lots of money."

Brockton shook his head. "You're crazy."

"Hey, we've got a legal search warrant," the cop continued. "I just hope you weren't lying when you told me that you didn't buy from these slime balls, or you're gonna have to find a new supplier."

"That's the least of my worries," Brockton said, his body still racing from the added adrenalin of fear.

"Just think how quickly your friends would stop using that shit if they knew they'd be spending tonight in jail. Or three to five in the pen with José and Lamar."

"The press ain't here, right?" The thought of the kind of publicity the media could give was frightening and he looked around quickly. There were no cameras.

"Maybe I shoulda' told 'em."

Brockton looked sharply at Leach, whose eyes gleamed brightly each time the lights from the sheriffs' cars reflected off them. The glow reminded him of the glow in Sienkewicz's eyes, weirdly.

"Well, I gotta help mop up," Leach said. He moved toward the cabin next door. "Hey remember this, Michael. It could have been you. And by the way, that woman you accused me of being with was a fellow cop. Nothin' dirty."

Brockton smiled weakly and retreated toward his cottage without responding. He'd better go tell the others to come out of the bushes. They were still hiding and that was suspicious.

It wasn't until the next morning that he could think about what happened the night before. Had Leach gone crazy? The guy had set up a drug bust that almost ruined the lives of a half dozen of his friends!

What also concerned him was his friend's eyes. The more he thought about it the more they had appeared like

Sienkewicz's when he started talking crazy. Maybe it had been the lights of the police cars but they had scared Brockton. They were zealot's eyes.

There was a similarity between Leach and Sienkewicz. Neither one realized that you had to set boundaries on your actions. You could fight what you thought was injustice but you had to know when to let things rest. If you didn't, the little battles would get to you. Sooner or later you'd drive yourself crazy. *And* get in trouble.

Brockton rolled out of bed and slipped into his sandals. He couldn't sleep anyway with all the residual cocaine running through his body and Stephanie and the kids would be arriving soon to help clean up.

Leach was heading for nothing but trouble with this attitude. Brockton had never thought of his friend as a troublemaker, but last night he'd gone too far. He had lost it over this drug thing. Leach should have chosen a different night to schedule the raid.

Maybe it was his home situation. He was letting his marital difficulties get to him. Brockton had seen a lot of guys start acting crazy when their marriages were falling apart. And he didn't believe his friend's so-called fellow cop story.

Brockton's relationship with Stephanie could have gone the same way if he hadn't put a lid on certain feelings. At one time he'd blamed her for his not making the pro ball circuit. He could have continued to blame her, even accused her of getting pregnant on purpose. Instead he'd made the best of the situation. And he had a family to be proud of as a result.

He heard the sound of a car entering the drive below and went outside to greet his family. Stephanie was carrying several large McDonalds bags. "Breakfast," she said. Everyone followed her inside.

He declined food, saying he had already eaten breakfast to cover up the fact that the coke had taken away his appetite. He watched his family eat, thinking how much they meant to him. He was crazy to be snorting, taking chances like that. He needed to quit the Extrajudicials.

"Michael, is something wrong?" Stephanie asked.

"No, nothing." He snapped out of his daze. "Just a little hung over."

"You've got the camp all cleaned."

"I had a lot of energy this morning." After the excitement had died down and everyone had left, he had cleaned the entire cottage. Still wired, he had lain down and tried to sleep, wishing he'd brought his briefcase so that he could work a few cases. Finally, around sunrise he had fallen asleep for a couple of hours.

"Dad, I met that guy's daughter," Michele said.

"Which guy, honey?"

"That teacher you're defending. You know, the one that's in the papers."

"Mr. Sienkewicz?"

"Yeah."

"What's she like?"

"She's weird."

"What do you mean she's weird?"

"She never talks to anyone. She just likes to be alone."

"Maybe she's shy," Brockton replied. His client probably couldn't raise a normal kid.

"Did you play ball last night?" he asked his son, remembering Michael had a game.

His son nodded, his mouth full of food.

"Did you win?" His son's eyes told him yes. Michael held up two fingers.

"Two homers!" Brockton said enthusiastically. "The Babe is back! What did the coach say?"

"He hugged me, said I was the greatest!" his son said proudly and Brockton threw a triumphant glance at Stephanie. He had been right all along. Michael had learned his lesson but he'd also made a point with the coach. He was too valuable to be left on the bench.

"Dad, can we go to the ball game tonight?" Michael asked.

"Home team's out of the race," Brockton replied. "They're losers this year and we can't cheer for losers, right?"

"Yeah," his son said, only partially convinced.

"Can we go sailing?" Roger asked, getting up from the table and looking out at the lake.

It took Brockton everything to suppress the groan that rose to his lips. "You don't want to go to the park and shag flies?"

"Yeah!" Michael said, looking to his sister for support. She shrugged her shoulders noncommittally.

"We'll do both," Brockton said. As lousy as he felt, he needed to get active, punish his body for snorting so much coke. "Since your father cleaned the whole camp, allowing your mother time to relax, we'll have enough time. Get your gloves and we'll go to the park first. The wind usually picks up after noon."

Roger couldn't hide his disappointment at playing ball before sailing, but he didn't whine. That was something

Brockton liked about his younger son. He never whined or threw tantrums. Stephanie had done a good job raising the kids that way.

"I heard there were police up here last night," Stephanie said.

Brockton looked up quickly. "Where'd you hear that?"

"Brenda called me this morning. She said Chuck was involved."

"I didn't know they were talking," Brockton replied, a hint of sarcasm leaking out.

"They are. He's trying to patch things up with her."

"Why do you stick up for him?" Brockton replied. "That marriage is over. Why try to hide it?"

"I'm not sticking up for anybody. Michael, what is wrong?"

She was right. He'd better watch himself. He was still irritable and jumpy. "It was the neighbors," he said. "The cops did a number on them. Okay team, let's get the equipment! Michele, you help Mom clear the table and the boys and I will get the bag out of the car. Let's go!"

While the kids ran to get the baseball bag out of the car, Brockton described the bust to Stephanie, leaving out his involvement. She didn't even suspect he was sniffing and he planned to keep it that way. He was going to put an end to it anyway. Maybe Leach's not so subtle warning was the excuse he needed to quit the Extrajudicials. Maybe his friend had done him a favor. He'd just have to be a little more careful about how he reacted to Stephanie, especially when she talked about Chuckie.

20

Monday morning Brockton arrived at his office ten minutes early. Candy wasn't in yet so he leafed through the messages on her desk and took his. Going to his office, he sat in his swivel chair and turned to look out the window. Everything looked the same: courthouse; DA's offices; light traffic. The blue sky was a nice touch.

Last night he'd dreamt that he was in court giving closing arguments in Sienkewicz's case. For some reason he had agreed to argue the case the way his client wanted him to and was telling a jury that Sienkewicz was a good man who had worked his entire life for the betterment of kids, but had made one mistake, had succumbed to a fatal flaw. What began as a well intentioned desire to help someone had turned into tragedy when he fell in love. Should he be judged on this alone? Should not the fact that this man—his client—was taking care of someone no one else cared for be taken into consideration by the court? Yes, he had a sexual relationship with the girl but it was not abusive. He had never beat her.

Brockton turned to the judge, a skull-like thin white man with a swastika plastered to his forehead. This brought up an interesting point, he said. Who exactly had been the victim? There was more to this than the prosecution was letting on and the jury should think of that while deliberating.

A groan arose from behind the judge. There, facing the witness stand chair, Sienkewicz stood with his pants around his knees. He was fucking someone. Brockton looked to see whose face belonged to the white, adolescent, naked body under his client. He couldn't discern the features but he knew it was his client's daughter. He was fucking his own daughter.

Brockton walked up to the bench, bent his head over one of several lines of white powder and snorted. He pulled his head back and the judge smiled at him. Brockton walked over to his client, now full of energy. "Why are you doing this?" he asked.

"Because I love her," Sienkewicz replied.

"But that is your daughter."

His client looked up. "This is what I mean by love. You have to live it. You have to practice it." The groaning continued as if piped into the dream. Brockton looked back at the judge, who smiled and pointed once again to the small lines of cocaine.

The telephone rang, causing Brockton to pull his thoughts from the dream and to the reality of his client's folder, which lay in front of him.

"Mr. Brockton, a Charles Leach on the line," Candy said through the intercom.

He picked up the phone. "Good morning Chuckie," he said, careful to hide his feelings about the weekend.

"Hey Mike, what are you doing tonight?"

"Nothing. What's up?"

"I want to take you somewhere. We're going to make a buy."

"Are you joking?" Brockton asked.

"Nope. I want you to see what's really happening out there." Brockton didn't reply and Leach continued. "Can you be ready around eight?"

"Let me check in with Stephanie, but I'm thinking that'll work. Where you picking me up?"

"Meet me in front of Siponi's Deli."

"Okay." Brockton thought quickly. "Is there anything special I should bring?"

"Wear black," Leach said, then laughed. "No, you don't need nothin' but an open mind."

Brockton hung up the phone. This sounded like the old Chuckie he knew.

That night at eight an unmarked compact pulled in front of the Siponi's. It was raining lightly and Brockton stepped out from under the deli's awning. A car door opened and he stooped to get in quickly.

"Hey Mike!" Leach greeted him enthusiastically. "How's the weather out there?"

"You still going to do it?" Brockton replied.

"Of course. A little rain won't scare away these wolves. Sarge, this is Michael Brockton, another sleazy lawyer. Mike this is Sergeant Lee."

Brockton reached across the seat and shook the sergeant's hand as Leach drove away from the deli and toward the center of town.

As they neared the north side, the landscape changed from tall, modern style buildings to smaller, two story houses.

"North side deal?" Brockton asked.

"You got it. It's worse than the west side for drug sales now." After a few minutes, Leach continued. "I tell you Mike, this is not exactly the place for a white boy from the suburbs."

"Then what are you doing here?" Brockton replied. Leach laughed. "What's happening, anyway?" Brockton asked.

"Our man's established himself as a mid level coke dealer. He met a Mr. Big who's supposed to have an unlimited source. We've set up a buy to see if the guy's telling the truth. If things go right, we may make a bust. But we want to be patient, cultivate this guy."

"Who's buying and who's selling?"

"Both."

"We'll buy to find out who's selling," Sergeant Lee explained unnecessarily, making Brockton feel foolish.

"He's going to buy under the premise that he's selling somewhere else, not using," Leach added. "We don't use the stuff."

"I know, Chuckie," Brockton said, keeping the irritation out of his voice. "I worked with you guys for several years, remember?"

"Yeah, those were the good ol' days. Why don't you go back to that? We could be on the same side again."

"Maybe with the new DA," Brockton lied.

"Right," Leach said. "Anyway, our man is going to present himself, go in there and try to set up a deal. We'll wait to see if the sale going down is big enough to warrant a bust. Hopefully, we'll nab Mr. Big and Mr. Bigger."

The sergeant cruised aimlessly for another few minutes, then pulled onto a side street near an apartment building. He parked the car behind the building's main entrance. "Uncles, come in," he said into a walkie-talkie he had picked up from the seat.

"Uncle One."

"Uncle Two."

"Uncle Three."

The voices came over the walkie-talkie clearly. One was a female, the other two males. Two sounded black.

"Are you situated?"

Rogers came from all three Uncles.

"Uncle Two, is Uncle One with you?"

"Roger."

"Then proceed to the store and have a look at the tape."

A few minutes later, a voice came over the walkie-talkie. "Ready to try the tape, boss."

"Proceed. Go look at it. If it doesn't look right, don't take it. If it looks good ask about the VCR."

"Got it. Go look at the tape, then ask about the VCR."

"Right. If it doesn't look right, don't take it."

"Here it comes now. Ten-four boss." The walkie-talkie communications stopped.

"Uncle Two is back," Uncle One's voice returned suddenly.

"What happened?"

"He asked if I wanted a VCR right now and I said no, I only wanted a tape," Uncle Two replied.

"How was the tape?"

"The tape looked good."

"You should have said you wanted to look at the VCR. Like I said, if the tape looks good, look at the VCR."

"Right boss, but that would have meant I went inside where I don't have any contact."

"You can do that. Just have Uncle One remain outside with the radio."

"Yeah, but she won't know where I'm at while I'm in there." Uncle Two sounded scared.

"Ask him where you're going before you go in there, so Uncle One knows," the sergeant explained.

"Good idea, boss."

The sergeant shook his head, turning off the walkie-talkie for a second. "It's hard to find good help in this city," he said. He flicked the walkie-talkie back on.

"...black male approaching. About thirty years old, five nine," Uncle Three was saying. "Nephew's wearing tan pants, black waist length jacket. He's reached the dumpsters, heading toward Uncle One."

"That's okay," said the sergeant. "He's on the other side of the river."

"Do you want me to go in, boss?" Uncle Two asked.

"Yes, go in. Leave your radio with Uncle One."

"You mean my gloves?" Uncle Two said, reminding the sergeant of the code word.

"Right."

"This is Uncle Three. Nephew's approaching from the south. He keeps looking back, I don't know why. He's wearing a green baseball cap, a black jacket, dark tan pants."

"Get that down," Sergeant Lee said. Leach pulled out a book and started writing.

"Describe again, please," Lee said. As the description came over the walkie-talkie, Leach checked it with what he'd written.

"He's heading toward the river now. He's about thirty-five feet away from me, looks in his early twenties."

"Is he happy?" the sergeant asked.

"He looks happy."

"Might be a lookout," Leach said.

"Uncle Two is back," Uncle One said.

"Uncles One and Two be aware of the happy black male crossing the river," Sergeant Lee said.

"Roger. Don't see him yet."

"Uncle Two, how did it go?"

"I told him it looks like business is taken care of. I wanted to get about five VCRs from him and he said when I'm ready to do business, let him know. He said he didn't have them in the store but he would be getting them soon."

"Roger," Lee said. He turned toward Brockton. "Doesn't look like tonight's the night."

"Uncle Three pursuing suspect!" a voice burst over the walkie-talkie. "I'm goin' in!"

Sergeant Lee swore and he and Leach leapt out of the car and started running toward the front of the apartment building.

21

Brockton sat in the car for a moment, then decided to follow. As he got out of the car, he noticed someone standing in the shadows at the rear of the apartment building. He was about to approach the man when the building's rear door burst open. A man ran out, then stopped when he spotted the car and Brockton. The man turned and started in the opposite direction. The person in the shadows jumped out and tackled him. Brockton watched the struggle until the man was cuffed. He walked around to the front of the building, hoping to find Leach and tell him they had captured someone in the back.

By the time he'd gotten to the front door there was a small crowd gathered. He pushed his way through people and walked up the stairs,

Sergeant Lee was talking with another officer, emotionally. It was Tulley, the cowboy. Brockton had seen him in court several times and recognized him immediately. He spotted Leach and walked over to the group of policemen.

"He ran, Sarge. I saw him pull out the stuff and exchange it with the other perp and when I started to approach him, he ran."

Aware that people were gathering, the sergeant drew the conversation away and Brockton decided to wait outside. He could get the story from Chuckie after it was over.

Brockton sat with Leach in a small bar on the outskirts of the city, listening to his friend describe what had happened inside the building. According to Leach, Tulley had chased the suspect into an apartment where a family sat watching television. By the time he entered the apartment the suspect had disappeared. The cop heard the toilet flush and had broken down the bathroom door. Instead of finding the suspect he had encountered an old man standing over the toilet, watching the water swirl his feces into the city's sewer system. At the same time their man at the rear door of the apartment had captured the suspect.

"The son of a bitch will probably get off with probation," Leach said, setting down his beer and reaching for the small basket of over-salted popcorn on the table.

"That should be the least of your worries," Brockton replied.

"What d'ya mean?"

"You raced through this family's house just to catch someone with a couple of grams of cocaine. They aren't going to forget what you did and that stuff gets around. It's not gonna sit well with the Hispanic community I can assure you."

"Hey, did he have cocaine on him?" Leach demanded. Before Brockton could answer, his friend said, "Yes, he did. So he's guilty."

"That's not the point."

"What is the point?"

"The point is you disrupted that family's household. That's what people are going to hear about."

"Reasonable suspicion. The guy was selling and we had to follow him. He might have ditched his stash somewhere in the apartment."

"Like the toilet?" Brockton asked sarcastically. "You sure shook up that old codger in the bathroom. He could've had a heart attack."

"You know as well as I that's the first place they get rid of their drugs. Follow the path of toilet water and you'll find cocaine."

"What about the shit? How much of that family's shit would you have to pick through to find your cocaine?"

"Everyone makes mistakes. But mistake or not, we got the guy."

"Well you sure shook up that family in order to get your man. They all sit down for some after dinner television, probably to watch some police drama and a half dozen cops burst through the front door, trampling through their home, shaking up grandpa. A man can't even take a shit in his own house these days."

"The son of a bitch with the drugs disturbed them first. We just followed him."

"That's not an excuse, is it?"

"We apologized. Said we were sorry."

"Who's gonna fix their door? Are you?"

"Hey, what's buggin' you? Whose side are you on?"

"I'm on the side of the law."

"Don't give me that shit. Either you're for drugs or against them."

"As I said, I'm on the side of the law. As it is written."

"You know, you can't be satisfied," Leach said. "We're not perfect, but it's dangerous out there. Sometimes we have to act quickly. And all you can do is criticize us. Well, if you can do a better job, go right ahead."

"It's the way you do your busts, without thinking."

"When the hell are we supposed to think? We're making a bust. Next time, if it was up to you, we'd stop and blow our whistles, say 'Excuse me José, wait a minute. I gotta think about this.'"

"If you did a better job initially, you'd have a better chance in court."

"If you can do a better job, go right ahead. Meanwhile, we plan to keep makin' busts. Each time we corral one 'a these guys we're sending the message south that we mean business. This isn't The City, where drug dealers can operate without fear. The streets are still ours here."

"And the mules will keep coming," Brockton said. "There's always another one looking to make a few bucks."

"The mules will keep comin' as long as your coke sniffin' lawyer buddies keep buyin' the shit. Some of the same ones who make their money defending these criminals, by the way."

"We also make money off situations like tonight. That family could sue you."

"What did you do, give them your business card?" Leach snapped.

"If I were an opportunist I would have."

"You are an opportunist," Leach said. "You all are." Brockton ignored the comment and Leach continued. "You know you've been criticizing us since we got here. You got a bug up your ass, then say it."

"If I have a bug up my ass, it's because you find it so easy to criticize us but look the other way whenever it concerns a cop. Don't you think there's a little hypocrisy there?"

"What's that supposed to mean?"

"You know what it means," Brockton said.

"No I don't. What are you talking about?"

"I'm talking about O'Connell, that's what I'm talking about. You let me hang my balls out there for a guy like that."

"Hey, you're defending a sleaze ball and that's all there is to that."

"That's my job, Chuckie. I'm getting paid to defend that sleaze ball. You're not getting paid to defend O'Connell."

"He's a cop. You can't start going after cops."

"I could say the same thing about lawyers. Crooked is crooked."

"There's a difference. We're out there risking our necks. You sit in your offices in your suits and ties and make deals to get the slime out of jail. Well, things have changed. This stuff is taking over the streets and we have to do something about it. Why can't you see that! Why can't you see what's going on out there!"

"As if I don't see what's going on. You forget I'm part of the justice system, too. I know what's going on."

"Then why the hell do you keep doing what you do? Why are you making our job that much harder?"

"Exactly because of what I saw tonight. What I saw was Sergeant O'Connell Junior. I saw a cop who breaks into an innocent family's home, causing the same kind of problems O'Connell did. And I see you protecting him. I thought you told me that O'Connell was a dying breed."

"You know, I brought you out tonight so you could see why we need a few guys like Tulley. So you could see how bad it's gotten."

"Then let's just say it didn't work," Brockton said.

"I don't know what's got into you, Mike. You sound like a completely different person. You sound like all you want to do is go after us."

"Who says I'm going after you?" Brockton replied. "I thought it was the other way around."

"It's around what you're trying to do. Nobody's stupid."

Brockton signaled to the bartender for two more beers. "So why are you protecting him? He set me up."

"All we're trying to do is protect the law abiding community," Leach said.

"By running roughshod over anyone that gets in your way."

"You saw what happened tonight. Police have gotten killed in those situations."

"I know one who I wish would have."

Leach stood up. "I ain't gonna listen to that! You're going too far, Mike! You're crossing a line!"

"What line?"

"The line of common decency. You're crossing the line of common decency!"

"Me?"

"Yeah. As soon as you start talkin' like that about cops, you're crossing that line!"

"He's out of control!" Brockton replied heatedly.

"You're out of control is who's out of control," Leach said. "That shit's got control of your brain and you ought'ta do something before it gets worse."

"What shit?"

"You know what shit. That white shit you're sucking up your nose."

Brockton sat back, feigning shock. "You think I'm doin' cocaine?"

"It's obvious. And too much of it. You might not think it's obvious, but I've noticed a change. Your behavior has changed, Mike. Your wife even says so."

Brockton shook his head. "You know, you're amazing Chuckie. I mean you are amazing."

"Hey, it happens to a lot of good people. And the first stage is always denial. That's part of the disease. We had a cop get lost in it. He's in rehab now."

"Is that the same as marital rehab?" Brockton replied.

"Leave Brenda and me out of this."

"Oh, you can discuss my alleged cocaine abuse—with Stephanie no less—but you don't want to talk about your problems. How would you like it if I were to discuss your girlfriend with Brenda?"

"I never mentioned cocaine use to Stephanie. And there's a difference between cocaine use and what I'm doing, which is nothing as if it's any of your business."

"What's the difference?" Brockton asked, clinging to the comparison.

"Cocaine is illegal, Mike."

"So is adultery."

"Which isn't happening. Nor is it illegal. And it's especially not a felony. Christ all I'm doin' is tellin' you how serious a cocaine charge is. You have things mixed up. Call me when you're ready to get some help. Any time." Leach stood up and left, a full bottle of beer on the bar.

22

"The people would like to call Ms. Margaret Lobdell," Ritter said. A middle aged woman dressed in a navy blue skirt and jacket walked stiffly to the witness stand. Her hair was tied behind her head in a bun that was so tight it appeared the wrinkles on each side of her eyes were caused by the hairdo pulling the skin tight. She had black hair, which contrasted sharply with her pale white skin.

More obvious were the woman's breasts. They were large, obviously so, and stood out straight and firm from her chest, refusing to be overlooked. Brockton's gaze remained on them longer than usual and Sienkewicz noticed.

"Be careful," his client whispered to him.

"What?" Brockton asked, momentarily distracted.

"Be careful you don't stare at her breasts. She has a problem with people staring at them."

Brockton didn't respond, embarrassed that his gaze might have been that obvious. He glanced at the woman's face. She was looking at him defiantly. Maybe she had noticed.

"Would the witness please state her name for the court," Ritter began.

"Margaret Lobdell," she replied stiffly and for a moment Brockton wished he had a jury in the courtroom. This woman would not be treated sympathetically.

"Ms. Lobdell, would you please state your occupation."

"I am a registered nurse."

"Are you currently employed?"

"Yes."

"Where do you work?"

"I work at Millwood Treatment Center."

"Ms. Lobdell, as a nurse at the Center what are your principal duties?"

"I monitor the progress of the patients in the substance abuse unit."

"All the patients?"

"The adolescent girls."

"Ms. Lobdell, in the course of your duties as a nurse on the adolescent unit of the Millwood Treatment Center, did you ever have the occasion to meet a patient named Larisa Moran?"

"Yes."

Brockton sat quietly, jotting down notes while Ritter established the identity of Sienkewicz's victim. The assistant DA had rebounded today, he thought. He was asking better questions.

"Ms. Lobdell, how well did you know Larisa Moran?"

"Objection," Brockton said. "The question calls for a subjective response."

"Sustained," Judge Holmes said. "Rephrase the question, Mr. Ritter."

"Where did you meet Larisa Moran, Ms. Lobdell?" Ritter asked.

"She was a patient at the Center. I was one of several nurses who supervised her for the four months she was there."

"Ms Lobdell, do you know a Mr. John Sienkewicz?"

"Yes I do."

"Is he in this courtroom?"

"He is."

"Would you point him out for the court?" The woman pointed to Brockton's client. "Let the court note that the defendant Mr. John Sienkewicz is occupying the seat at which Mr. Lobdell is pointing."

"So noted."

"Let the court note that my client is the only blonde-haired, blue-eyed person in this room," Brockton said, not bothering to stand.

"So noted." Judge Holmes used her courtroom voice this time.

"Ms. Lobdell, how did you meet John Sienkewicz?" Ritter continued.

"He has tutored students at Millwood Treatment Center. I met him there."

"How long has he done this?"

"He has been working at the Center for a couple of years."

"Did he tutor Larisa Moran?"

"Yes, he was her tutor the entire time she was at the Center."

"During the time Mr. Sienkewicz tutored Larisa Moran, did you ever suspect him of making any sexual advances toward her?"

"Objection. Conjecture."

"Your honor, I'm simply asking a yes or no question," Ritter said.

"It's conjecture, your honor. Suspect him?"

"Overruled."

"Ms. Lobdell, would you like me to repeat the question?"

"Yes."

"During the time Mr. Sienkewicz tutored Larisa Moran, did you ever suspect him of making any sexual advances toward her?"

"Yes," Ms. Lobdell replied without hesitation.

"When?"

"The first time occurred when I came upon him in her room. He was staring at her breasts."

Brockton almost laughed, but kept himself in check. He would tear this woman up in good time.

"Do you remember any other incidents?"

"I remember something that wasn't sexual in nature but which I thought was rather strange and led me to believe that something existed between them."

"What was that?"

"Mr. Sienkewicz once gave Larisa several gifts."

"What kind of gifts?"

"Clothes and perfume."

Sienkewicz leaned over and whispered something in Brockton's ear. Brockton nodded and jotted down a quick note. It was about time Sienkewicz told him something useful.

"Ms. Lobdell, in the time you were working with Larisa Moran at Millwood Treatment Center, did she ever speak of being physically or sexually molested?" Ritter asked.

"Objection!" Brockton said. "Leading the witness."

"Your honor," Ritter said, "I'm looking for a simple yes or no."

"I'm going to allow the question," Holmes replied.

"Allow me to repeat myself, Ms. Lobdell. In the time you were working with Larisa Moran at Millwood Treatment Center did she ever speak of being physically or sexually molested?"

"Yes, she did."

"Under what context did that occur?"

"After group, which is a daily session during which the girls are encouraged to speak about their problems. Larisa revealed to one of her fellow patients that she was involved in a sexual encounter with an older man. That patient told one of our nurses what she had said and the nurse told me."

"Did Larisa Moran mention any names?"

"No."

"Did she identify the older man in any way?"

"Yes."

"How?"

"She said it was her teacher."

"Who was her teacher, Ms. Lobdell?"

"Mr. Sienkewicz."

"In her entire time at the Center, did she have any other teacher besides Mr. John Sienkewicz?"

"No."

"Thank you, Ms. Lobdell. That is all."

Holmes turned to Brockton. "Would you like to cross examine the witness, Mr. Brockton?"

"Ms. Lobdell," Brockton said, dispensing with any preliminaries, "or is it Mrs.?"

The woman stared at him without answering. He was going to have to shake her up a bit before he got down to business. "Molly, how long have you worked at Millwood?"

"My name is Margaret," she replied coolly.

"Right Molly, how long?"

"Your honor," Ritter protested. "The man is out of order."

Holmes looked at Brockton, but before she could say anything he apologized, then continued.

"How many years, Miss Lobdell?"

"Seven."

"And you've seen how many teachers pass through the doors of Millwood?"

"I wouldn't know."

"Approximately?" Brockton prompted.

Ms. Lobdell shrugged her shoulders.

"Over a hundred would you say?"

"I guess so," Ms. Lobdell said.

"And you mean to tell me that of those hundreds of teachers, you have never seen one present a gift to one of their students?"

"Rarely."

"But you have."

"Yes."

"Did you ever stop to think that one strategy a good teacher uses is to present a gift to someone, to motivate them to work harder?"

"I have, but usually they notify us in the office that they are doing this."

"So it's a problem of control," Brockton responded. "You wanted to control what my client was doing."

"I didn't say that. I simply said that teachers usually notify us when they are giving patients gifts. Mr. Sienkewicz did not notify anyone as far as I know."

"Have you ever taught, Miss Lobdell?"

"Objection!" Ritter said. "Irrelevant."

"Your honor, it is important that I establish why the gifts were presented. There is a reason."

"Then please get to the reason Mr. Brockton," Holmes replied. "Overruled."

"Have you ever taught, Miss Lobdell?" Brockton repeated.

"Yes. In nursing school."

"I don't suppose you ever gave any of your students a gift?"

"I don't recall ever doing so, no."

"So you thought that what Mr. Sienkewicz was doing was strange."

"I explained to you what I thought. I felt it strange that he not notify anyone on our staff about what he was doing."

"Did you ever think to speak to him about this strange behavior?"

"No."

"Well maybe you should have. You see it was Larisa's birthday when he brought the gifts. Thank God someone celebrated it."

After a long moment of silence, Ms. Lobdell said, "We do celebrate our patients' birthdays. But you must understand that Larisa was a difficult—"

"—Excuse me, your honor," Ritter interrupted. She looked at him and he shook his head.

"In what way was she difficult?" Brockton asked, picking up on the miscue. The nurse sat tight-lipped and Brockton decided to move on. "Miss Lobdell, you said you saw my client staring at the alleged victim's breasts, is that correct?"

"Yes it is."

"Where did this happen?"

"In her room."

"What was my client doing in her room?"

"He was supposed to be tutoring her."

"Do teachers usually tutor their students in their rooms?"

"No."

"Then why was Mr. Sienkewicz in the room with his student in the first place?"

"She had been restricted to her room."

"Was anyone supervising these tutoring sessions?"

"Of course. I was."

"And where were you when my client was allegedly staring at these breasts?"

"Right there. I saw him."

"You were in the room the entire time?"

"No. I was supervising several students."

"So you were not supervising Larisa Moran the entire time my client was in the room."

"I never said I was."

"Why not, Miss Lobdell?"

"There is an awful lot to do at the Center, Mr. Brockton, and we cannot possibly assign a personal supervisor to every patient."

"So you happened to stroll by and saw my client staring at the alleged victim's breasts."

"Not exactly."

"Could it have been that he was looking at her whole person, and when you passed by his gaze was passing over her breasts?"

"No. I was not passing by. I was going to Larisa's room to give her medicine."

"How do you know he was staring at her breasts and not something else?"

"I told you. I saw him."

"Miss Lobdell, how far away from my client were you when you determined that he was staring at her breasts?"

The flush of the toilet behind the curtains interrupted the cross examination and the entire courtroom was silent for a long moment. Brockton hoped the smell wouldn't follow. "Do I need to—" he began.

"—I was in the doorway," Ms. Lobdell replied.

"How far away is the doorway?" Brockton continued.

"I don't know. I never measured the distance."

"Approximately how far?"

"Ten feet perhaps."

"And how far was my client from the alleged victim?"

"Not far enough," the nurse said, venting her feelings a little.

"Would you have preferred that he tutor her from the hallway perhaps?" Brockton retorted. She didn't respond and he continued. "Was he, say, five feet away?"

"One or two feet."

"How was she standing in relation to him?" Brockton asked, moving close to the nurse. "Was she standing next to him?"

"She was sitting," Ms. Lobdell replied, growing uncomfortable with Brockton hovering over her. "He was standing over and to her left." As she described what she was saying, the nurse held out her hand, forcing Brockton to move back a step.

"About this far?" Brockton asked, moving closer again.

"Yes."

"Yet you could tell that he was staring at her breasts, not her shoulder, face, or perhaps her homework."

"It was obvious what he was staring at."

"Why, was she bare-breasted?" he asked and at this moment an idea struck him. He stayed as close to the nurse as possible.

"No."

"Did you ask him what he was staring at?"

"Of course not."

"Maybe he was admiring her shirt."

"If he was, he couldn't have missed her breasts as she was wearing a low cut blouse. That much I do remember."

"Why was she wearing a low cut blouse, Miss Lobdell?" Brockton asked, seizing on the woman's slip.

"I don't know why," she replied. "Why don't you ask her?"

"Do you think that was appropriate attire for a tutoring session?"

"No, I don't."

"And as a supervisor of this tutoring session wouldn't it have been incumbent upon you to see that my client's student was appropriately dressed?"

"Objection, your honor," Ritter said. "Why is the defense wasting the court's time on whose job it is to dress the victim? That is not the issue."

"Your honor," Brockton said, "There is a great deal of significance in this witness's testimony if it can be established that the alleged victim was wearing a low cut, loose-fitting shirt rather than something less revealing and more appropriate."

"That much you have established, Mr. Brockton," Holmes said. "Whose job it is to dress her is insignificant. Sustained."

"Miss Lobdell," Brockton said, turning back to the witness. "Did you say anything to my client at that time about what you perceived he was doing?"

"No."

"Why not?"

"By that time I was aware of the allegation of sexual abuse and by law I was prohibited from speaking to him. It may have endangered the patient."

Brockton glanced at the clock. It read 7:45, but he knew the day was drawing to a close. It was time to let the fur fly. He stepped closer to Lobdell and turned his back toward the judge. "Endanger the patient, Miss Lobdell? Granted staring at a person's breasts is not a part of a teacher's job description, but endangering her? I mean, what would you do if someone stared at your breasts? Wouldn't you speak to them about it?"

"Objection!" Ritter yelled, jumping out of his chair. But he was too late. The nurse's mouth dropped open and at that moment Brockton let his eyes drop to her breasts, then back to her face. He winked.

The nurse hissed, then swung at him. He backed away quickly and instead of hitting him the nurse's hand struck the statue of the woman holding the scales of justice. The statue toppled off the judge's desk and one of the plates on the scales flew into the air and struck the clock. As the plate clattered to the floor, the clock started running.

23

After leaving the courtroom, Brockton returned to his office to change into his jogging outfit. Holmes had closed the day's testimony after the nurse lashed out at him, leaving him time to run, and the court officials to pick up the scattered pieces of the Scales of Justice. As he changed, Brockton chuckled to himself. It couldn't have happened more perfectly. Unaware of what he'd done, Holmes had grabbed the gavel and was about to slam it down when she noticed that most of the people in the courtroom were gazing at the clock. She noticed that it was working and her hand stopped in midair. Not only had he rocked the nurse and Ritter, he'd made Judge Holmes hesitate. The judge had recovered enough to lecture the nurse, then warn them all not to turn the trial into a circus, but he'd made her hesitate. Of that he was especially proud.

The nurse deserved it. She was a pompous-assed bitch. When she stepped down from the witness stand she'd directed the most murderous gaze he'd ever seen at him, but he shrugged it off, looking at her as if to say she was crazy. Which she was. And the crazier a person was, the easier to find her weakness.

He'd knocked Ritter back on his heels, too. The little weasel deserved it.

As Brockton stretched, he reviewed what he had coming up in the case. He'd lined up a couple of character witnesses to appear in defense of Sienkewicz and he'd uncovered several small discrepancies in O'Connell's testimony, but he didn't have what he needed for the sure win. He'd been hoping something would come up during the course of his questioning Ritter's witnesses. It hadn't yet. He needed to find out more about the cop. A guy like that had to have a weakness to exploit and blow up his testimony.

Thinking about O'Connell reminded him of the evening with Leach earlier this week. That had thrown him. What was really going on? Why did Leach continue to defend him? The guy was crazy. And why was Leach talking about cocaine use so often? His friend was always looking for a reason to divert attention from the real issue: a crooked cop. First he'd given him that 'something was coming down and tough cops were needed' bullshit, as if this hadn't always been the case. Then, when he saw that wasn't working, he started talking about lawyers using coke. All he'd done was make Brockton even more suspicious that something else was going on.

Was O'Connell scared? Was that what this was about? And did Leach really know he was doing coke, or was he just trying to warn him off a cop? If Leach knew, who told him? There might be a leak in the Extrajudicials, a mole even.

Brockton reviewed each of the lawyers in the group. The most obvious talker was McCormick, who knew O'Connell. He had passed on the offer for a better plea bargain, even if he'd done it indirectly. Maybe he was doing more powder than he let on and had gotten caught. Or maybe he'd caught another Diwi and they told him they wouldn't overlook this one unless he cooperated. No, Brockton thought, he was being paranoid about the whole thing.

The intercom lit up. "Mr. Brockton, a young girl is here to see you. She says it's very important."

Brockton absentmindedly pressed the intercom's Speak button. "Who is it?"

"She says her name is Larisa Moran."

He jumped. What was she doing here? Grabbing the papers on Sienkewicz's case, he jammed them into the folder and pushed the intercom button again. "Send her in." So much for the jog.

Just before the door opened, he spotted the dictaphone light on his desk. It was on. He pressed the Record button.

A slight framed girl appeared in the doorway. She had large brown eyes and a classically-shaped nose. Brockton's eyes fell to her figure, which was fuller than it should have been given her age. McCormick had been right, she was naturally seductive. And looked older than fourteen.

"Hello." Brockton centered his gaze on her face. He stood and extended his hand toward one of the plush leather seats in the office.

"Hello," she replied in a rough, almost masculine voice. She sat in one of the seats, a small, leather bound book on her lap. Her eyes held Brockton's and he suddenly felt weird, like he had when he first met Sienkewicz,

"What can I do for you?" he asked, pulling himself together.

"Ms. Washington sen' me."

"Has she decided to testify?"

"No. I tol' her I want to take back what I say to the police. She tol' me come see you."

"Why?"

"She tol' me you could get Mr. Sienkewicz free."

Brockton quickly reviewed the ramifications of what the girl was saying, noting that she had pronounced his client's name correctly. "Would you be willing to put this in writing?"

She shook her head.

"If you're serious about what you're saying, I would need something in writing, an affidavit."

"This the best I can do," the girl said, holding out the leather book she was holding.

Brockton took it. "What is it?"

"His diary. When I tol' Ms. Washington the story, she show'd me this and said bring it to you. She said maybe you could help him."

"Does he know you're doing this?"

"He don't know nothin' 'bout it. We don't talk—I tol' him we had nothin' to say to each other."

"I need more than this. I need something from you, in writing."

"You gonna have to do without me signin' no paper."

"It's not me that's gonna have to do without," Brockton replied. "It's Mr. Sienkewicz, who you say you want to free. Given what the district attorney's office has done so far, I'm not gonna be able to help you do that without a recantation."

"Most of it the truth, so I ain't signin nothin'."

"If it's true and he did rape you, why shouldn't you want him to go to jail?"

"Mister, he didn' do no different than what happen before. And he love me. He stood up for me, even used a gun to defend me."

"Then why did you turn him in?"

"He turn't hisself in. And when I found out, I was angry wit' 'im so I didn' say nothin'. I feel kinda sorry for him even if I don' love him."

"Feel sorry for him?" Brockton said, unable to keep the disbelief out of his voice. The girl started to withdraw and he tried to recover. "He...raped you."

"I tol' you he didn' act no different than most. I hoped he different is all. He was nice, never bothert' me for a long time."

Brockton thought about the tape that he was recording and decided he should press her about the story. Her visit itself might save his ass but it would be an even greater coup if he could get her to crumble on tape.

"Why didn't you just refuse?" he asked, switching into his courtroom mode.

She didn't respond immediately, just looked at him as if he didn't understand. "He expect it," she said, finally.

"He expected what?" he pressed.

She didn't say anything.

"Couldn't you just tell him no?"

"I gotta go," she said and stood up.

"Listen," Brockton said quickly, "I think there's something you're not telling me. Is someone pressuring you?"

The instant he said it, the girl's whole demeanor changed. She looked around as if expecting someone to step out of the closet. "Everything I tol' you the truth. I can't tell you no more."

"If you agree to sign an affidavit, I'll talk to the district attorney and make sure nothing will happen to you."

At this the girl stood up to leave. "Ms. Washington warn me 'bout this, said I'd be gettin' myself into more trouble."

"Look, why don't you sit down and start from the beginning. Tell me what's really going on. Start with who sent you here and what they told you to say."

The girl looked at him, confused. Brockton stood up and leaned over his desk. "Larisa, I'm going to be frank. I don't believe you're telling me the truth. Believe me, you won't be the first—I'm used to it—but I think you're hiding something serious. Who's threatening you? Who's pressuring you?"

"I gotta go," she said, turning to leave. "That the best I can do."

He straightened up quickly. "I can put you on the witness stand and make you talk. Do you want that to happen? I can put you out there and bring up your whole past. I can talk about Sergeant O'Connell."

At the mention of the policeman's name, she darted a scared look at him and turned and left, practically running.

"Shit!" Brockton pounded his hand on his desk, pulling his gaze away from the empty doorway. He pushed the Stop button on the dictaphone, then pushed Rewind. The machine didn't make any noise. He opened it. There was no tape inside. "Shit!" he swore again. A great chance to get some information and he didn't even have a fucking tape in the machine. What the hell happened to the tape?

He thought about Larisa Moran. The girl was every bit as sensuous as Bart claimed. Her eyes screamed innocence and sexuality at the same time and her voice only added to the attraction. Nor was she a stranger to the ghetto.

What an interesting mix of simplicity and sophistication, he thought. While she responded to some questions like he'd expect from a child, she also realized a lot of things about life, things that made his own daughter seem like a five year old. That was the crime, he reminded himself. This kid was only fourteen and she had to deal with scum like Sienkewicz. And O'Connell. After seeing the look on her face when he mentioned the cop's name, Brockton was sure he was involved in some way.

He opened the diary and idly leafed through it. The thought of a girl signing an affidavit recanting what she had said had excited him for a minute, but that didn't seem possible after talking to her. Someone was pressuring her.

After reading a few paragraphs, he closed the diary. What kind of shit was this? Who the hell was Vladimir? Would this help him defend Sienkewicz or further incriminate him? He cursed again at not having had a tape in the dictaphone. Who the hell had removed it?

He tried to think what this meant with regards to the trial. Until he knew what the book contained, he'd have to be careful not to mention it specifically. He'd finish up what he had to ask the nurse tomorrow morning, then request that she come back next week in case he found anything else on her in this book. Instead of going home tonight, he'd call Stephanie and tell her he was going to grab a sandwich in town, then read it. He looked at the clock. If he hurried his jog, he could still get it in and read the diary, then meet the boys at O'Malley's. He pressed the intercom.

"Yes?" Candy responded.

"Candy, why is there no tape in my dictaphone?"

"You gave it to me earlier today, to transcribe the Doley case."

"Right. Listen, take messages for me for the rest of the day." He turned off the phone and restarted his stretching routine.

24

After he had jogged and showered in the downtown Y, Brockton called home and told Stephanie that he was going to work late. Back in the office, he leafed through the notes his secretary had left for him, but there was nothing that needed immediate attention. He had some time to read. If nothing else his client's diary might provide him with a couple of good stories for the boys tonight. He opened the book.

My Little Carmen
Monday, March 18

Dear Vladimir,
I met a new student today. She is a young girl, almost as young as your Lolita. However, my little Carmen is in a drug treatment center, recovering from alcohol abuse. I have been assigned to tutor her.

There is something special about her. She is not one of those finely bred children who, raised under the stigma of some hidden abuse, begins drinking to deal with it. My little Carmen is a product of the ghetto. She knows the streets. She has been forced to fend for herself and because of this, has developed a personality that is all her own.

She is also beautiful. I have been teaching for years and have taught many pretty girls, yet no one has attracted me as she does.

I know what you are thinking, Vladimir. You are saying to yourself, 'Aha! He wants to seduce this girl.' You are thinking that I am in love with her.

It is understandable that you would think this way, for you know how easy it is for a man of sophistication to fall in love with someone so young, so innocent. Yet you are wrong. This girl is special to me for an entirely different reason. Fate has sent me to her. How I came to live and work in this city has always been a mystery to me, but now I know why. I have been chosen for a special task. I cannot tell you about that yet for it would be getting ahead of myself. I must first be sure the suspicions I hold are true.

- John

Brockton set the diary down. His client was further out there than he thought. Besides writing a letter to a dead author, he was talking about a fourteen year old girl he'd raped as if she was a pawn in some cosmic game. He was going so far into this fantasy world that anyone reading this would think him guilty.

Christ, how many teachers got this weird? His daughter had had a couple of strange ones over the years, but none of them were this far out there.

For a moment Brockton considered skimming the diary instead of reading it entirely. Introduced as evidence this kind of thing might incriminate his client even more. Then his lawyer's sense took over. He'd have to read it carefully to satisfy himself that he hadn't missed one small detail that he could use. As fucked up as Sienkewicz was, the diary might give him something to work on, something that could get the case thrown out of court. There were plenty of irregularities—he just needed some details to build his case for a dismissal around them, and he had plowed through enough boring law texts to get what he wanted. He'd have to treat this the same. He'd have to put the time in. He picked the diary up again.

Wednesday, March 20

Dear Fyodor:

I must tell you of a girl I am tutoring. My little Carmen is a very special girl. Let me tell you why:

I was discussing the importance of literature with her today and quoting you, Fyodor, to illustrate how timeless classic literature is. I told her what you wrote about your century not being a century for the thinking man and how relevant that thought still was today. My little Carmen listened quietly while I expounded upon this concept and then, when most students would lose interest, she said she knew just what you were talking about. Surprised, I asked her what she meant and she said if she stopped to think about what was happening to her, she would go crazy, and it was better not to think about it at all. Imagine my incredulity at hearing this type of insight from a fourteen year old!

But that was only the start. She went on to say that many peo-
ple she knew went crazy because they let themselves think about life
too much and most times it was better not to. I asked her why not
and she told me because it meant that they would have to deal with
the truth, which they could not handle. She said that she was afraid
of the truth.

I didn't know what to say. While most teenagers live a life of
video excess, my little Carmen was displaying an interest in classic
literature. She surprised me further by saying that she wanted to
read one of your novels, that she loved to read. She is not a typical
student, Fyodor. She is a jewel! After our lesson I went to the library
and took out The Brothers Karamazov, *one of my favorites of yours.*
Not waiting until the next day, I brought it back to the center. I left
it at the front desk, where the receptionist promised to deliver it to
her as soon as she went on break.

Now that I am taking the time to write this down, Fyodor, I
discover with horror that I completely overlooked my little Carmen's
subtle plea for help! How could I be so blind! Am I that caught up
in my work that I cannot see what she was hinting at, what I sus-
pected yesterday? (I'm sure Vladimir has told you about my suspi-
cions.) She said she was afraid of the truth and I let that statement
slip right by me! What truth is she afraid of? Is it the same evil that
fate has sent me here to destroy? And now that I have ignored her
cry for help, will she ever bring it up again? Have I lost this battle
before it even started?

Brockton set the diary down again. How long was it going to take to get to this 'great evil'? And did it have anything to do with O'Connell, or reality for that matter? The

diary was believable enough, but he would need something more to go on than obscure references to some 'evil." He skimmed the next couple pages and caught Margaret Lobdell's name.

Thursday, March 28

Dear Vladimir:

I apologize for not writing to you in so long, for keeping you in suspense about my suspicions, but something has complicated my quest. I should say someone because it is the daytime head nurse, Ms. Margaret Lobdell, who has made life difficult for me. She has decided that she does not like my little Carmen. The feeling is entirely mutual; my little Carmen hates her. Unfortunately, their dispute has become a battle of wills, which both of them are determined to win. Nurse Lobdell has made it her personal mission to dominate my little Carmen. I don't think it is a question of treating her any longer. She wants to break her down in the coolly cynical way that only a therapist can do. My little Carmen is just as obstinately determined to oppose anything the woman says and all the resistance she has developed to survive in her harsh environment has been summoned to fight this battle.

The nurse is a disgusting, alabaster-skinned woman with thick, dark hair and entirely too much makeup. The contrast between her skin and hair makes me think of a statue of the virgin Mary wearing a fluffy black wig. The nurse's most noticeable features are her breasts, which stand out straight and firm like giant bastions of Christendom. When someone asks her a question, she takes a deep breath and sticks them out to intimidate the questioner. It usually works because you are forced to look the other way rather than be accused of staring at them. The nurse runs her floor of the treatment center with those breasts, Vladimir. I wonder what would happen if someone were to stare at them instead of look away.

Brockton stopped reading long enough to congratulate himself at Sienkewicz's last sentence, reminded of the court-room scene that afternoon. It had been a great move.

One of the nurse's favorite control displays is to make the girls wait for long periods of time during group sessions before she allows them to urinate. She says it helps them learn control. One girl even urinated in her pants rather than risk the nurse's wrath. Of course she didn't apologize to the poor girl, instead castigated her for a lack of control.

My little Carmen immediately tired of that rule and, of course, got in trouble. She left a group session to go to the rest room without being given permission (If only I could help her deal with these pressures!) and was given a week's restriction. But I stray from my point. I was apologizing to you because I haven't written in so long, and trying to give you some explanation. What has happened is that my little Carmen has become caught up in what is happening to her here, and is battling the nurse and staff to the detriment of my probing. She is even talking about leaving. If she does, I may never be able to confirm my suspicions.

How can I help her to survive here and not get lost to the streets? To me? Perhaps you think she should break out now, but I assure you that time hasn't yet come. My little Carmen still needs to learn how to deal with people, how to differentiate between those who help her and those who want to hurt her. If she leaves now, she will end up back here within weeks like so many of them do. She must wait and choose the right moment. When she is ready to leave, I will be the first to help her.

When I talk to her about staying, however, she grows depressed. My little Carmen is fragile, which no one sees because she acts so tough. Never given any guidance, forced to direct her own life, she battles those around her the same way she always has, by being nasty and rebellious. She has put up this front for so long just to survive that she cannot let it go. But this tough exterior hides a huge streak of vulnerability that I see clearly. Each of her battles is another feeble attempt to hide her vulnerability. I see her fall into the trap time and time again, and my heart aches for her. I see her snap at the nurses, then watch the tears roll down her cheeks when they leave. I want to take her in my arms and soothe her. Instead I play the role meted out to me. I tell her she is doing well. I tell her I have never met anyone as unique as her. (Sometimes I think this is all too much and I should get away. What would happen? Would she be hurt or would she shrug it off and survive, become even harder than before?)

But again I stray. I wrote to you to tell you to have patience. I still intend to draw out of her what has happened. It is only that my task has become more difficult. In addition to being an inhibiting influence on my progress, the head nurse is very astute. The other day she came to me with her giant bastions of Christendom waving and asked if I had been talking to my little Carmen about her troubles. "You're not to talk to her about those topics," the nurse said. "We have therapists who are trained to do that."

What can I do now but continue to teach this young flower, try to prevent her from wilting within the lifeless, antiseptic walls of this *institution? I must wait with the patience of the Sphinx for her to speak again, for I fear that someone will find out what I am doing if I question her too directly.*

Monday, April 1

Dear Fyodor:

How clever is fate the way it reveals what must be done! The alienation I wrote to you about last week has worked right into my hands! It all began over the weekend, when my little Carmen got into trouble for taking late night walks alone in the recreation area outside the center. Although the area is fenced in, patients are forbidden to go there without supervision because they are afraid someone will try to slip over the wall. Last night one of the nurses discovered my little Carmen there after curfew, when the girls were supposed to be in their rooms. When she was asked why she was out of her room my little Carmen told them I had given her a book to read for homework and that she hadn't finished it. She showed them the novel I'd gotten for her at the library and told them she had gone outside to read it because she couldn't have a light on in her room. She used the flood lights to read by. She then grew so nasty that they placed her on one month's restriction to her room.

A nurse approached me about the incident and I covered for her. I told the nurse that I was unaware of all the activities she was required to participate in at the center (a lie!) and thought the book would help her pass the time.

You think it is wrong that I lie, Vladimir? Do you not see how masterful this move is? My little Carmen is furious and the focus of her anger is now directed at the staff. She sees herself as innocent and clings to her innocence like a drowning person clings to a life raft no matter how ridiculous it sounds to those around her. But more importantly, she trusts me. I stood up for her. She said to me today, "I will never tell them what they want to know! I would tell you first!" She trusts me, Fyodor, and I can once again pursue my suspicions. Because she hates the staff, I can be reasonably sure that she won't tell them what we are discussing.

Tuesday, April 2

Dear Vladimir:

Plato wrote that the normal man contents himself with dreaming that which the wicked man does in actual life. I have discovered who that wicked man is. I have found the villain, for today, our first day alone together in her room, my little Carmen revealed his identity to me. It is who I suspected.

It all happened quickly, without any of the breaking down that you would expect to happen when someone reveals something she has repressed. And it happened as a direct result of her anger with the center's staff. She was complaining about them and saying that they were no different than the people outside. Playing the role of a teacher I reminded her what she had said the day before, telling me what they wanted to know, and she told me, without hesitation, that someone had beaten and raped her, then threatened to kill her if she said anything. I asked her who this someone was, holding my breath, and she said, "a policeman they call Donkey Dick." This is the name he used when I knew him at Palmerola! This is the man fate has sent me to destroy!

Brockton set the diary down. This was it. He'd hit pay dirt. If this was true and the diary provided enough details he could nail the son of a bitch. He had no doubt it was O'Connell that his client was talking about. His reaction when they met at the Thruway stop had given him away.

He had to make some decisions. How should he approach this? Should he question Sienkewicz about the diary, tell him that he had it and try to flush out more answers? The girl had said that Sienkewicz didn't know she had his diary and as scared as she was, she probably wouldn't tell him. She had said she wanted nothing more to do with him.

It would be smarter to keep the whole thing secret for now. Sienkewicz had kept all this from him so why should he feel obligated to say anything to him?

Should he tell anyone else? No, he wasn't ready yet. He'd just ask Holmes for some time, tell her that new evidence had been brought to light and leave it at that. That would shake them up a bit. If he asked for a week, he was sure Holmes would give it to him. That would allow him enough time to finish the diary and pursue anything he needed to get the case thrown out. If Sienkewicz could substantiate his charge, they'd have to drop the case, he was sure of it. And his client would never even know. He'd just call the son of a bitch and tell him he was free.

He liked the idea. He'd call Sienkewicz now and tell him not to bother coming to court tomorrow, that he'd be in touch with him as soon as things were resolved. He wouldn't tell him any more than that, just leave him hanging. He didn't deserve to know anything anyway as uncooperative as he'd been.

25

As soon as Brockton entered O'Malley's, Bart McCormick waved him over to where he and several other lawyers were drinking. Brockton waved back and walked the other way, toward the rest rooms. While washing his hands he thought about what he was going to say. They had probably all heard what happened at the courthouse; that kind of news traveled fast. He was going to enjoy telling them about it in detail. He'd keep the diary secret.

"Hey Rooster!" McCormick yelled, moving back to make room for Brockton once he'd made it to the bar. "Here. Here. Right here! Rooster, you've got the city's whole law establishment buzzing. What the hell did you do?"

"What do you mean?" Brockton asked, feigning ignorance.

"What do you mean! The DA's office is pissed! I saw Ritter at the courthouse and he was so mad he couldn't even talk about it. All he could say was that you played dirty!"

"Paybacks are a bitch."

"What happened?"

"He put someone on the stand that he never should have."

"Who?"

"Some nurse social worker."

"What happened?"

"The woman—and I use the term loosely—took a swing at me."

"She actually swung at you? What the hell did you say to her?"

"Nothing. She went crazy and tried to hit me. Missed, of course. Instead she knocked over The Scales of Justice, sent 'em flying."

"Wait a minute," McCormick said. "Don't be modest, Rooster. Did you ask her out for a date? Insult her mother? What did you do? Something must have set her off."

"I didn't say anything. I think she got a little upset when after her testimony about my client staring at this kid's breasts I thought I'd try it out on her. She wasn't too happy about that."

"You stared at her tits? How the hell did you get away with that with Holmes?"

"She didn't catch it. I turned my back so she couldn't see me."

McCormick whistled. "What about afterwards? She didn't do anything afterwards?"

"I told you, she didn't see me. I had the bitch so fired up that Holmes thought she was crazy. And Ritter didn't know what to do. He was stunned. That's why he's so pissed. The son of a bitch sat there like a fuckin' rock."

"The witness said nothing?"

"She didn't have time to. Holmes closed it up right there. But get this. One of the scales that went flying hit the clock, which started working. That was the clincher."

"We heard. We heard the clock's working now. You ought 'a send them a bill."

"It still doesn't tell the right time," Brockton said.

Sidney Greene shifted in his chair, almost falling off. He was drunk already. "Shit, I wonder how Holmes took all that talk about tits. She's got a nice set herself under that robe. You ever seen her out of that robe?"

"I see them every month," Bart said. "She goes to the symphony on the same night Cheryl and I go. I mention them every time to Cheryl. She gets jealous and I get laid."

"Talk about knockers," Sidney said, "Did you see the ones on that babe I left with last Thursday?"

"Yeah, who was that girl you walked out of here with?" someone else in the group asked.

"Name's Beverly," Sid said.

"She has a nice set. I'd put down twenty to see them."

"Beverly Big Breasts," Sid said.

"Who is she?"

"Just an old friend."

"Sure, Sidney, just an old friend."

"Okay, since it's out in the open I might as well admit it. I was leaving the bar and noticed her. She was in town for work, some corporate job. I told her I thought she was pretty and she followed me to my car."

"Bullshit."

"No bullshit. We went out to my car and I got head. She said I was funny, brought back old memories."

"What memories? You being a funny guy?"

"Wait till she finds out you're married."

"She knows."

"So you gonna bring her home for dinner?"'

"The wife would kill me if she saw me with another girl. But old friends don't count, especially if it's just a blow job."

"Yeah, right," Brockton said. "Tell your wife that." Sid was spilling too much information, from drinking too much alcohol.

"It's the twelve year itch," Sid said. "Comes right after the eleven year one."

Brockton shook his head. Sid noticed. "You're not trying to say you never cheated, are you Rooster?"

"Never."

"Bullshit."

"No bullshit."

"You say that here, in front of us, cuz you gotta be political but I know you've had a secret screw."

"Never," Brockton repeated.

"Rooster!" Bart said. "Don't do this to me! All my illusions falling before my eyes!"

"I been loyal since day one."

"Now I know you're cheating," Sid said. "No one talks with that much conviction unless they're trying to hide something."

"Sounds old fashioned but it's the truth," Brockton replied.

"Not even a blow job?" Sid continued. "I don't know anyone who hasn't gotten at least a blow job."

"I get that at home."

"I don't let my wife blow me," Sid said.

"So how you gonna get any head?"

"Not my wife. That's sacrilegious."

"You're getting a little hypocritical aren't you Sid?" Brockton said.

"It's dirty is all," Sid replied. "I can't ask my wife to go down there."

"Wash yourself once in a while."

"I do. I just have a little more respect for my wife is all. That's why I don't use her name, either, when I talk about sex."

"But think of how much better it would be to have Diane give you head. You wouldn't—"

"—Hey don't use her name like that. Don't use my wife's name."

Brockton smiled. "Sid, you're a ball of contradictions. I don't think a roomful of psychiatrists could figure you out."

"It's that Catholic school education," Bart added.

"I get enough," Sid replied. "But let's get back to the big news of the evening. If you're telling the truth about your own fidelity, which I'm sorry to hear about, I want to go on record as wondering whether we need a new Rooster. Bart, what about it? We need an active Rooster."

"There's only one Rooster," Bart replied. "He's just having a weak moment."

"Well, in case the weak moment lasts too long we have to have someone who's ready to step in."

A new round of beers arrived at the end of the bar and there was a moment of quiet as they were passed around.

"Sid, you're fucked up," Brockton finally said.

"Why?"

"Not only are you cheating, you're broadcasting it. Most people have a little more discretion."

"Wait, I didn't do anything with her. I walked out to the car with her, we made out for a while and I went home. I was the one to pull away. I felt guilty."

"What happened to the blow job?"

"I was lying," Sid said.

"Once you start that shit you don't stop," Brockton said.

"Why are you picking on me?"

"I guess I thought there was some hope for you."

"Jesus, Rooster, what's the matter with you? You're sounding awfully self righteous."

"I'm just saying you're fucked up is all," Brockton replied.

"What can I tell you? I drink too much, earn too much money, and made out with another woman. Then lied about it. I have to live with myself, though. But I'm funny, Rooster, you gotta admit that. I'm funny, right?"

Brockton still said nothing.

Sid got off his bar stool and set his pint glass on the bar. "Hey, maybe I had a little too much to drink, but let me just say that I, for one, am not going to become one of those guys that never gets any. Sit down with any group of males and listen to them. Any group. What do they talk about? They talk about how little they're getting. They stare at all the girls coming into the bar and talk about how much they want them. And odds on that most of the ones talking are married.

"Now I ask you, why are married men always talking about pussy when they have everything they need at home? Because they ain't gettin' it, that's why. Freddie from the DA's office was in here the other day saying that he only gets laid once every three months."

"Freddie said that?"

"Yeah. He said it's like a dividend that pays quarterly. He's a funny guy."

"Why does he even bother?" Bart asked.

"Don't think you're so far removed," Sid said. "I remember when I accused my wife of giving the dog more attention than me. Get this, I said to her, 'Honey you never forget to walk the dog twice a day. So why do you forget me?' She said it was because the dog would shit in the house if she didn't walk her. So I said, 'Is that what it would take? Should I threaten to shit in the bed?'"

Everyone laughed and Sid took a long drink from his beer.

"Poor Freddie," Bart commiserated. "Once every three months? That's dismal."

"I told him that and you know what he said? He said he was glad to get it that often, that at least it kept the pipes from rusting. Yes, I may be fucked up, Rooster, but I'm going to enjoy sex while I can. I seen too many couples that stay together but are nasty to each other. Like what's his name, that old lawyer that only does traffic violations. Jensen. He's always talking about trying to please his wife. He said he gave up on the physical desires. I ain't givin' that up no matter where I gotta get it."

"Do what you want, Sid," Brockton said. "It's a free world and you are free to do what you want."

"Right," Bart agreed. "A free world. Hey, by the time I convinced Cheryl to have a third kid she was sick of the salamander. It'd be the right time and she'd call me and say hurry up, get it done. Then lay there while I plugged away. I've always said that's why Mandy looks so much like me cuz I did all the work."

"Just because your marital life has fallen to pieces doesn't mean everyone's has to," Brockton said.

"Falling to pieces?" Bart said. "Who said anything about falling to pieces?"

"You're always complaining," Brockton replied.

"I worry is all. Just the other day I came home and Cheryl was alone, sleeping in bed. The kids were at her parents' home. So I'm thinking she wants out, the Big D, and sent the kids away while she tells me. I was ready to go into the study and pull out the papers. Instead, she pulls me into bed. She just wanted sex."

"Sounds like a check fuck to me," Sid said. "My wife used to do that all the time. I'd come home late and she'd be up. She'd fuck me to check that I wasn't cheating on her. Sometimes she'd even smell me first."

"Sounds like a great way to get head," Brockton said, winking at Bart.

"Speaking of crazy wives, I'm defending this guy whose girlfriend found him in bed with another woman. She goes into the kitchen to get a knife but instead of going after him she goes after the chick. She stabs the girl right there, in the bed. In her own bed!"

"Not a good move."

"Why did they arrest him?"

"While she was stabbing the girl my client puts his arm up and catches a piece of the blade. He gets pissed and tears the knife out of his girlfriend's hands and stabs her. She's pressing charges. Says since she never attacked him and he stabbed her, he's guilty of assault."

Bar noise took over the conversation for a while, the discussion having been worn out.

"So what's Ritter gonna do next to fuck up this case?" Bart asked after the short silence.

Brockton shrugged.

"I can't figure out why he's using all these hearsay witnesses," Sid said. "He's got a police report, which is all he needs."

"He's afraid of the Rooster," Bart said. "He's afraid you're gonna pull something out of your hat and discredit the report."

"He's probably at home right now preparing for all the shit you're gonna dump on him."

"Shit, he doesn't have anything to worry about tomorrow," Brockton said, careless from the beer. "After I finish with the nurse, I'm gonna put this case behind me."

"What d'ya got?" Bart asked.

"Nothing much," Brockton replied, trying to cover up. "Just some evidence that should take care of things. I'm going in there tomorrow and ask for more time just so I can see the looks on their faces. I'm gonna fuck 'em up."

26

The next morning O'Connell wasn't in court as Brockton hoped he'd be. He'd served the cop with a subpoena and told Ritter he planned to put him on the stand early in the trial, so it was odd that he wasn't there. Perhaps he'd come late, Brockton thought, disappointed.

Once Judge Holmes had seated herself and the formalities were over, Brockton continued his cross examination. "Ms. Lobdell, yesterday you testified that while at Millwood Treatment Center the alleged victim, Larisa Moran, mentioned being molested."

"Yes I did." The nurse appeared to have fully recovered, sounding more confident than ever.

"Did she mention this to you specifically?"

"No."

"To whom did she mention it?"

"To another patient at the center."

"Who was that other patient?"

"I'm not sure I can tell you that information, if it should be confidential or not."

"Let's forget about who the patient was for now. It was another patient in the unit I take it?"

"Yes."

"So some patient told you that Larisa Moran told her she had a sexual encounter with someone."

"I said she said she had a sexual encounter with her teacher."

"But she didn't mention his name."

"No."

"So she had a sexual encounter with some teacher."

"With her teacher, who was Mr. Sienkewicz."

"But she didn't mention his name."

"At that time he was her only teacher."

"But he isn't the only teacher she's ever had."

"I doubt that."

"And she never mentioned him by name." The nurse didn't respond and Brockton asked, "Did you know her teacher's name at that time?"

"What do you mean?"

"At the time some patient told you that Larisa Moran had a sexual encounter with her teacher, did you know her teacher's name? Or was he just another teacher?"

"I knew Larisa's teacher, and that his name was Mr. John Sienkewicz."

"Yet isn't it true that for weeks you actually called him Mr. Smith?"

The nurse's face clouded. "I don't recall that."

"Think about it, Ms. Lobdell. My client even came to you and corrected you. Do you remember that?"

After an initial hesitation, Ms. Lobdell said, "That's possible, but if I did, you must understand that there are quite a number of tutors at the center. It is easy to get a name mixed up once in a while."

"You didn't know Mr. John Sienkewicz's name?"

"I said it is possible that I mixed up his name. I do know that during his time there I correctly connected his face with his name even if I did misspeak it."

"You do recall that he has been working at that facility for almost two years."

"Yes."

"But you didn't even know his name."

This time the nurse didn't bother to reply and Brockton remained silent for as long as Holmes would permit. Then, with as much incredulity as he could muster, he said, "Do you mean to tell me, Ms. Lobdell, that you suspected my client because someone mentioned to someone else that she had a sexual encounter with someone, and that none of these some ones bore my client's name?"

"I don't mean to tell you anything, Mr. Brockton," the nurse replied evenly. "I am simply here to state what I observed." Although it was obvious that she was insulted by Brockton's question, the nurse was keeping firm control of herself today. Ritter must have counseled her.

Brockton looked at his papers, sorting through the questions he'd jotted down. "Ms. Lobdell, isn't it a law that you have to file a report for all disclosures of physical and sexual abuse?"

"Yes."

"Did you file a report?"

Margaret Lobdell hesitated, then said, "No."

"Why not?"

"Larisa Moran left the center shortly after the disclosure, within days."

"Whether she left or not, you should have filed a written report, correct?"

"Not necessarily. The disclosure was second hand and I wanted to be sure it was not frivolous. Having worked with drug dependent children for some time I am aware that sometimes they say things they later retract."

"Did this someone retract what she said Larisa Moran told her about being sexually abused?"

"No, however adolescents are sometimes confused about sexual abu—"

"—Did you question her again?" Brockton interrupted.

"Who?"

"Either girl."

"No."

"Why not?"

"As I already said, Larisa was released."

"But this is a serious allegation, Ms. Lobdell. Don't you think it is one you should have followed up on given that level of seriousness?"

"I was following up on it."

"With a written report."

"Adolescents sometimes say things in order to manipulate people's emotions, and to get attention. As trained nurses we assess what has validity and what should be screened out."

"You honor, this is unnecessary," Ritter interposed.

"Your honor, this is not only necessary it is as relevant as anything can be."

"Continue," Holmes said.

"So you screened out what Larisa Moran said to someone about being sexually abused. And you did nothing about it."

"I didn't screen anything out. I started to check up on whether the disclosure had merit. I do not work at the center around the clock, however, and while I was following up on the report, Larisa was released. Since Mr. Sienkewicz was no longer coming to the center I felt that I did not have to worry about his being near our other clients."

"He might have come there again."

"It's not likely given all that has happened."

"Would it have been at all within the realm of possibility that he might have tutored at the treatment center again given that he had been tutoring there for two years?"

"It's not likely."

"But not impossible. And you were willing to let this alleged sexual abuser continue to tutor your patients."

"Objection," Ritter said. "Conjecture."

"There's nothing conjectural about it, your honor. I said alleged."

"He's stretching this to the point of unbelievability, your honor."

"Allow me to correct the assistant district attorney. Under federally mandated reporting procedures and the treatment center's own internal regulations, his witness was required to submit a written report to the center's medical director within forty-eight hours of the disclosure taking place."

"Which is an entirely different point than the defense attorney is making, one that we are all aware of," Ritter added. "And as the defense attorney knows, the center did not first report the abuse."

"Sustained."

"So from there, Ms. Lobdell, you dropped the whole matter," Brockton continued.

"As a matter of fact, I did not. I also called Larisa's case worker. She told me that Mr. Sienkewicz had been charged with sexually abusing and assaulting Larisa."

Brockton looked at the woman in front of him. "Ms. Lobdell, do you consider yourself a good nurse?"

"Objection!" Ritter said.

"Sustained." Judge Holmes gave Brockton a warning look, but he was glad he had thrown the insult at her. It had shaken her a bit.

"Do you know that about ninety-five percent of children's disclosures are, in fact, true?"

"Are you quoting me statistics, Mr. Brockton? Because if you are, I am already aware of them."

"But being aware of them didn't make you think that this disclosure was true," Brockton continued, ignoring the retort.

"Not entirely, no."

"Then the disclosure must have been dubious in the first place considering everything you neglected to do."

"I made a mistake."

"A mistake, Ms. Lobdell?" Brockton walked over to the witness stand, suddenly wanting to hurt the woman. "Let me sum up the mistakes, just the major ones. From a distance of at least ten feet, you saw my client staring at some breasts. This gave you to think that he may be doing something wrong. Then you heard about a possible case of sexual abuse involving two people and you neglected to follow up on it with a written report, a report that the law requires you to write. Of course you never bothered to speak to my client, whose name you didn't even know, a man who for all intents and purposes could have returned to the center to abuse other patients. And now you have the nerve to claim that you truly suspected my client of having abused this girl."

"You may choose to highlight certain actions of mine as mistakes, Mr. Brockton, but considering what has happened since the police have become involved, I prefer to think that they were, in general, correct."

"Or maybe the police have just continued to make more mistakes, Ms. Lobdell. Isn't that possible?" She didn't reply and Brockton said, "Have you ever witnessed the police questioning a suspect after a disclosure?"

"No."

"They don't question people the way nurses do. They don't sit back like you and listen, then screen out what seems to be unfounded. And they don't bother to check to see if a disclosure is frivolous, as you say. They come at you. They know just what they want to hear, and they dig for it. So—"

"—Objection!" Ritter snapped. "Your honor, this is irrelevant."

"So please don't think you're the only one making mistakes, Ms. Lobdell," Brockton continued. "If the police had listened to the alleged victim a little longer before acting, she might have retrac—"

"—Objection!" Ritter yelled again.

"Retracted what she said to them. Perhaps it is the police who made the biggest mistake and should be the ones apologizing." Brockton turned toward Judge Holmes. "Those are all the questions I have, your honor."

"Mr. Ritter?"

"Thank you, your honor. Ms. Lobdell, I understand it's hard to admit making mistakes, but would you agree that this is one time you missed a warning sign, that there was a lack of—"

"—Objection, your honor. The man is leading the witness."

"Sustained."

Ritter stood quietly for a moment, then asked, "Ms. Lobdell, to the best of your judgment, was Larisa Moran telling the truth when she said that she had been sexually abused by her teacher?"

"Yes, I believe she was telling the truth."

"And who was her teacher at the time she disclosed this information?"

"Mr. John Sienkewicz."

"The same Mr. John Sienkewicz that is sitting in front of you today?"

"Yes. And how his attorney can defend such a man says something about his moral character," Ms. Lobdell added.

Brockton shrugged.

"Thank you," Ritter said. "That is all."

"Anything further, Mr. Brockton?" Holmes asked.

"Your honor, I'd like to request that this case be thrown out due to the incredibly large number of contradictions that I have made apparent."

Judge Holmes looked at Ms. Lobdell, then at Brockton. "Request denied. Do you have anything further Mr. Brockton?"

"Yes, your honor, as I mentioned to you earlier, just yesterday I obtained a piece of evidence that I believe is key to my client's defense. I will need some time, however, to look it over."

"How much time?"

"A week would be fine."

"Do you have any problems with that, Mr. Ritter?"

"No, your honor," Ritter said immediately, but Brockton was sure the assistant DA sounded uneasy.

"Very well," Holmes said. "I'll give you until a week from next Monday, Mr. Brockton. That's more than sufficient time. Any problems with that?"

"That's fine," Brockton said.

Ritter quickly scanned a date planner in front of him. "That will be fine, your honor."

As the judge slammed the gavel down, Brockton walked over to Ritter. "Where's Donkey Dick?" he asked.

"Who?"

"Your cop. O'Connell. Donkey Dick." He walked away. He wouldn't have the pleasure of seeing O'Connell sweat out that new bit of information, but Ritter would tell him. The son of a bitch would be sweating soon enough.

27

Brockton didn't have time to read more of the diary until that evening. After supper he excused himself from the table, begging off his usual play time with the kids by saying that he had work to catch up on. He locked himself in the study. He had a week to put this case to rest and hoped that was all it would take.

Monday, April 8

Dear Fyodor:

I have become one of your characters, Fyodor. I am the cowardly little mouse who scurries back into his hold, the humiliated man who watches others because he is afraid of himself. I am the one who takes notes from underground.

You object to my self portrait? Your character was only a clerk and I am a teacher, you say? Yes, a teacher can play a greater role than a clerk in our world, but he can also be wretched and cow-

ardly. When he loses the ability to affect the young minds around him, Fyodor, a teacher can even become wicked. He can make life miserable for his students and seek pleasure in it.

Do not mistake me. I have not become your despicable little man because I torment my students. I treat them with a good deal of respect. Yet I have gone underground, more deeply than your clerk ever did. And I have done this because I am a coward. Like your clerk, I have become a spineless creature amongst a world of brutes. I watch the brutes around me make fools of themselves while being entirely envious of them. And because I can only watch—and envy—them, I suffer from the same disease your clerk did, lucidity. I see very clearly the depravity in man.

To what am I referring, you ask? I am referring to our secret, the evil my little Carmen has revealed to me. For instead of acting on what she has told me, I have done nothing. I listen attentively and express the proper amount of empathy yet rather than seek help I hide what she tells me from everyone else. I do not want to become involved.

Do not think my cowardice is without reason. It is the very same authorities to whom I would speak who would hurt my little Carmen. If I were to expose this evil they would come with all their truth-seeking machines and attempt to break down her story. Then they would start looking for a scapegoat to save themselves. And who is a better scapegoat than I? So you see, Fyodor, why this must remain our secret. We share the knowledge that there is an evil man out there, who can hurt us.

I've told her the seriousness of speaking to anyone about our secret. At first I was afraid she would give us away by boasting about the candy and other gifts I smuggled in to her (you know how easily one thing leads to another), but she assures me she doesn't have anyone to talk to at the center.

I worry about the nurse. She hovers near my little Carmen's room all the time, as if waiting for her to break some petty rule. I often wonder if she knows what we talk about, what I am trying to do. Will she betray us?

I apologize. You want to know if I have discovered anything further. I can only tell you that I have confirmed my suspicions. The evil I must destroy is Richard O'Connell. But before I tell you how I know this, let me tell you about him so that you understand the magnitude of my task.

I first met him amidst a table of GIs, in a whorehouse. He was telling them about a prostitute he hired, a young girl. He made her kneel in front of him by pointing a gun at her temple, then told her to give him a blow job or he'd shoot her. This story brought a round of applause from the table until he said that he wanted, before he left, to shoot one of the prostitutes in the act. He was concerned that he could shoot and pull away before she 'bit the donkey' as he termed it. No one laughed at this, Fyodor, because they knew he meant what he said.

So you see why I am fearful. This brute, this evil man, will do whatever his selfish soul desires. He plods along his path of evil without stopping to observe the effects he has beyond himself. If he stopped, he would despise what he saw; perhaps that is why he does not. Like all brutes, his capacity to ignore the pain he causes others allows him to continue on this destructive path.

What I mean to say, Fyodor, is that we all entertain wicked thoughts, yet only the brutes pursue them. But you know this. You, who captured the soul of your people, know how selfish our actions really are, even acts of love.

So while the brutes carry on, covering up the results of their evil deeds with self-righteous doublespeak, I remain silent. I listen to my little Carmen speak of this man and I do not expose him. I have become an observant little package of misery.

I watch everything I do and say. I hide in my miserable hole, hoping that our secret will not be revealed and that someday I will find the courage to act. My empathy is a facade, while hidden below the surface, waiting for the word or motion to set it free, is a brute. We all wear masks etched from our moral code, which hide our true nature. Those who truly know the soul of a man know what I mean.

Brockton lay the diary down before reading the next entry. Sienkewicz was getting his characters mixed up. What did he mean he was a brute? And when was he going to supply him with the details he needed?

He heard noise in the front room where his kids were watching television and decided to get a beer. He might be at this for a couple of hours. Minutes later, he returned to his study and continued reading.

Monday, April 15

Dear Sigmund:

An interesting series of events has occurred over the past week and our friend Vladimir suggested that I write you for advice. For several weeks I have been tutoring a young girl who is trying to resolve her problems, many of them psychological. Because she has chosen to confide in me and not the nursing staff at the treatment center, we have become very close. Lately, however, I have become concerned with the sexuality behind many of her actions. She brushes her body against me during the course of her lessons. She pretends that it is accidental, but I suspect she does it on purpose. Until this point I have not discussed it with her. Does she understand, at her age, what a man thinks when a female acts like this toward him? Is this an unconscious action of desire on her part?

Perhaps you cannot answer me with so little knowledge, but allow me to describe to you something that happened today. My little Carmen and I were discussing our weekends and after she told me how she had spent hers I mentioned that I had taken my family shopping. I continued talking, oblivious to my little Carmen's reaction when she suddenly told me that she hated my wife.

The comment took me as unawares, Sigmund, and since I didn't know what to say, I ignored it. She has never met my wife, has only heard of her in a peripheral sense. Yet she expressed this great feeling of hatred for her. Because you deal with these types of things with your hysterics, I'm sure this would be familiar to you. What might I have done?

I'm sure a psychologist would have explanations for why my little Carmen acts this way. She never received enough love and affection as a child and she is seeking it from me. She was sexually abused when young, they would say, and the closest thing to real affection she experienced was that abuse. She is seeking affection and at the same time lashing out at others, whom she sees as competition. I would be warned to be cautious given the sexuality hidden just below the surface, ready to explode.

I cannot let those fears impede me! My little Carmen looks to me for support and to withdraw from her would send her into a down-

ward spiral. I'm sure you experienced this in some of your patients, and see the dilemma I am in. My desire to help her has exposed me to emotions that are very powerful and exert great influence on us both. Most people who work in a human service field experience this and protect themselves by detaching their emotions from the job. But don't you see what a copout that is?! My little Carmen, like so many others, would immediately detect any detachment. I cannot abandon her.

This path is dangerous, Sigmund. I am being sucked into this relationship like into quicksand, one step at a time until I cannot remove myself. Yet while I fear the emotions I am experiencing, I am also strangely excited by them.

Perhaps I reveal too much. That is possible, is it not? You, at certain points in your writing decided not to reveal your past because, and I quote, "the personal sacrifice which this would involve is too great". I, too, have a career and thoughts like this could cause me to lose my job. You, at least, were protected by the mantle of scientific research. I work in a field where the dangers of sexual encounters are only too well known. The countless hours teachers spend with students make them inevitable. Yet the punishments are great in my profession, as great as the temptations.

I sometimes think this relationship has gone too far. Should I inform the nursing staff? Should I express the fear that my little Carmen's sexuality is breaking loose? For while I understand that this is natural to a girl in her position, I wonder how I will react, how much control I can exhibit if things go too far. To succumb to it now would endanger my talk. But if I tell them, they might remove me from the situation and push my little Carmen away. I have earned her trust—how can I sink to their level by betraying it?

Friday, April 19

Dear Fyodor:

I write to you of something of extreme secrecy, yet something I can no longer withhold. For since it happened I have felt emotions that I haven't felt in years. I have spoken often to my students of uncontrolled passion yet always in a vicarious sense, skeletons rattling about in dust-covered literature books. Now, a skeleton has emerged and its power has overcome me. I have stripped off my mask.

I don't have to remind you, Fyodor, that this must remain a secret. My teaching career is at stake, for if anyone ever found out what happened I would no longer be allowed in a classroom. I wouldn't be allowed to see my little Carmen.

When I arrived to tutor her Tuesday afternoon her door was closed. The head nurse told me, in her usual brusque manner, that she didn't feel well, then left me standing there. I decided to peek into her room and drop off some homework papers I had corrected.

She was lying on her bed, asleep. I whispered her name and she didn't respond. I entered the room, planning to leave the papers on the desk. The door closed silently behind me, not all the way but enough to block anyone from looking into the room. I did not push it shut, that much innocence I can claim.

She lay so quiet and beautiful that after I placed the papers on her dresser I went over to her just to gaze at her lovely face. As I gazed at her my eyes were confronted with the soft curves of her shoulders and neck. She was wearing a low cut shirt, Fyodor, and I was drawn in, my eyes lingering over her beauty. I was overcome by the sight and my hand reached for her. I was seized with an intense desire to kiss and caress her. She looked so helpless and inviting.

This desire has possessed me before, but I have always been able to fight it off. Once I touched her I lost control and began to kiss her face, her bared shoulders and her breasts. I wept while I kissed her, Fyodor, for her and myself, heedless of the price I would pay if I was discovered behaving like this, like some teenager with uncontrolled hormones directing me.

Suddenly she opened her eyes and looked at me. I drew back, but instead of being frightened she acted puzzled. I remember thinking that she must be drugged (they have been giving her all sorts of pills to try and control her behavior), because she didn't say anything, instead lay her head back on the pillow and went to sleep. I started to withdraw but when I turned toward the door noticed that it was open and there, standing in the way, was the nurse. I was sure she had seen what happened and was going to question me. I tried to engage her in conversation. She smiled and said nothing and I slipped past her and hurried out.

Did she see what I did? I have heard nothing from the center since this incident. I do not know whether they are keeping her from me, or telling the truth when they say that she is still sick. I cannot know what they suspect.

I have experienced an emotional reawakening since this happened. I feel exhilarated. I have even become a better teacher, injecting new vitality into what I teach. The passion that has been dormant in my life now overwhelms me, so much so that I am afraid to return to my little Carmen. If they were to allow me to see her again, I might not control myself. The brute grows stronger each day.

How long can a wistful pedagogue subject himself to the beauty and innocence of a youth such as she? You say that a student has a

propensity for falling in love with a teacher, Fyodor, but is not the
opposite as likely? How can I witness her emotional outpourings,
her most vulnerable self, without falling in love with her? How can I
hide from life's strongest emotion without feeling cheated? I love her
as much as a man can love anyone. Will it free me, this maelstrom
of emotions, or will it imprison me? Will I become like your charac-
ter, a man turned to hatred because I am filled with love?

Brockton put the book down. It was obvious that he was-
n't going to be able to introduce this in court. His client had
incriminated himself in anyone's eyes, especially with this
last admission. And he was headed in so certain a direction
that Brockton could predict where it was going to end.

Resisting the temptation to jump ahead and see if he was
correct, he jotted some notes that would help him focus on
how he needed to approach this. He was glad he'd been as
vague as he had about new evidence. He'd probably said
more than he should have. He needed to get something firm
to sink his teeth into and something, he couldn't tell what,
told him it would be in this diary. He needed to keep reading.

Wednesday, April 24

Dear Sigmund:
I trust you have been communicating with Fyodor and have
read about what happened this past week. I am writing again be-
cause I realize that I never told you how I discovered that the evil I
seek to destroy is none other than Richard O'Connell. I apologize

for this oversight. Sometimes memoirs this personal require us to go in an entirely different direction than anticipated. I will try to make it up to you now.

You do not know much about this evil man I am pursuing, so let me tell you about him. It was in the back room of a whorehouse outside Palmerola when I decided that someone needed to destroy him. The door to the room was open, something prostitutes do for safety reasons and he entered the room carrying a rifle. He called the girl's name, then, in the most unforgettable moment of my life, he turned to the crib next to us and bayoneted her sleeping child. She screamed—I will never forget that scream—and he hit her with the butt end of his gun and left.

I could to nothing. I jumped up and cowered in the corner while others raced to the scene to pull the dead child from the bloodied arms of its mother. But that day I vowed to put an end to this evil.

He came to me later to talk about this obscenity, as if to expunge himself of guilt. He told me that a certain Communist traitor had been responsible for the death of a GI, a friend of his. They had been unable to find the traitor to avenge his death, but while investigating had discovered that a prostitute had given birth to his child. He had killed the child to avenge his friend's death.

Whether this is true or not, Sigmund, I cannot forgive him. Fate chose me to avenge his sin when it allowed me to witness the look on this evil man's face when he turned, with the blood of a dying chile on his bayonet. I remember it as if it had happened yesterday. He was smiling.

I am sorry to have taken so much of your valuable time. You wanted to know how I am sure the man I seek to destroy is this same man. Although I have known all along, I only confirmed it this evening, as it wasn't until then that I found the courage to call him.

I waited until the stroke of midnight to call, and he answered. I recognized his voice as if I had last spoken to him yesterday. I froze for a minute and he almost hung up. "I know what you did to her," I finally was able to hiss and that caught his attention. "Who is this?" he said. "Someone who knows you," I replied. "But you have nothing to fear if you leave her alone. I love her." I hung up.

You may have guessed what my plan is. I intend to keep him away from my little Carmen and to do this I will pretend that I am a jealous lover. I will not tell her I did this when I see her again. I do not want to frighten her. But he is a dangerous man and would kill her without hesitation without my protection.

Once I free her from this operation I will devise a way to destroy him. I know this will take time and that I must plan. First, I must find my little Carmen so that together we can do what must be done.

Brockton looked up from the diary. This was dragging. Besides naming O'Connell, the diary hadn't said anything new and it hadn't even provided the proof his client claimed had been forthcoming.

He glanced at the grandfather clock Stephanie's parents had given them as a wedding gift. It had stopped at two o'clock. He'd forgotten to wind it. Something clicked. Two o'clock in the morning, the time O'Connell was supposed to have spoken with Larisa Moran at the hospital. He said in court that he had been working the graveyard shift for some time. But Sienkewicz's diary read that he had called O'Connell at midnight. He leafed back through the diary. This happened on a Tuesday night, when he would have been working. Brockton was too aware of what happened in court to immediately think he'd discovered a flaw in O'Connell's testimony, but it would be worth checking into where the cop had been that evening. And the evening of the hospital incident for that matter. He doubted the cop would be that stupid and lie about something so easy to verify, but it was worth checking.

He jotted down a rough version of the request he would present. If nothing else, it would stir things up down at the station, maybe throw a little hot water on O'Connell. If there were any irregularities, he'd know Brockton was closing in on him.

28

Brockton didn't start for O'Malley's until late that Thursday because he was hoping the DA's office would deliver the information he'd requested in the morning. He hadn't had time to finish reading the diary, but since he planned not to introduce it, he could afford not to. Instead, he prepared his strategy from what he knew.

He'd imagined the DA's office buzzing in panic at the request he'd made and permitted himself several chuckles at the thought. But when dark closed in, they still hadn't sent him anything. He should call and ask them how it was going, just to get a little feedback. Instead, he called home to check on his family before heading out for a beer.

O'Malley's was on the edge of the city, in a neighborhood that remained segregated for the most part by zoning ordinances that prohibited larger apartment buildings from being created. Two family houses with a high percentage of owner occupied homes meant trimmed lawns, quiet streets and domestic disturbances that occurred inside rather than on the streets. A number of cops lived in the neighborhood.

Brockton eased up on a Stop sign two blocks from the bar, then, glancing to his right and left, entered the intersection. He spotted the police car parked half a block up the street to his right, but it was too late to stop so he coasted slowly through the intersection. Seconds later, flashing lights shone in his rear view mirror. He swore and pulled over, keeping his hands in the ten-two position that made law officers feel safe.

He looked out the window. It was a female cop who he didn't recognize. "Did I do something wrong, officer?"

"You don't know?" she replied.

Brockton resisted a sarcastic reaction. She had him dead to rights.

"Do you know what a Stop sign means?" she continued.

"Sure, in this neighborhood it means an influential person lives on the block."

The officer hesitated a moment, surprised at the response. "What about a seat belt? You too influential a person to wear one?"

"No, I live on the other side of town."

"Let me see your license and registration."

He gave them to her. Ten minutes later, when Brockton was about to get out of his car and ask what was taking so long, the officer approached his window. She looked at him for a long moment as if trying to decide what to do. "Nice car," she finally said.

"Thank you."

"You Brockton? The lawyer?"

"I'm driving a BMW, ain't I?" he retorted.

"Troublemaker."

"What trouble is that?"

"You know what trouble. I heard about you at the station. You been hasslin' one 'a our best."

"Your best? Then we can't be talking about the same person. The guy I know is scum." As good as he felt for saying it, he knew he had stepped over the boundary.

"All right, get out of the car," she said.

" Are you serious?"

"Let's go!" she snapped, stepping away from the door. Her voice sounded hard enough for Brockton to do as she said. "You wanna cause trouble for us, we'll treat you just like the criminals you defend. Get your hands on top of the car. Now!"

Brockton complied as slowly as he dared. As he did so, he couldn't help picturing the same move being performed by any one of a dozen of his clients over the years.

"Spread the legs."

"Don't you need a male officer for this?"

"One more joke from you and the only thing you'll need is an ambulance," the cop replied. "All right, let's start with running the Stop sign. No seat belt is next." She walked to the back of the car, pulled out her nightstick and smashed his rear light.

"Hey, you assho—"

"—Get your hands on the car!" she roared, turning toward him and raising her nightstick. "You think I'm kidding? Try me!"

Brockton glanced around him quickly. No one was in sight. He put his hands back on the car.

"Broken tail light," she continued. That's three tickets. Should we try for another?"

"Do you know what you're doing?" he asked. "Do you know I can slap a lawsuit on you that'll have your head spinning?"

"You threatenin' me, Mr. Brockton?" the cop retorted.

"I—"

"—Save your breath. You got about as much credibility as the people you take money from. Now get in your shit can and wait, before something serious happens."

Ten minutes later the officer handed him three tickets, then took off. Once she had left Brockton crumpled the three tickets up and threw them on the floor of the car, swearing. Measly payback shit from a city cop who thought she was something.

His eye caught the diary that lay on the seat next to him and he froze. Since last week he had been carrying it around with him as if it was a second wallet. He hadn't let it out of his sight. If the cop had pushed things further and searched his car, she would have found it. In the wrong hands, it could easily have been lost as well as put his client in deep shit. Stowing it under the seat, he headed to O'Malley's.

He remembered when he'd put someone in a similar situation. The guy was a drug dealer who he'd only taken on because he was a relative of McCormick's. The case had put him in an uncomfortable position because Leach had been shot at during the bust and wanted the guy in jail.

Brockton had cited all the right cases to get the evidence suppressed even though the guy had been carrying, but the weekend before he presented the case he decided to play a joke on his client. He told the guy, a mid-level drug dealer with the usual inflated ego, wants to meet him downtown. The turd had acted complacent through the whole thing so to shake him up he'd handed him the paperwork to his case and told him not to lose it, that it was the only copy he had and he wasn't going to rework the case. Before the guy could react, Brockton told him that was the way he operated. Read it over the weekend and have it in his office Monday morning at eight, he'd told the guy, then warned him not to make any copies and ushered him out of the office.

He had spent the weekend laughing with his friends about what he'd done, imagining this guy carrying his case around with him, even sleeping with it to make sure he didn't lose it. The turd had deserved it.

Now he was in a similar situation with this diary.

"A ticket for not wearing your seatbelt?" McCormick said. "Jesus, Rooster, sounds like they're gunnin' for you. What else did she get you for?"

"The bitch smashed my tail light, then gave me a ticket for it," Brockton replied. "Fuckin' bitch."

"Female cops are worse than men," Greene said. "Like they gotta prove something."

"Did you get her badge number?" McCormick asked.

"Yeah," Brockton lied, not wanting to let the boys know he hadn't even thought to do that he was so shaken by the experience. "Bullshit tickets, too. The only one that was legit was runnin' the Stop sign."

"That's points."

"You should ride home with someone tonight, Rooster," McCormick said, slipping off his stool. "They could be waiting for you outside, ready to pop you with a Diwi. Expensive."

"I should get a ride with you?" Brockton said. "You're half fried."

"I'm not on their shit list. I'm not pushin' 'em around. Wait! They could stop me and see you in the car. Shit, you can't ride with me, I can't afford to get busted. I gotta take a leak."

Before McCormick returned, Brockton found his way to the rest room. Once inside he checked the stall, then went to the urinal next to McCormick.

"I heard you met Larisa Moran." Brockton looked sharply at McCormick, who kept his gaze on the urinal in front of him. "What d'ya think?"

"How'd you find out I met her?"

"She told me. That's not smart, you know. Talking to her."

"She came to me."

"You should've sent her home."

"I tried to tape her. That would've gotten this case thrown out. The press would've eaten it up."

"You're going up against the wrong people."

"Who?"

"You know who. They're crazy; that's why they hold the cards."

"So?"

"You get any new evidence?" McCormick asked.

"No," Brockton said, no longer trusting his friend. In fact, he was reaching the point where he trusted no one.

"You know O'Connell's not that bad a guy."

"Bullshit."

"I know he's a little strong-minded about some things, but he's a cop. He has to be. And he's certainly not the worst of them."

"What are you trying to prove, Bart, besides that you're ignorant?"

"I'll ignore that comment, Mike. What I'm trying to say is that you've never done anything wrong? You don't have anything to hide?"

"Just a few unpaid parking tickets to add to tonight's hat trick."

"Come on, Mike, nothing? No deals?"

"Nothing that wouldn't embarrass them any less than me. I get it. You're a message boy aren't you? You—what the hell are you tellin' them?"

"Nothing."

"And what the hell are they tellin' you?"

"Nothing, I said."

"Well you tell them if they have something to say, say it to me directly not through some chicken shit messenger."

"You think I'm delivering a message? Come off it, Mike. I talk to people like anyone down at the courthouse does. I'm down there a lot. Yesterday, Ritter comes up to me and says he's worried about you. He says you're pissing off a lot of people. And, he adds, you don't have the cleanest life yourself."

"What's that supposed to mean?"

"I don't know, you figure it out."

"What are they talking about? The coke? Did you tell them about that, too?"

"Fuck no. The coke is obvious to them by the way. You hang around a group of people who sniff it. They see that and make some obvious assumptions, like anyone would. They know I do it. Ritter even told me that once. He never mentioned the Extrajudicials, but he knows who we are, more or less."

"So I have the little shit by the balls," Brockton replied. "Listen, I'm not the one who decided to agree to a bench trial. That was his mistake. He would have had a much easier time with a jury."

"He had something solid, thought it would be an open and shut case," McCormick said.

"That's his problem. Now he's stuck with it. Maybe he should have thought twice before choosing that route with me."

"I'm just saying the DA's office is concerned, which means the cops are behind him and want a result they can live with. He can't much help that."

"Ritter's a dick head. He's just pissed because I'm gonna mop up the floor with him and O'Connell."

"It's gone further than just them. Listen Mike, I wouldn't even mention this shit except I'm your friend. You can choose not to believe that, but it's the truth. I care about your career in this city and the way you're headed right now is not good. You may win this one, but you'll lose in the long run.

"You remember how they harassed Dixon until he moved?" McCormick continued. "He didn't have to move—no one was threatening his family—but they made his life so miserable in this city that he left. Shit, what am I telling you this for? You were in the DA's office then. You know what happened. The blue gets a hard-on for you and you might as well move to another country."

"That was different. Dixon was wrong."

"What does wrong have to do with it? Wake up, Mike! What happens when one of your kids gets in trouble? Instead of givin' him a break they'll start a rap sheet. They'll build one just like they do with every ghetto rat. Shit, the fact that I even gotta say this tells me you're weirded out."

Brockton didn't reply, just glanced over at McCormick and for the first time saw his friend as he really was. The guy who spoke so piously to the urinal was a balding, skinny wimp whose small shoulders and arms made the bulge of his stomach even more noticeable, one step short of disgusting. His tie was still tightly wrapped and hung off the bulge, accentuating his ridiculousness.

Brockton finished pissing and washed his hands. As he went out the door McCormick said, "Think about it, Mike. If we don't cooperate, we can't expect much from them."

"What were you two guys doin' in there, comparing dicks?" Sidney Greene said when they returned to the bar.

"Yeah, except Bart couldn't get hard," Brockton replied. The group was silent.

Moments later, a young, shapely woman entered the bar and after looking around, spotted the people she was there to meet. She walked over to them, passing by the group of lawyers. All eyes followed her across the room.

"Ooo..." Sidney cooed.

"She's too young," McCormick said, happy the conversation had switched to something he was more familiar with.

"She's old enough to be in a bar," Sidney replied.

"She's young enough to be your daughter," another of the lawyers said.

"Could be, but she's not."

"She's someone's daughter."

"That used to bother me until I decided that I wasn't gonna get laid as often if I started getting picky."

Brockton excused himself, bored with the conversation. Waving off a warning to avoid the city cops, he left the bar. He still had some reading to do and wanted to say good night to his family before they went to bed.

29

Once Brockton had said good night to the kids, he told Stephanie he would be up late and brought Sienkewicz's diary to the study.

Wednesday, May 7

Dear Vladimir:

Today was the first day I noticed the signs of spring. Late, yet so appropriate for what has happened in my life. After a long winter, the buds have broken forth with passion. The plants are soaking up the sun's warmth, the rays of energy nourishing their life like my soul is being nourished. Like those plants, my soul appreciates anew the reasons for living. I feel! I love! I exist!

Vladimir, you must know who has done this to me. I have written too often for you not to guess that it is she who has wrought this change. Just as I was about to give up hope of ever seeing her again, my little Carmen and I have spoken.

Let me update you. The morning after I called Richard O'Connell, I called the treatment center to inquire whether my little Carmen could be tutored. They told me she had left.

Rationally, I knew it was better that it end this way. When I reread the diary and realized what I had done to her, I saw how I had lost control of my actions. Her leaving the center rescued me from a scandal, possibly saved my career.

But when they told me that she had left I also felt great sorrow. She had been taken from me. After all that had happened, our special relationship had ended. Would I ever see her again? And if I did, would it only be a chance encounter, a passing in the street when neither of us would have the time or courage to exchange more than pleasantries?

For weeks I thought of little else. I searched for her everywhere, trying to relieve the heavy weight on my soul. Unable to concentrate on my work, I spend my free time driving the streets of her neighborhood, hoping to see her. I looked up her address in the school census and passed by her house, leaving unsigned notes for her to contact me. The house was abandoned, but I foolishly hoped that she might return there.

Yesterday, as I was driving by the huge, abandoned house I noticed a car parked in front. An older man was sitting in the car, talking to a group of teenagers. Thinking he might be the landlord, I stopped and asked if he knew the people living in the house. I told him who I was looking for.

The man I spoke to, who I know only as Don, told me he knew my little Carmen. He said she had lived at that address but had moved. He didn't know where she was living now, but said he saw her often. I gave him my telephone number and name and he prom-

ised to have her call me. He left me with a knowing wink, thinking, no doubt, that he knew my intentions. I played along. It matters not what he nor others think since they know nothing of my task. It is only important that they do not intrude.

I know it sounds like a frantic hope, Vladimir, but as you see, my hopes have been rewarded. When I got home from school today there was a message to call a telephone number I didn't recognize. I called the number and she answered!

She wanted to see me, she said, but couldn't talk over the phone. I told her I would come to her right away, but she said she could not do that. She would not even tell me where she was, so I agreed to meet her tomorrow evening, downtown.

Now I am wrestling with my feelings, Vladimir. I had finally begun to live with myself again; should I allow myself to fall back into that emotional maelstrom? What happened at the treatment center almost ruined my life. It is foolish to subject myself to those temptations again.

Yet how can I ignore her! She needs help! What if her dilemma is linked to that of the evil I must destroy? I can't ignore the task I have been called upon to fulfill. I must go.

Thursday, May 8

Dear Vladimir:

I saw her this evening, Vladimir, and she is more beautiful than I remembered. Like a plant that begins to etiolate, she had started to lose her natural vigor under the domination of the treatment center nurse, but she is growing again. She has regained her color.

I drove downtown late that evening and she was standing along on a street curb, wearing a tattered white dress like some kind of

*forgotten angel. She said she had been job hunting all day. I took
her to a diner on the outskirts of the city, where we could talk without being recognized. She is pregnant and wants to get an abortion.
Because of her age she needs a parent to accompany her and wants
me to go.*

Brockton looked again at the date of this entry. The social worker had testified that Sienkewicz took the girl to
Planned Parenthood for birth control pills. It didn't seem
possible that they would mess this thing up, yet someone
was wrong. He jotted down a note to investigate this, then
continued reading.

*I didn't know what to tell her. How was I to help? She is too
young to have this done without parental consent. She said all I had
to do was say that I was her father, that I could pass for her white
half. What she needed was an identification card with the same last
name as mine and she asked if she could use my daughter's, who is
her age. She assured me that this would work and my daughter's
name would be kept secret. She said she had friends who did this
before. My little Carmen knows the ropes, Vladimir.*

Brockton was unaware of Stephanie entering the room
until she touched his shoulder. He set the diary down and
looked up.

"Watcha doin'?" she asked.

"Trying to find information to win this case," Brockton
said.

"In that book?"

"It's a diary. I'm thinking there may be a clue in here that will help me get the case thrown out."

"You've been preoccupied with the case," Stephanie said. "More than most."

"It's a weird one," he replied. "Trying to win but not really liking any of the options." After a moment, he asked, "Did you want something?"

"I want you," Stephanie said. "When is that going to happen?" She smiled.

"I'm sorry, baby," Brockton replied. "Let me finish this up and come to bed."

"Wake me," she said and kissed his forehead.

Once Stephanie disappeared, Brockton contemplated the situation. The last thing he wanted to do was upset his marriage. He would not allow himself to get wrapped up in someone else's—or many people's—perverted behaviors, legal or otherwise. And that included the Extrajudicials and all their pissing and moaning about marriage and its travails. He was lucky and needed to remember that, not let his job interfere with family. He picked the diary up again.

When she first told me that she was pregnant, I asked her if Don was the father. She laughed and said he is just an old man. He lives in the neighborhood and gives her and her friends rides places, she says. I don't trust him. I know this man and others like him. They do small favors for these kids but I see the depravity in them. They are unpaid taxi drivers, taking kids where they want to go while they wait for the right moment to approach them for sex.

Sigmund knows what I mean. These men are the father figures which so many of these kids lack, yet they expect the reward of sex.

The attraction between father and daughter is readily apparent. My little Carmen said Don asks her for sex all the time, but she tells him no. He continues to ask. And she continues to ask him to drive her places. I told her to call me instead, that I grow angry each time I see her riding with him.

Friday, May 9

Dear Vladimir:

Planned Parenthood is a depressing place. As your love for Lolita was forbidden, pushed into secrecy, so fares this agency that houses the city's public abortion clinic. The interior of the building is colorless and unappealing. It makes you feel like you are doing something sinful as soon as you enter. One gets the feeling upon entering that it is a besieged institution.

Even the abortion procedure sounds medieval. Physically scraping a woman's uterus and the pain that must involve is almost designed to discourage repetition. No matter what side of the choice issue you are on, Vladimir, it is hard to remain blind to this sad but inevitable result of our society's ignorance.

As my little Carmen predicted, no one questioned my claim that I was her father. I was asked to stay in the waiting room with all the other uncomfortable people while the abortion was performed. My little Carmen was pregnant the entire time she was in the treatment center, Vladimir, and they were unaware of it! To protect myself, I told her that if anyone recognized her, that she was to say that she was there to get birth control pills. She agreed to this. If she keeps this promise, I am one step closer to my goal.

Sunday, May 11

Dear Vladimir:

How clever are the workings of fate! That I should have doubted them at all shames me., I know why my little Carmen has returned to me. My task is not finished. I know now that I must destroy this man and that my little Carmen will help me do this.

She told me the story of her rape this evening. She was picked up in a police roundup on Winthrop Ave. She swears she was not prostituting, that she has never done that and I believe her, but since she was there and wearing revealing clothing the police picked her up. She got into a car and he was driving.

When he recognized her, he took her out of the city to a darkened parking lot. Once there, he waved a ten dollar bill at her. Then he lay it on his zipper and told her what she would have to do to get it. She refused, she said, even though she admitted to being a little drunk. He said it wouldn't take long and there was more money where that came from.

You must remember, Vladimir, that my little Carmen was living day to day at this point. She was staying where she could at night and this wasn't the first time prostitution was mentioned to her as a way to get money. Yet before she could respond he took out his gun and told her to get out of the car. He put it to her temple, she said, and I do not have to tell you any more except to say that when she finished, he hit her across the face with his gun, bruising her. She was afraid to tell anyone what happened and made up a story about falling down to account for the bruise.

While she was telling me this it all came back so clearly, what he used to do at Palmerola. She could have been the one, Vladimir. She could have been murdered by this evil man. Am I so cowardly that I can still do nothing, knowing this? I must do something. I can no longer sit back.

Yet this man is powerful. I don't wish to sound like a coward, but I must tell you, Richard O'Connell is a leader of the dreaded Mazorcas.

This is something I have never written about, Vladimir, because of the danger it brings to anyone who speaks of them. I fear for my life each time I think of them, yet I can no longer remain silent. I can no longer watch as my little Carmen is tormented by this man. I must reveal everything about him.

The Mazorcas was an elite group of soldiers created at Palmerola Air Base, ostensibly to deal with the growing quantities of drugs flowing through Central America and into the United States. I say ostensibly because the group's other mission was more self-serving. They were also to extinguish the growing number of independent runners who were profiting from the drug trade, thus draining funds needed to support the war against neighboring Nicaragua, which was going badly at the time. It wasn't difficult to identify these runners and liquidating them caused little notice when hidden amongst the great number of "disappeared" at that time.

Brockton looked up from the diary. What was all this about? Was all that went on in the courtroom a result of things that happened this many years ago? Or was it a dispute between a pervert and a small city cop, nothing more? Was his client making up a story? Sienkewicz was really stretching things this time. He was over the edge.

I know of this because I was the interpreter they assigned to the first group. Being multilingual—and white enough to be trusted—I was assigned to teach them rudimentary Spanish. I was a good sol-

dier, Vladimir, and served my country by teaching them well. I said nothing about the Mazorcas' other mission at first, but when I witnessed them using the same drugs obtained from the military leaders they were allied to and secretly working against, I reported to my superiors. (You must know, Vladimir, that the military is a drug pipeline into our country.) I was told to keep quiet and I did.

But the Mazorcas grew uncontrollable. They began to liquidate anyone in their way. Their own commanders finally had to disown them, even shipped some of them to other countries to finish their tours. I was stripped of my job as an interpreter and given a quick discharge.

They have re-banded. They have begun operations in this country. They carry out these operations under the guise of combating the drug war, carrying identification that allows them to work unmolested. They continue to communicate with each other, enacting atrocities on our own citizens. This force is ripe with scandal.

How do I know this? The immunity these men have makes them careless and he is no exception. In order to have his way with my little Carmen, he told her many things to scare her. He revealed himself and I have pieced together the fragments of his boasts.

After a drug raid in the middle of a cocaine distribution area on this city's south side, police turned three drug runners from New York City over to the Mazorcas. The drug runners—two Latino males and one female—were lined up and shot, then dumped into the metalwork of a bridge nearby that was closed for repairs. To hide this atrocious act, they poured cement over the bodies.

They did this, Vladimir, for the same reason they operated in Palmerola. Hiding behind the local police's desire to send a message to New York City dealers that they wouldn't tolerate drugs entering this community, their real objective was to eliminate competition that cut into their own profits. You see, I know these villains.

You do not believe me? You do not believe a massacre really happened here? Then explain to me why this bridge, after being worked on for less than ten days, was suddenly reopened. It was reopened, Vladimir, to cover up this heinous act. And now this very same bridge has been closed again, for further repairs. What more proof do you need? Closing down bridges is a tactic taken directly from the Mazorcas. They often closed off avenues of escape in the villages they raided so they could cut down on the number of people who escaped, and prevent witnesses. They are doing the same thing here that they did years ago in Central America. They are liquidating people.

Brockton looked up. He knew what bridge Sienkewicz was talking about: Stewart Ave. He used to drive to work that way when he lived in the city. And he remembered the construction happening two different times. But his client had hit new levels of fantasy in concocting this story. The bridge had been reopened the first time because in the heat of a mayoral election the challenger had tried to make an issue out of the city's poor roads and had scheduled a press conference there. The mayor found out and sent city workers to repair the bridge right in front of the TV cameras. The bridge was kept open until after the mayor had won the election, then closed again for repairs. His client's story was preposterous.

His claim that the girl had obtained all this information was also dubious. Larisa Moran was fourteen, not forty. She wouldn't have been able to relay that kind of information to Sienkewicz even if O'Connell had been stupid enough to brag about it. Brockton thought about Stephanie waiting for him, then decided to plow ahead.

30

Saturday, May 18

Dear Sigmund:

What is love? Is it not something we must experience if we are to avoid being pulled under by the lethargy of materialism and desperation? Is not passion something we should pursue if only to prevent our emotions from dying before old age and physical weakness set in? And does not this pursuit often involve throwing off the constraints of a society that has turned us into frustrated, sterilized inhabitants of a fertile planet? So many people live lives of self righteous misery, waiting for someone else to do something immoral so they can cluck about it like frustrated hens. These people will never understand passion.

From whence come these thoughts, Sigmund? From a dream so vivid that I am still trapped in it. The emotions are still with me. I feel like one who has just experienced something tragic, like the death of a loved one. I'm not sure if what I'm living is real right now, because feelings of self preservation have taken over. I dreamt, Sigmund, about my little Carmen's seduction.

She was living alone in the abandoned house I first knew as her address. Her mother had kicked her out and she called me to ask if I could get the heat working. I started a fire in the old fireplace to keep her warm while I looked at the furnace. Naturally this meant I would have to remain in the apartment until the fire was just ashes. I asked her if she expected company and she said no.

Once the fire was started and I was assured that the house wasn't going to burn down, I sat back on the couch and watched the flames lick away at the wood. My little Carmen knelt in front of me, watching the fire as if mesmerized. My eyes feasted upon her. I watched her head, her body, the small of her back. I noticed the way her hair moved when she turned her head ever so slightly.

She began to cry. I asked her why she was crying and she told me it was because she did not have a child, that she wanted a child. It was then that the thought of making love to her overtook me. She had never experienced love before and I wanted her to experience its pleasures.

I knelt behind her and began to massage her shoulders. She let this go on for a while, then turned, reached up and pulled me down on her. After we kissed she took off her shirt and lay on her stomach. "I want a child," she said.

Brockton set the diary down. This sounded familiar. It was—he had read it in the police report. He pulled Sienkewicz's folder out and scanned the report. The girl had alleged that before Sienkewicz raped her, he told her, "I want to have your child." Was it coincidental that both statements were that similar? Or was there something else to this? The holes in this diary were looking larger than ever.

I didn't respond. She had just aborted a child and must be experiencing feelings all females undergo after such trauma. Yet she wanted to make love to me, Sigmund. Your research has demonstrated the sexual attraction the young have for their parents, or parent surrogates, and this is what I sensed was happening.

At this point you can see that the dream was beginning to take on more aspects of reality. I had visions of an earlier time and place, that of Palmerola, when I lay with other girls. I remember thinking, "How much should I pay her?", as if my little Carmen was just another prostitute. What did ten or twenty or fifty dollars mean for such a priceless experience? I would have paid hundreds for this moment!

Once I recognized that I was dreaming I began to control it. You know how one can escape looming disasters by subconsciously manipulating a dream? I brought it to a conclusion. We spent ourselves on the floor while the fire spat its fury.

When Vladimir writes of love, he describes a possessive act, a physical thrill disturbed only by the small itches of conscience. For me, love is a total giving. I have never felt closer to God. I would do anything for my little Carmen. I was slow, and calmly built toward an urgency that would please her. Yet that never happened. She was unresponsive, as if unable to fathom what I was doing. I remember thinking, "She has never received before, only given., How can she know how to receive?" before I awoke.

Am I any different than the others, Sigmund? I have searched my soul for reasons why I am. I have read and reread your treatise, The Interpretation of Dreams, and the following statement leaps out at me: "But this is meant even sexually and because desire is unwilling to check itself before the thought of doing wrong, as the philosophy of carpa diem has reason to fear the censorship and must con-

ceal itself behind a dream." Haven't I the same goal as the old man who combs this neighborhood looking for sex? I have controlled this desire in the past, but it now seems out of control.

What a mole I am! I have undertaken to seduce this girl no matter what the cost and dressed it up even to myself! Is not the seduction of a young girl as great a crime if it's done deceptively as with violence? He hurt my little Carmen, but he could also claim to be seeking passion. And she has no illusions about him, whereas my deceptiveness may cause her greater harm. I am taking her childhood from her.

But I love her! I am talking about her as if I didn't love her! How was I to know this would happen, that it would go this far? I did not plan this, and however it ends I have that innocence to fall back on. I will help her, not abuse her as others have done. I will take care of her better than any man would.

Now that I have taken an irrevocable step toward seducing my little Carmen, I feel exhilarated. The line between helping and hurting someone becomes so fine at times that it disappears. I am not like Fyodor, who hides behind excuses. I cannot blame this on brain fever as he does, Sigmund. In that way I am like our friend Vladimir, for we both know what we are doing. Only Vladimir knows what depths we plumb. We are truly brothers, he and I.

Tuesday, May 21

Dear Fyodor:

How many times have I dreamt of holding her! And now that I have touched her, felt her close to me, I can think of nothing else! I cannot stop seeing her! I must get closer, make her see that our love is the only one worth pursuing! The emotions are too strong to resist! I have come to the realization that I love her, must have her.

Yet you know, Fyodor, that I am a timid man. I do not have the courage to approach her openly. I have agonized over this, knowing that she won't consent to open herself to me simply because I suggest it, as Vladimir's Lolita did. I am more realistic than our friend. A young girl, no matter how much she has seen, does not open herself up easily to a man three times her age. My little Carmen grew up defending herself in a harsh environment and she will struggle. I must ready myself. I must move at just the right moment, when she is at her most vulnerable. And I must be ready, if she refuses, to dissimulate.

How will I do this? I will trick her, as your little clerk tricked his prostitute. You see I have learned much while hiding in my little mouse hole. I have learned how to manipulate people, how to play on their emotions. I have learned how your clerk played the game. And like him, I am a sick man...a mean man.

A plan occurred to me the other day. My little Carmen telephoned and she was crying. She told me her mother had come home drunk again and that she had spent money she promised to give her for cleaning the house. I told her I would give her ten dollars to go out, as I usually do when she needs money. I was about to hang up when without prompting she told me she hated her mother. She said her mother had neglected her for years, that whenever she had money, she spent it on liquor instead of food and clothes for her family. She told me several stories about her mother's drunkenness, about one boyfriend who had beaten her several times. My heart went out to her, Fyodor. I wanted to help her, to hold her and take her pain away.

At the same time my mind worked in a more devious direction. I will connive to make her love me, I thought. The wider the split between my little Carmen and her mother, the more she will have to depend on someone else, and that someone could be me. Lolita's

mother died fortuitously, allowing Vladimir the opportunity to se-
duce his love but there are more ways than one to peel away a pro-
tective cover. I will make her need—and thus succumb—to me.

People will recoil in disgust if I tell them this, so I tell only you. I
love her and feel I can go no further without expressing my love. If I
approach her from this sinuous path, she will give herself to me
without having the chance to refuse. I know you understand. You
know how much I love her. You know that we have become so close
our union is inevitable.

Brockton looked up, puzzled. If Larisa Moran had read
this, why did she think that Sienkewicz loved her? Wouldn't
she have been angry about what he had written? Would she
even have given him the diary? Or is this what love meant in
her life? With the shootings, stabbings, the misery around
her, was this an acceptable condition? Maybe a girl like
Larisa could have missed Sienkewicz's underlying intent,
hidden as it was behind all the crap about love. Or maybe
she hadn't even read it.

What about Mrs. Kennedy? What had motivated her to
send this to him? Brockton had called her again and she told
him that she would deny ever having sent it. He let her response sit in his mind for a while, but he couldn't reach any
conclusions worth noting. He returned to his reading.

Thursday, May 23

Dear Vladimir:
Today my little Carmen told me that her social worker asked her
if I ever touched her. She said no, that I would never do that, that I
was helping her get her life together, but this woman warned her to

be wary of men who worked with young kids, that they often did it in order to get close to them for sexual reasons.

What a bitch this woman is! She is the same one who has abandoned my little Carmen time and time again and now she is trying to step back into her life. Why? Does she suspect me of something?

I should have known she would ask my little Carmen about me. I should have seen through her facade when I first met her. She is one more human service worker who thinks she can make a difference by showing up at the last minute and feigning concern when in reality all she is looking for is someone to condemn. And her suspicions must be giving her the extra charge she needs to stick her nose into our business.

I know you say I'm a hypocrite, for I have thought everything this disgusting woman is implying, but do not put me in the same category as yourself. Do not scoff. I am different. I have helped my little Carmen. I have done more than anyone for her. And this social worker, who has done nothing, is trying to turn her against me!

As for your insinuation that I had my little Carmen's seduction in mind from the start, is there not an element of sexuality in all relationships? Sigmund would say yes, even between parent and offspring. Do not protest your innocence, Vladimir; although you were pursuing a child not of your own blood, Lolita was really about the sexuality between father and daughter. I know how you acted toward her, buying trinkets and pandering her in order to seduce her. I too, have read Greek mythology, so keep your accusations to yourself.

I am tired of people who assume to know my motives. Who are they to judge me? Where were they when she was putting any drug she could get hold of into her body? Where were they when she needed a pair of shoes to go to school? Which one of them gave her food when she was wandering the streets with no place to stay be-

cause her drunk mother had locked her out? These wagging-tongued hypocrites would roast in hell if they were ever judged on what they had done for others.

As Brockton read the diary, the weird sensation he'd experienced when he first met Sienkewicz overcame him. The man was helping a girl who no one else cared for. He was doing it for her. He shrugged off the sensation. A lot of good his help had been when his real objective was to have sex with her. He started reading again.

And this social worker, this nosey female who asks so many questions about me, is just one more clucking hen who deals with her own frustrations by prying into other people's affairs. Is she only making sure no one else does what she would like to do? Or does she have darker motives? Let me tell you, Vladimir, I have heard through the grapevine that this woman is a lesbian, so it would not surprise me if she were lining my little Carmen up for herself. Why else would she continue their relationship so long? At least I have admitted to my despicable nature.

Brockton put the book down again. Why hadn't he thought of that when he had Winston on the stand! He could have had a field day insinuating that she was after the girl herself. Then, when she denied it, he could have compared the relationships' similarities. He might even have put her over the edge, exposed her as a lesbian. He cursed the missed opportunity, then looked at the time. It was late and he'd promised Stephanie he'd join her. He had a free morning when he could finish this up.

31

Brockton beat Candy into the office again that morning, refreshed and relaxed. Immediately, he started to read.

Friday, May 24

Dear Fyodor:
I finally overcame my fear and confronted him. I couldn't stand by any longer. It had to stop. She was always talking about him, Fyodor, and I could no longer bear the strain. She was afraid to walk the streets.

I drove to his home late one evening to speak to him. He had just gotten home and still had his police uniform on. Although I surprised him, he recognized me immediately and invited me in. He took me into a large room, which contained a huge fireplace and several expensive Oriental rugs. On the wall above the fireplace was a giant moose's head, framed by two shotguns. Scattered around the room were pictures of his overseas adventures, several from his time at Palmerola. One in particular caught my attention. It was a solid gold eagle, framed, with a red background. The eagle was adopted by our government from the northern Aryans of the Old World. It was also the insignia of the Mazorcas.

He saw me looking at the eagle and patted the gun still strapped to his side, then pointed to his zipper. "Remember Palmerola?" he said, and winked.

I controlled myself, Fyodor. I remained outwardly calm and rational. I had never stood up to him before and it would be foolish to do so now. I had been a participant in his past destructiveness and could not pretend innocence.

When he asked me why I had come, I told him that I was my little Carmen's friend and that she wanted me to ask him to leave her alone. I assured him that she had done as he'd asked and that I, myself, had taken her to get the abortion. I told him that I had been the one who called him, hoping to help avoid trouble between them.

At first he didn't respond to my plea. He called her a whore and made several other deprecatory remarks, then repeated his belief that women needed—no liked—to be taken by force. He had always maintained, Fyodor, that although women rebelled against the use of force it was a part of their ancestry, that intrinsically they wanted to be raped. While he talked he started to finger his gun.

Finally, he said what I already knew, that she had gotten pregnant by him and he couldn't allow that. He was morally opposed to miscegenation (He didn't use that language, Fyodor, but that is what he said in so many words).

When I heard the word 'moral' issue from his lips, I almost broke into a rage. I wanted to reveal my love for her, tell him that I would no longer allow this to go on without taking personal vengeance. I wanted to tear the gun from his holster and make him get on his knees and beg for his life as he had done with so many others. I wanted to kill him.

Instead, I dissembled. I am not a brave man and I was afraid of him. I started to cry. I suggested that he let her live her life without fearing him, that she should be able to love whomever she wanted. I told him that she loved me.

This last confession was too much for him. He pounded his fist against the wall, causing pictures to rattle. "I told her to get rid of it!" he screamed. "I told her what to do and she hasn't done it! I've been taken advantage of and have to do something about this!"

There was no point in continuing the conversation. I had witnessed his emotional rages before and was beginning to grow overly emotional myself. I could not bear his abuse without reacting. He continued to say he didn't believe her, that he wanted proof. I told him that she had used my last name, so getting proof was impossible. He demanded to see proof of this and I showed him a slip with my daughter's name on it. This was not good enough, in fact, put him in an even greater rage. He started pacing. Again he said he didn't believe her (He studiously avoided calling me a liar, Fyodor) and that he would have to do something drastic. He said that even if she did get an abortion, she could cause a lot of trouble, so he would have to do something anyway.

I didn't know how much more I could take. With tears streaming down my face and my sanity about to abandon me, I suddenly thought of a way out. I told him I would take the blame for the whole thing. I told him I would confess to raping her, Fyodor, and that if she ever decided to talk she could blame me. I even agreed to put this in writing.

He leapt at my suggestion. At first he only wanted a signed confession from me, then, fearing she might turn on him, he said she would have to sign a statement, too. He would write it up and keep it as insurance that she wouldn't change her story. He would take care of the details, to see that I wasn't unjustly accused. Even if she turned on me, he said, the worst I would get was some bad publicity because her case would be too flimsy. He said I wouldn't even lose my job. I told him she wouldn't betray me, that I was sure enough of her love not to fear that happening.

I know you are shaking your head in disbelief, Fyodor, but you do not know the love I hold for my little Carmen. You are too selfish to understand this intensity of feelings. He promised to leave her alone if I were to do this, so I agreed. Looking back, I see how I have endangered myself, but I did not see that at the time. I was blinded by my desire to protect her. I couldn't see beyond the gun at his belt, nor the thought of that gun at her temple as she knelt in front of him.

Brockton set the diary aside and tried to imagine this being true. How could anyone, even someone as crazy as Sienkewicz, put himself in this position? Brockton had dealt with a lot of criminals, but the one unbreakable principle they kept was not to voluntarily incriminate themselves. When it came down to paying for their misdeeds, even the scum knew how to cover their asses.

Maybe his initial reaction to Sienkewicz had been on target. The guy was so far gone in his dream world he didn't even realize what he was doing to himself. That was why he behaved so weirdly. He didn't understand that the justice system would lock him up when he acted like this.

At this point there wasn't much he could do with the diary. Thoughts of a knockout punch were irrelevant at this point. Sienkewicz had virtually convicted himself without admitting anything. Brockton decided to continue reading. He was nearing the end and Candy could take his calls until he'd finished the diary.

Saturday, May 25

Dear Vladimir:

I am crestfallen. I finally had a chance to reveal my love to her and as misfortune would have it I could not even do that right. My little Carmen knows that I want to possess her and she rejected me.

I was taking her to a party when it happened. We were alone. She had dressed up for the evening and looked beautiful even though she was wearing too much makeup. I had resolved to keep my feelings to myself when she noticed a man walking on the street. She had been talking about something inane, but when she saw this man she turned and whistled out the car window, then made a comment about his ass.

Because this conversation is so essential to me in what it says about our relationship, I will write the rest of it exactly as it happened. Do not think there is one word left out, Vladimir, because I have gone over it in my head a thousand times, searching for some sign that she may love me. I find none.

I began by substituting myself in the role of the man she had whistled at, and asked:

"What if he were to approach you?"

"Who?"

"The man you just whistled at."

"He did once. I turned him away."

"But you like his body."

"He asked me to go steady with him." I laughed.

"Why did you laugh?"

"Because that's old fashioned. That's not how you ask someone in the nineties."

"How would someone ask, then?" (Sly, I was. So sly, Vladimir.)

"Ask what?"

"Ask to go out with you?"

She changed the topic. *"You can't treat guys like that, go out with them just because they ask you. Most only want to pull your card when you give them the chance, to see what you're about. Sometimes they fall in love with you, but if they don't, at least they can say they got you."*

"I would fall into the former category. I would fall in love with you."

She didn't respond.

"Does that embarrass you?"

"What?"

"My comment."

"No."

"I apologize if it did. I have always felt that way about you, but I was always too courteous to bring it up." (I said this so smoothly, Vladimir, hoping to cover up my original intent. She remained silent and I rambled.)

"I have always liked you. I just didn't want to force that on you. You know my situation. I have a family. I felt you might not want

to handle this. I have always taken that into account with you." (I was coy, Vladimir, using 'this' and 'that' wherever I could.)

"I know how embarrassing it can be to have to reject someone's approaches. I've been in that situation before, having to reject someone, and it isn't pleasant." (Do you see how careful I was in my approach?) "Do you feel that way?"

"What?"

"Do you feel embarrassed about me approaching you this way?"

"Mr. Sienkewicz, you're married."

"That's over. I no longer love my wife. We live together for the children." (She wasn't able to understand this. As crazy a life as she has led, she understands and yearns for a traditional existence and the stability that brings.)

"Well, you're still married. It ain't right." (She sounded like a goddamn counselor, Vladimir, and I almost started telling her one of the dozens of stories I had fabricated for just this occasion. I almost started to tell her about an unfaithful wife and how I was tortured by her affairs. Instead, I dissembled.)

"If I thought you could love me, I would divorce my wife and live with you." (I said it matter-of-factly so that in the future I could claim I was joking, but this must have taken her by surprise, because she turned away from me and stopped talking altogether. When we reached the apartment where she was going, she thanked me for giving her a ride. I didn't respond, just kept looking straight ahead, the way I do when I am displeased.)

"I'm sorry, Mr. Sienkewicz, I can't let you cheat."

"Oh, don't think you'll be stopping me from cheating. You'll just stop me from loving you. (I thought this would devastate her, Vladimir, but it was impossible to tell. She got out of the car too *quickly and I kept my gaze straight ahead until she disappeared into the building.)*

I have read and reread these words, Vladimir, until they blur in front of my eyes, hoping that they will speak to me, tell me what I long to hear. Are they telling me she loves me? Or is this the pipe dream of an old man? Do I disgust her? I cannot think that way. If my suggestion lingers with her long enough she may decide that I am not as bad as her other options. She isn't able to accept my love now, but she may come around.

I am not worried about being caught. Because of the way we parted, I don't think she will tell anyone. My little Carmen is too sophisticated to close off the option of choosing that path.

Monday, May 27

Dear Vladimir:

My little Carmen called to ask me for a ride tonight and I told her no. I felt good saying no. I told her I was angry about what happened the other night and let her know that I planned not to let it happen again. I told her I was glad that she had been honest, but that she should have had more principles than to call me for a ride to a party, then talk to me the way she had. I told her I was through giving everything and receiving nothing.

I grew very emotional, Vladimir, although I knew it was the wrong thing to do. I said she had abandoned a friend—practically family—and she would probably end up getting pregnant by someone who only wanted to screw her.

She tried to explain herself, but I didn't listen. I told her that I wasn't a door mat she could trample on. It was time she thought of someone else once in a while, I said. Just because her hormones told her she would rather have sex with some ghetto punk, she shouldn't abandon the one person who has listened and stuck by her so long. I hung up before she could reply. I know I was rude, but I cannot help it. She has forced me to be this way. I have decided not to answer her calls for a while, to show her how much she needs me.

The telephone rang and Brockton picked it up before Candy could. "Hello?"

"Mr. Brockton, this is Milton Ritter. Do you have a minute to talk?"

32

When Brockton entered O'Malley's, McCormick was already there, a half drunk beer in hand. The bartender brought two more pints and left.

Brockton looked around. The pub's decor was the same, but it was especially pleasant tonight given the circumstances. The soft light and clink of glassware provided a great scenario to his latest victory.

"So what happened?" McCormick asked.

"They caved. Instead of giving me the information I requested, I got a call from Ritter. He offered a sweetheart deal."

"You take it?"

Brockton looked around again before answering. He wanted to remember this moment. He gazed at the glasses hanging upside down over the bar and above the glasses, perched on the wood supports, dozens of bottles of liquor and mixers. He surveyed the rows of liquor bottles and the antique cash register facing him and listened to the noises of the partially filled restaurant. He smiled, taking in the noises as if they were applause. "I'm gonna do what I said I'd do. I'm gonna stick it to 'em."

McCormick didn't respond, just stared at his beer. Finally, he looked up. "You told Ritter that?"

"I did. What's to eat here? I'm starving."

"You want to sit down and eat?"

"No, something quick. At the bar."

"Food's lousy. I'll order a pizza from next door."

"Good idea." Brockton watched McCormick disappear to find a bartender, almost hastily it seemed.

His friend was gone for almost ten minutes and after ordering another beer, Brockton decided to call Stephanie. He found McCormick at the telephone. "Look, I can't argue all night," his friend was saying. "I gotta go. I got a couple of business calls to make. I'll call you later." His friend hung up and dialed another number. "Hello, can you deliver a pizza to O'Malley's? Yeah, Jake said it's okay, I'm a regular. How long? Good. Just a minute." He turned to Brockton. "Pepperoni okay?"

Brockton nodded.

"Pepperoni and peppers. Yeah, fine. I'll be at the bar, in the back next to the Red Rooster. Yes, Rooster, the big red one. Just ask Jake to point out the Rooster. Phone number? Just a minute." He looked up and read the telephone number into the receiver. "The Rooster? Don't worry about it, I'll see you come in the door and signal you. Come thirsty 'cuz the first beer is on me."

"Who were you talking to?" Brockton asked.

"I just ordered a pizza."

"No, before that."

"Shit," McCormick said. "The wife's after me."

"You cheatin'?"

"No, but she thinks I am. Never had so much sex. And all the rest of what comes with it."

"Like communication?"

"I can't believe how much I'm having to express 'my feelings'. Sometimes I just gotta make something up."

"You listen to Sid and you'll end up the same as him," Brockton replied.

"You heard?"

"Heard what?"

"About Sid. Diane's filing for the big D."

"What happened?"

"She got a phone call from that young thing he's been screwing. What a scene."

"What happened?"

"He told the girl this story about how his wife neglected him and the kids, how she was never home because she was running around with half the neighbors' husbands."

"Diane? His wife? She's a saint!"

"Yeah. Can you imagine?"

"She found out?"

"Sid did too good a job of it. This girl felt so bad after she heard his story that she called Diane to tell her to treat her husband better. She told her the story he'd been feeding her and it came out that she was screwin' him. Now neither will speak to him. And he's facing the big D."

"He deserves it," Brockton said.

"Well I don't plan on losing Cheryl even if it means I have to communicate."

"Sids's whole family is fucked up," Brockton replied. "And don't think it wouldn't happen to you."

"I don't listen to him, I just feel sorry for him," McCormick said.

"What about his family? Do you feel sorry for them? Has anyone mentioned his son? Do you wonder that maybe his getting in trouble is due to Sid's situation?"

"Easy Mike, that's not fair."

"Why not if it's true?

"First of all, it's not even a sure thing that he's guilty. He was seen around the scene is all."

"I'm saying consider it. Do you see Sid playing ball with his kids? Taking them fishing? Or anywhere else for that matter? Have you ever talked to the kid? He's weird, believe me."

"You need to take it easy Mike."

"I need to take it easy! You're the one who started talking to that bimbo the other night. You don't think I heard about that? No wonder your wife's worried."

"I didn't do nothin'!"

"You should have walked away.

"Hey, I'm fucked up, okay? I'm a fucked up person. Is that what you want me to say? Is that what you want to hear? Okay?"

Brockton shrugged, saying nothing.

"Look, I gotta piss," McCormick continued. "I'll meet you at the bar. You're not going to tell anyone about that

call, right? I can't have people thinking there's trouble between the wife and me."

"I said I wouldn't."

"You're all right, buddy. You're the Rooster."

After his friend left, Brockton set down his glass and dialed home. Guys like Sid would never know what it took to
make a marriage work. And Bart, for that matter. A little
communication wasn't too much for a stable family.

It took four rings before someone answered the telephone, unusual in a house with teenagers. Stephanie finally
picked it up. "Hi hon, how are you?"

"Fine. Where are you?"

"At the pub, havin' a beer. I'll be a little later than I
thought. I have to talk to Bart about a case. How are the
kids?"

"Fine. Roger's on Cloud Nine."

"Why?"

"He finally got that ride in a police car. They picked him
up right at school. He's been talking about it since he got
home."

"Chuckie took him?"

"No, another officer. A sergeant."

Brockton felt a sudden chill. "What was his name?"

"O'Donald, or something like that."

"Sergeant O'Connell?"

"Yes, that was it."

"That son of a bitch!"

"Michael, what's the matter?"

"What the hell is he doing?"

"I told you, he—"

"—I'll be right home," Brockton interrupted. "Where's Roger? Is he home yet?"

"Of course he is. I told you that. He's right here."

"He better be! That...I'm coming home."

"What's wrong, Michael?" his wife asked again and Brockton detected the fear in her voice. He got hold of himself. He needed to hide this from her.

"What is Roger doing taking rides from someone he doesn't know?" he asked.

"He's a police officer, Michael. He's a friend of—"

"—I don't care whose friend he is! Roger doesn't know him! How many times have I told the kids not to take rides from strangers, persons they don't know!"

"Michael, what is wrong with you? It was a policeman! He had a great time. And don't think you're going to launch into another tirade when you get home. Roger didn't do anything wrong."

"I'll be home soon." It had worked, he knew it would. If he redirected his anger to Roger, Stephanie would defend their son and forget the issue.

Bart wasn't at the bar when he got back. He sat down to wait for him. What was going on? Was this supposed to be a warning? He was going to shoot the bastard. O'Connell didn't know who he was dealing with. The son of a bitch was dealing with a crazy man when he started playing around with his family. He'd find out his address, drive over there, take the shotgun off his hearth and blow his head off.

He could play the midnight game, too. O'Connell would deny it but with a gun pointed at his head he wouldn't sing that tune for long. Tough guys were the biggest criers once they were beat, he'd learned that on the baseball diamond. He'd make the son of a bitch get on his knees and beg for his life.

Five minutes later Bart hadn't returned and Brockton couldn't sit still any longer. Leach was the one he really had to deal with. He returned to the phone and dialed his number.

"Hello, Leach residence," his friend said, his usual way to answer the phone.

"Bob," Brockton said.

"Who is it?"

"Bob, what the fuck do you think you're doing?"

"Oh, Mike. What's up? What's wrong?"

"You know what's wrong. What are you trying to do, get yourself killed?"

"What are you talking about?"

"O'Connell. My son. You know. I'm a cunt hair away from taking a midnight ride to his house and blowing him away. Are you guys crazy? You're messing with my family!"

"Hey, slow down buddy. Slow down and tell me what you're talking about. Hey, let me get on the other line in my study. Just a minute."

Leach put down the phone and Brockton heard him saying something. A woman's voice replied. Brockton slammed the phone down. He'd show the motherfucker what fear was.

He remembered the conversation with Stephanie. She must be wondering what was up. He'd have to call and calm her down. She couldn't find out what this was all about. He redialed his number. Stephanie picked up the phone. "Hi honey, how is everyone?" he asked.

"Fine, Michael. What's wrong?"

"Nothing. How's Roger?"

"He's fine. I just checked on him."

"Good. Listen, if Chuckie calls, tell him I'm still at work. He wants to find me and I don't want to see him. Will you do that?"

"Michael, are you drunk? Who are you with?"

"Everything's fine," he said, intentionally slurring his response. "I'll be home soon. I'm taking a taxi."

"What is going on?"

"Just trust me," he said. After saying good-bye, he hung up.

By the time he had returned to the bar, Brockton's hands were shaking. He saw McCormick signal to him from the end of the bar, but ignored him.

He remembered the time he had come home with Stephanie from the theater after trying a new babysitter. When they got back to the house, Roger was crying—howling—as if he had been dropped. The babysitter was red-faced and said she didn't know what was wrong. Brockton lit into her. He told her she was lying and screamed at her, then said she had better get out of the house before he hurt her. Stephanie had had to stop him. She took the girl home, then hadn't talked to him for nearly a week. But she hadn't hired the girl again. People didn't mess with his family.

He picked up his beer, grasping the glass tightly to stop his hand from shaking. He had better get a hold of himself.

He thought again about going to visit O'Connell. He should just get in his car and go there. He'd burst into his house and shoot him, right in his trophy room. He wouldn't give him time to beg for his life. There were certain things that just weren't allowed.

For a second Brockton let himself think if it had been Babe. If it had, he would have lost control immediately. He needed to get hold of himself, he thought again. As much as he wanted to let himself be guided by his emotions, he needed to be rational. He pulled his jacket off the rack at the corner of the bar near where he stood and held it in his other hand, still undecided about what to do.

"Rooster, what's up?" McCormick asked, interrupting his thoughts.

"My son took an unexpected trip to the police station."

"Why?"

"That's what I need to find out. And more importantly, why was he with O'Connell?" He almost choked on the bastard's name.

"You know he asked me the other day what your kids' names were," McCormick said.

Brockton dropped his jacket and shoved McCormick into the bar. His friend hit it with his back and his head snapped up. "Hey!" he yelled. "What the f—"

"—What the fuck are you doing talking to the cops about my family?" Brockton snarled, then stepped in McCormick's face and grabbed his tie. "Don't ever do that!"

"What the..." McCormick was about to continue, but the look on Brockton's face caused him to remain silent.

The front door to the bar opened and someone yelled for the Rooster. It was the pizza delivery. Brockton let go of McCormick and bent to pick up his jacket.

"What's wrong with you!" McCormick said, straightening out his shirt and tie. He left to get the pizza.

Brockton, given a little time, calmed himself down. McCormick returned. "Look, things have been pretty tense for me lately," Brockton said. "I've got a lot going on."

"I'll say."

"I'm sorry." Brockton waved to the bartender. As much as he wanted to go home, he had to calm down before he saw Stephanie. In this state, she would know something was wrong and the one thing he was sure of was that he had to conceal this from her. She'd never forgive him for getting so involved in this.

He needed a good reason for why he had acted the way he had on the phone. And he needed to placate McCormick, as much as he despised him right now. "What's a good Irish whisky, Jake?"

"Jameson," McCormick answered for him. "You got any?"

"Got a bottle of the twelve year old," Jake replied. "You want a couple shots."

"Gimme the bottle," Brockton said.

"It's not cheap. Three seventy five a pop."

"Figure out the cost on the bottle and set it up." Brockton pulled out his wallet and laid it on the bar.

"Yeah!" McCormick responded. "Jameson Twelve! Only the best for the Rooster."

Jake left and Brockton turned to McCormick. "Let's do some drinking. That's the problem, I just haven't put on a good drunk in too long."

It was a good idea. If he came home drunk, he wouldn't have to talk to Stephanie and she might think his calls were a product of the liquor. Anything was better than going home to face her now.

The bartender returned with the bottle, two shot glasses and a silver bucket of ice. "Water?" he asked. Brockton shook his head and handed him a credit card.

Two hours later they had finished two thirds of the bottle and were drunk. Still standing at the bar, McCormick was beginning to slur his talk. Suddenly, he stopped. "Shit, I forgot to call Cheryl." He went through his pockets, but couldn't come up with any change. "You got a quarter?"

"No, I gave all my change to Jake earlier."

"Shit, I gotta call." McCormick looked around him and spotted a Leukemia Society coin board at the corner of the bar. He walked over and worked a quarter out of one of the slots.

"You're gonna get busted for a Diwi because of that move," Brockton said. "God will make sure of that."

"I put a quarter in there last week," McCormick replied. "I'm borrowing it back."

When he left, Brockton picked up his coat and slipped out. Bart would finish the bottle. He needed to get home.

He didn't remember the trip home, but he arrived safely. He'd driven the roads enough times that he knew the trip blindfolded and when he drank, he drove more carefully. Staying well within traffic regulations had been a good enough way to avoid a Diwi until now. He followed them to a T when he was drinking.

Pulling to the curb, he almost swiped the neighbor's garbage cans, which reminded him that he hadn't taken the garbage out yet. He groaned, but circled the house. Fumbling, he lifted the garage door and let it slide up. He pulled the garbage cans out, then started back around the house. He hit a muddy spot and slipped. He dropped one garbage can and held out his hand to keep from falling on his face. "Shit," he mumbled. Standing up, he wiped his face, transferring the mud from his hand to his face. Dimly, he wondered what Stephanie would say when he entered the house. Good, it was good, he told himself. She wouldn't pursue his phone calls that night. She'd be too upset.

He started to carry the garbage cans down the driveway in a zigzag pattern, thinking how ridiculous he must look to any of the neighbors watching. Good thing it was late, no one was awake. This was something the gossipy bitch next door would have loved to talk about. These were ridiculous things to be thinking when his family was in danger.

By the time he got inside the house, his wife was awake and waiting for him. Seeing the mud on his face, she directed him toward the bathroom. He stumbled to the sink and turned on the water.

"Where have you been?" Stephanie asked, coming up behind him.

"I stayed for one more. Which turned into more than one. What time is it?"

"Two o'clock. What was all that about Roger? What's going on?"

"Nothing," Brockton said, then burped loudly.

"Don't tell me nothing. What's going on?"

"Drunk," he mumbled, then pushed past her into the bedroom. He sat on the edge of the bed and attempted to untie his shoes. He couldn't and finally just pulled them off.

"Something's wrong with you lately, Michael."

He grunted, glad that he was as drunk as he was. "Sorry. Roger's okay?"

"He's fine. Not for long, however, when tomorrow comes."

"Huh?" Brockton could feel his pulse quickening over the alcohol.

"I got the telephone bill today. He rung up over two hundred dollars in telephone calls this month."

"Roger?" was all he could say.

"He's been calling a telephone service to talk about bugs. He made three calls that cost twenty-five dollars each."

Brockton hissed, then chuckled drunkenly, relieved.

"Oh come on, Michael. This isn't funny. We may have to get counseling for him."

"Hey, at least it wasn't a sex line," Brockton said, and chuckled again.

"You're not funny," his wife shot back.

Brockton groaned and lay back. If that was the worst thing Roger could do, he wasn't very worried. It was the last thing he remembered.

33

Brockton was at his desk when Candy put the call through. "Mike?"

"Hi Chuckie, what's up?"

"You heard about the guy you're defending?"

"What?"

"He's back in the Pub."

"What happened?"

"We got a call that he was bothering the girl. We picked him up near her house."

Brockton didn't respond at first, shocked. "When did this happen?" he finally asked.

"Early this morning. He was carrying."

"A gun?"

"Yeah. The guy's a Looney Tune."

"Did he do anything?"

"No, they caught him before he could use it. She called the police. Hey, you got time for lunch today?"

"...Yeah."

"How about eleven thirty?"

"Siponi's?"

"Sure."

"See you there."

Brockton hung up and sat back at his desk. What the fuck was Sienkewicz doing? Just when he has them by the balls, the son of a bitch gets himself back in trouble. Brockton fumbled through the pocket of his coat and pulled out the diary. He hadn't read the last entries yet, but now he was curious. Maybe it would tell him something.

Sunday, June 16

Dear Vladimir:

How did you deal with post coital boredom when it is that of a child whose last barricade you have broken through? Did you not begin to see Lolita differently? You never wrote about this, perhaps because you were afraid she never loved you, but you must have felt what every man feels after the conquest, the feeling of depreciation that hides only from those caught up in the self deceptions of romance.

Ever since I seduced my little Carmen, I see flaws that were always evident in her. Her imperfect shape, the roughness of her nose, her cavity-ridden teeth. I see her childishness—something I once overlooked—and am annoyed by it.

Is it inevitable that we feel these things once the act is done? Will her flaws grow even more evident and difficult to bear? I often grow angry when she wants to do something typical for her age, like listen to music loudly or start with her incessant chatter. I find it impossible to sit quietly. I want to snap off the vulgar noise she calls music. I want to tell her to shut up. I grow bored and want her to leave.

She doesn't notice the change in me. She prattles on ignorantly, asking for things like a baby in a supermarket. Making love to her is the only time I can hide from her faults. Her young, naked body still excites me. I think how lucky I am and promise never to give her up. I will continue to play on her vulnerabilities to keep this deception alive, but how long can I continue this game? How long can I continue to strike her vulnerabilities, then, once she is crying, move in. Sex is always better after an emotional outpouring, but what will I do if she tires of this game?

I don't feel the possessiveness you wrote about, Vladimir. Perhaps it is because I know she will return to me, that I have what she cannot find elsewhere in her world. I was sly in providing these things, playing on her simple needs in order to break her down. How different this is from the way you felt about Lolita! Yet at the same time, how similar. Are we fated only to love those whose misery we can multiply?

Saturday, June 20

Dear Vladimir:

She needs to stop talking to people. Her carelessness will cause someone to find out. I spoke to her about this, but she shrugged me off listlessly. Something is bothering her. She said it wasn't me, but wouldn't tell me what it was. Has my time arrived? Has fate decided to unleash its powers which, like the relentless pull of gravity, will crush me to its breast?

This world can be so cruel and unforgiving. Why do we subject our youth to trials like this? Is there no compassion left for them? Are we only too interested in ourselves to think about the young? Are we products of that same uncaring environment, unable to change how we behave toward each other and our children?

Brockton looked back at the date of the last entry. It was the same week Sienkewicz was arrested. Had he known what he was going to do? What was his client's game?

Saturday, July 4

Dear Fyodor:

In the coming storm, individual players will experience tragedies for which they have been prepared but know nothing about. I have evolved a strategy to rid the world of an evil and am ready to face tragedy.

The task is not difficult. I have the information. What I need is someone strong enough to break the web of conformity and confront this evil. Someone noble enough to endure alienation for the cause of justice.

This person must believe me. I know there are things I have said that sound preposterous, but they are true. Every day we live through trials much worse than a liar can invent. Or a novelist, who is no more than a liar. Your writings, Fyodor, exposed some grave truths about human behavior, yet you invented. You lied. What has happened here is true. How can we ignore it?

Do not worry for me. I have done what is destined. If strong enough, I would have brought justice myself, but the very same love that made me follow this path, the love I hold for my little Carmen, disabled me. Who would believe I am being persecuted because I wish to expose scandal when I am so linked to scandalous behavior myself?

It is up to a more powerful person to strike the final blow. I will suffer from the repercussions, but in a society unwilling to deal with injustice fairly, there must be pawns. The time for vengeance has come. I trust you will contact our friends and explain this to them. Until our next communication, I remain yours.

Lovingly,

John

Brockton set the diary down. What should he do with it? If what his client had written was true, it was a dangerous document. Had Mrs. Washington sent it to him for that reason? Was she afraid someone would come after her? Or was it all bogus?

What did Leach want to say to him? Was he going to feel him out about what had happened this morning? Or was it about his wife, who had left him? He hoped he wasn't going to ask him to be his lawyer for that mess.

The intercom lit up. "Mr. Brockton, you have a call."

"Who is it?"

"Mike Schmidt, from the city desk."

"Tell him I'm busy and get a number."

"He says it's important, that it'll only take a minute."

"Put him through."

The line rang and Brockton pushed a button. "Hello."

"Mr. Brockton?"

"Yeah."

"This is Mike Schmidt, from the Herald."

"Yeah?"

"Listen, I have a letter on my desk from a client of yours. A Mr. Sienkewicz."

"I know him."

"It says you know something that we should know. About his case. Do you have anything that you could share with us?"

"No."

"Do you have any idea of—"

"—Listen, you said a minute," Brockton interrupted. "And you know as well as I do, Mr. Schmidt, that anything I have to say would have to be okayed by my client."

"I'm taking this letter to mean it's okay."

"I don't have anything to say."

"Off the record, did you know he was going to send this, or is he crazy? This sounds pretty crazy."

"Off the record, I have nothing to say."

"All right. Thanks for your help."

"Any time," Brockton said, hanging up. What the fuck had Sienkewicz done now? Brockton picked the phone up again, buzzed Candy and told her to hold all calls. He needed time to think this over.

If what the reporter was telling him was straight, at least Sienkewicz hadn't spelled anything out. What was he planning to do? Brockton would have to go to the Pub and talk to him. He'd play it cool, say nothing about the diary but ask him about the letter to the newspaper. He'd just have to wait to see what Sienkewicz was going to say before he responded. He didn't feel comfortable going into the Pub without knowing what he was going to say, but he was as quick on his feet as anyone. He'd just have to depend on his quick thinking once Sienkewicz revealed what he planned to do.

First he needed to talk to Leach and get all the information he could on what had happened earlier. He was going to need all the ammunition he could get before talking to his client.

Eleven thirty was early for lunch and the cafeteria was almost empty when Brockton sat down. Leach arrived moments later and the two sat without speaking for several minutes, waiting for a waitress.

Brockton didn't feel comfortable and it was obvious that Leach didn't either, because his friend didn't know how to start. He didn't have the best social skills in the world; that was one of the reasons he'd become a cop. It was easier to just tell people what you expected of them.

The question rose in his mind again: Did Leach want to talk about Sienkewicz, or his wife? Brenda's sudden move out of the house must be taking its toll like it did with everyone who didn't realize how good they had it until it was too late.

"How are things at the station?" Brockton finally asked, breaking the ice.

"Fine," Leach replied. "I'm up for a promotion."

"That's great!" Brockton tried to sound enthusiastic.

"It's more money. I could use that now, with all that's happened."

"Who's representing you?" Brockton asked. He felt free to talk about the divorce now that Chuckie had brought it up.

"Ain't gone that far. Brenda hasn't said a thing yet."

"Get a lawyer right away. You'll save money." It was the most direct way he knew to tell his friend two things, that he wasn't going to represent him and that Brenda meant business. From what Stephanie said, she wasn't going to change her mind and go back to him.

"It all turned out for the better with that scum bag you were defending, I guess."

"What do you mean?"

"He was carrying a gun. He's in jail where he belongs." Leach looked around, then pulled a sheet of paper out of his top pocket and handed it to Brockton. "That's a copy of the police report. Don't tell anyone I gave it to you."

"Thanks." Brockton put the report into his inner jacket pocket immediately. He was surprised, had thought Leach didn't trust him anymore.

"You gonna pursue that other stuff further?"

"I haven't decided yet."

"He did it, didn't he?"

"Yeah," Brockton admitted, feeling grateful enough to Leach to let him know that much. "But I wouldn't mind pasting the DA after what he did to me."

"He ain't gonna be around forever."

"It'll send a message to the next one."

"You'd go through all that just to pay him back?"

"It's not just him I wanna pay back."

"What d'ya mean?"

"O'Connell's involved in all sorts of cover ups. He's as dirty as they come."

"That's bullshit."

"No it's not."

"I'm telling you it's bullshit. We heard all those rumors and investigated it all. You're a fool to believe any of 'em."

"I'm gonna do more than believe 'em."

"Christ, Mike, haven't you done enough?"

"Done enough? You talk as if I brought this on. I was set up, remember? My family was threatened. Am I supposed to forget that? Am I gonna wonder every time my kids leave the house whether another O'Connell is going to give one of them a ride in his police car? I should have killed him."

"Shit, we went over that. Sergeant O'Connell never gave your son a ride. That's not even his beat."

"Stephanie said he did."

"I'm telling you he didn't. I checked into it, I told you, and the guy's name was McDonald. Like Old McDonald."

"Bullshit."

"Look, you want to bring Roger to the station and meet him? His name is McDonald and he's a good, honest cop. He saw Roger run into the road and gave him a ride home. You know, what really pisses me off is that you think I'd ever do anything like that, no matter what happens between us. I love your kids."

"What was O'Connell doing asking about my kids?"

"I didn't know he was. Who told you that?"

"Bart McCormick."

Leach made a noise of disgust. "That drunk? How could you believe anything he says?"

"I believe him. And I want an answer. If I find out O'Connell had anything to do with my family, I'm going after him."

"I don't blame you. I know what family means."

Brockton resisted the temptation to reply sarcastically. Instead, he said, "What about the bitch?"

"What bitch?"

"The one who broke my tail light."

"What are you talking about?"

"The cop. The female cop that smashed my tail light. I told you about her."

Leach shrugged. "You're on your own with that one. But let me tell you, there are a couple 'a girls on the force that even I wouldn't tangle with."

"I ain't afraid of them."

"You push too hard and you'll have every cop on the force wanting a piece of you."

"I've already been told that. By one of my own."

"Then listen to your own. We make some mistakes. So do you. Let's call it a draw."

"That doesn't sound like the same cop I talked to a couple of weeks ago."

"That was different. That was about drugs, an issue you can't ignore."

"It seems to be an issue you can't ignore."

"I'm not gonna get into another argument with you," Leach said. "Like I said, you gotta accept mistakes like we do."

"I didn't make any mistakes. I tried to settle a score. He deserved everything he got."

"I don't mean you you, I mean you lawyers."

"You're not talking about me and I'm not talking about you," Brockton replied, still angry. He decided to go for a long shot. "If I'm not satisfied, I'll have to think about bringing up the bridge closing."

For a moment he though he detected a flicker of surprise in Leach's eyes. "What d'ya mean?" his friend finally asked.

"I mean I got a reporter who's ready to bite and maybe I'll have to go that far to satisfy myself. Like I said, O'Connell's involved in some heavy shit. I could bury him."

"You won't do that," Leach said matter-of-factly.

"So it isn't bullshit. He is involved in something big."

"I don't know what he's involved in, I told you that a hundred times. I don't ask. Fighting drugs is the toughest job on the force. It's dangerous. And when you try to cut those guys down, you're putting yourself in a bad position. Chasing some bitch who smashed your tail light is nothing compared to what those guys will do." Brockton didn't respond and Leach added, "You know he's leaving."

Brockton picked up his sandwich and concentrated on biting into it, hoping to conceal his surprise.

"Says he can't handle the new philosophy," Leach continued.

"Where's he going?"

"Took a job in Arizona. He ain't got family here and it's a raise."

"I pity the people in Arizona."

"So you see, we are cleaning ourselves up," Leach said. He leaned back again and his voice took on a more normal tone. "As fucked up as he is, though, he pegged your guy the first day. His problem was that he ain't patriotic. He goddamn wanted to give the store away."

34

Brockton reached through the bars and took Sienkewicz's hand. His client's shake was limp. He seemed withdrawn and sat hunched over. He even seemed to have lost weight in the short time since Brockton had seen him.

"Did you send a letter to the newspaper?" Brockton asked immediately.

Sienkewicz looked at him, his eyes lighting. "Did they say they received one?"

"Yeah." Brockton suppressed a desire to curse at his client. He needed to remain cool. "A reporter called me saying he'd received a letter from you. I told him no comment, that if he wanted to pursue it to talk to you."

He was sure he saw hope fade from Sienkewicz's eyes as he spoke. Good. If the son of a bitch thought he could play him, he was sadly mistaken.

"The truth is all I seek," Sienkewicz finally said. "I wa—"

"—You fucked up," Brockton interrupted. "I may have been able to get you off before this. Instead I had to work out a deal with the DA's office. They're gonna drop the assault charge if you admit to sexual abuse, third degree. That's a Class E felony and you'll have to do some time. They wanted the maximum four years in a state pen. I talked them down to two in the county, because you'd never survive there. You'll never appreciate how hard that was for someone who did what you did, but it's safer at county. Especially for someone with your type of crime. It's almost a country club up there and with good behavior you can get out earlier, with three years probation after that. You'll have to stay away from the girl, too."

Brockton looked up. Sienkewicz was sobbing. "My little Carmen," he whispered. "I love my little Carmen."

Brockton felt the sudden urge to take a chance. "Is there anything else you've neglected to tell me about?" he asked. He regretted the question the moment he asked it. The son of a bitch could ruin everything.

"Nothing," Sienkewicz whispered, almost to himself.

A surge of adrenalin rushed through Brockton. He'd done it. He's asked the question, given his client an opportunity to bring up what was in the diary. If he wasn't going to bring it up, let him sink.

Sienkewicz straightened and wiped his tear-streaked cheeks. "I want to prove my innocence," he said. "I want to prove my love."

Brockton stood up. "She'll be old enough when you get off probation. If you really love her, you can wait. We go to court next week. From now on, let me handle your case."

"Let the record reflect that in the case of the State of New York versus Mr. John Sienkewicz, Mr. Sienkewicz is appearing on indictment for assaulting and sexually abusing Larisa Moran, a minor of fourteen years of age. Mr. Brockton, what does your client wish to plead to this indictment?"

"Your honor, my client has agreed to plead guilty to the second charge if the district attorney drops the assault charge."

"Has the district attorney agreed to this?" Holmes asked, turning to Milton Ritter.

"Yes, your honor."

Holmes was about to say something further, about why so much of the court's time had been wasted Brockton suspected, but she kept the comment to herself.

"Mr. Brockton, how does your client plead to the charge of rape in the third degree, which is a Class E felony?"

"Guilty, your honor," Brockton said.

"Is this correct, Mr. Sienkewicz?" Holmes asked, directing her gaze toward Brockton's client. Brockton held his breath, not completely sure what Sienkewicz was going to say.

"Yes."

"In pleading guilty, Mr. Sienkewicz, you understand that you are waiving your right to any further trial in this matter?"

"Yes."

Sienkewicz seemed distracted, Brockton thought, which was good.

"Did you have sexual contact with Larisa Moran, Mr. Sienkewicz?"

"Yes."

"Did you use force?"

Brockton half stood. "Your honor, given her age and the charges against my client, I'd like to suggest that the question is irrelevant."

"Mr. Sienkewicz, do you understand that what you did was wrong?" Holmes rephrased her question.

Brockton held his breath.

"You say that—" Sienkewicz began.

Brockton pushed the table in front of him and the scraping noise drowned out what his client was saying. He turned to Sienkewicz. "Shut the fuck up!" he whispered, rearranging the table at the same time so the noise would prevent his comment from being heard by others.

"Mr. Sienkewicz, do you understand that what you did was wrong?" Holmes persisted.

"You say—"

"—Your honor, my client has admitted his guilt," Brockton interrupted. "He is simply experiencing some difficulty in seeing how this will affect his life. Now it's been agreed that if he pleads guilty on the rape charge, the district attorney will drop the assault."

"Mr. Brockton, are you telling me that you want your client to forfeit the right to deny his innocence?" Holmes asked.

"No, your honor," Brockton replied. "He has already admitted his guilt. What I'm trying to do is prevent any last minute hesitation of his to stand in the way of a fair and expeditious sentencing."

"Even if that hesitation is a feeling that he is being railroaded?" Holmes persisted.

"With all due respect to the court, your honor, my client is not being railroaded. He has admitted his guilt and feels grateful that one of the charges is being dropped by the district attorney. He also understands that two years in the county penitentiary, which we previously discussed, is a fair deal for him." Brockton turned to Ritter, hoping for support. This was embarrassing. Ritter shrugged and Brockton turned back to Holmes.

"Mr. Sienkewicz, do you understand what you are agreeing to here?" Holmes asked.

"Yes."

"Do you understand that you will be facing a minimum of one year in the county penitentiary, possibly two, and that after that you will be on probation, during which time you will be expected to stay away from Larisa Moran?"

"Yes."

"And that if you violate the conditions of your probation, you will be incarcerated again?" Holmes asked.

"Yes," Sienkewicz said, his voice growing weaker.

"Do you have any questions regarding this trial?" Holmes asked.

Sienkewicz shook his head.

The toilet flushed. Brockton cleared his throat. "I think it's time to get out of here," he said. He smiled, then added, "Before the stink hits." He reached in front of him to gather his papers. This was the perfect excuse he needed to leave before anything else happened.

35

The Oriskany Battlefield was less than an hour's drive from his home and although Brockton wasn't that interested in history, Roger wanted to go. It was a good time of year to visit because there weren't many tourists in October. So at Stephanie's insistence, he agreed to make a family outing of it.

Brockton glanced at Roger through the rear mirror. His son was reading a book on the Revolutionary War. He had taken a keen interest in wars. Not just in playing the video games but in reading about them. It was a good sign that he wasn't still caught up in bugs.

"Hey Dad, get that one!" Michael yelled, pointing to a chipmunk in the road in front of the car.

"That's a leave," Brockton replied, slowing. "Chipmunks are okay, squirrels no." His gaze returned to the rear view mirror where Roger was still reading, undisturbed. He was still young and even if he wasn't into sports the way Babe was, Brockton loved him.

This was a good trip, he thought. Stephanie had accused him of neglecting his family last week after he missed Michael's piano recital. She claimed he'd changed over the past couple of months. He denied it but agreed to do more family outings, which he hadn't done since summer. Neglecting family was something he'd been accusing others of doing and he was guilty of it himself.

Maybe he had become too involved with the Sienkewicz case. He had put in long hours planning his next move, coming home later than usual, and staying in touch with his fellow attorneys. Then, when he was offered victory, he had wanted more. The DA's office had made him a face saving offer and he wanted to talk to a reporter.

Schmidt had called him again before the sentencing, but by then he'd decided to blow the guy off. As usual, the press was seven steps behind the real story.

O'Connell deserved exposure, there was no doubt of that, but just how smart would that be now that he was leaving town? Sure he'd get all sorts of press, but Leach and McCormick were right, he'd be putting himself on the wrong side of too many people. Did he really want to deal with that?

And what exactly was all this about Mazorcas, drug running and assassinations? Did he really want to explore that issue? In the end, he was not a hero aiming to mess around with a system that large. He'd read stories about this but it was well beyond his reach as a small city lawyer. Throw on top of that his own cocaine usage, which while recreational, he wasn't about to entirely give up and it was best to let sleeping dogs lie on that one.

A tall miniature of the Washington Monument rose from the area where the hill sloped down. It was where the American and British forces had clashed, Roger told him.

"Dad, who were the Loyalists?" Roger asked.

"What does it say about them?"

"It says they teamed up with the English and attacked the Americans here. And the Indians, but they were on both sides."

"Some Americans were on the side of the English," Stephanie explained. "They were called Loyalists because they were loyal to England."

"They were the bad guys," Brockton added.

"Why?"

"They didn't want independence," Stephanie said. "They wanted us to remain a colony of England."

"Oh."

A strong wind buffeted the car, trying to push it off the path. Brockton pulled into the small parking area. It was chilly outside.

"Hey Dad, let's toss a couple!" Michael yelled.

"Warm up with Rog, then come and get me," he replied. His two sons raced off into the field. He watched them run, then turned toward Stephanie and smiled. When she first became pregnant with Michael, he'd told her he didn't want to know what sex the baby was; he was too afraid it'd be another girl. Instead, he'd silently voiced every prayer he knew, and waited.

Finally, he asked her. He'd remember that evening forever. They'd gone out to dinner at a local Chinese restaurant
and he probably wouldn't even have asked except he was
feeling lucky that day. He'd won a case in court and picked
up sixty bucks in a football pool on the same day. Then, after dinner, while they were being served coffee, he'd opened
a fortune cookie with a fortune that read, 'Today will be
memorable for you.'

As soon as he read the fortune he asked his wife. She
smiled and told him it was a Michael Junior and he stood up
in the middle of the restaurant, raised his arms and howled
like a college kid. He put the fortune in the album with Michael's baby pictures.

Even then he cautioned Stephanie not to tell anyone.
Medical errors weren't unknown and he didn't want to get
caught with his balls hanging out there if the doctors pulled
out another girl.

Besides being the emotional high of his life, having a son
had inspired Brockton. He'd started working out again, in
earnest. After Michele, he'd put on a few unwanted pounds.
Nothing most people would notice but a lot for his wiry
frame. But he was going to be in shape for his son. By the
time Michael was born Brockton was down to his semi pro
ball weight.

The birth had been the watershed of his life and he remembered it like it had happened yesterday. In the waiting
room he promised himself that by the time his son was old
enough to know what it was all about, his father would be
the best hired gun in the city. And if Michael ever grew dis-

306 • BILL METZGER

couraged, he would tell his son about that moment. He'd push him to be number one.

Brockton had lost it in the delivery room. When he heard his son cry, he had grown so emotional that he'd started to cry, then almost fainted. One of the nurses had to support him while he gazed at his tiny, kicking son. He'd missed Michele's birth, but he wasn't going to make that mistake again.

When you got down to it, having a kid was like being God. You were creating something perfect. That was why he could never understand his friends losing this for a little pussy. How could they gamble like that?

Greene and Leach, even McCormick spouted all sorts of rationales for their actions but the single, most common flaw Brockton saw was neglect of family. They could say all they wanted, but he would tend to what was most important first, his own.

Leach was so crazy about the fellow cop he was screwing that he'd forgotten all about his wife and kids and hadn't even seen what was coming. He came home one day and Brenda was gone. She'd planned to move out and he hadn't even known. She wasn't going to let him know, either, because she was afraid of what he'd do.

Brenda leaving him was only the first step. The agony of a legal battle hadn't even begun yet. Brockton had represented too many spouses not to know the nastiness of that battle. He'd been accused of screwing female clients more than once by ex-husbands simply because he was getting the women what the law said they deserved.

Chuckie was in for some rough times. Sure there were a lot of ups and downs in a marriage, but now he lacked something essential: emotional fulfillment. You got that from family and as soon as his family abandoned him, they created a hole that he could never fill with a bimbo. That had been obvious from their last meeting.

The girl wasn't even that good looking. She had a mysterious air about her, but she wasn't anything to give up your family for. And he had to work with her. The worst part was that Leach could never go back. Cheating on Brenda was as final as the moment a child was born.

Greene was in just as deep shit. He was still living at home, but it was a lousy situation. Trying to hide infidelity from his wife wouldn't last long, especially with his wife, who was no dummy. She put up with his drinking, but she wasn't going to let him get away with this stunt.

Brockton reached out and pulled Stephanie to him. "Who is Frederick?"

"Who?" his wife asked.

"Frederick. Fried-rich, something. Sounded German. He's a writer, like that guy Naboko or whatever his name is."

Stephanie laughed. "Nabokov," she corrected.

"You were the lit major, not me," Brockton said.

"I really don't know what you're talking about."

"One of my clients used the name and I was wondering what he meant. He said something about a judge and a hanging. What was he talking about?"

"He was probably talking about Friedrich Durrenmatt. He's not as well known as Vladimir Nabokov, but he's a respected German author. He wrote a book called 'The Judge and his Hangman', one of his more critically acclaimed novels. An old man gets revenge on another, evil one, but doesn't involve himself because he's too weak. He gets others to do the heavy lifting for him. It's a good story."

Brockton sat on a bench near the Battlefield's small gift shop and leaned against the arm rest. It was decisions about family that were important, not the bullshit work he did at the courthouse. That just paid the bills. Taking out the garbage on the right night was more important, frankly.

He thought about the other evening. He'd paid a price for that night. After picking up the driveway trash, he'd returned to the house and traipsed mud all over the place. He hadn't found out about that until the next day, when Stephanie made a federal case out of it. After making him work through his hangover, shampoo the rugs and pick up the garbage scattered across the back yard, she'd sat him down and quizzed him relentlessly. She'd acted like she didn't trust anything he said. He told her a flimsy lie—that he'd gotten friends to drive him and his car home—and asked Bart to back him up. It bothered him to have to ask Bart, but he'd had no choice.

It was that next day when Brockton decided that he wasn't going to say anything to the reporter. He didn't feel bad about Sienkewicz's sentence, either, even though he could have gotten a better deal. When all was said and done his client wasn't innocent. He had had sex with the girl no matter what the situation, and that was illegal. She was fourteen. It was even possible that he'd gotten so caught up in his passions that he had beaten her and the diary was a way to try to escape punishment. The guy was weird.

O'Connell had abused the girl, too, but if she wasn't willing to speak out, then why should he? She could have reported what happened to the therapists at the treatment center, when she had her chance. They were trained to deal with situations like that. But she hadn't said anything. He'd deep-sixed the diary she gave him, and let Leach know in case anyone was interested.

Brockton gazed at his sons again. Sienkewicz could have avoided this all if he had taken care of his family. He'd neglected them. He'd even used his own daughter's ID card, involving his family in the sordid affair. That was inexcusable. That was where he went wrong. Like his friends, his client had neglected the health and success of his own and now they were paying the price. Brockton liked being known as the best, but when it came to sacrificing his family he knew when to pull out.

He got up. "Babe, come here!" As his two sons ran toward him, he walked over to Stephanie and grabbed her around the waist.

Michael reached him first and he pulled him to his side. "Record this, Mommie," he said. "On this day in October, on the windswept knolls of the Oriskany Battlefield, Michael's old man publicly stated that his son will not only be a major leaguer, but rookie of the year. He will return meaning to the nickname Babe."

He tousled his son's hair, then pulled Roger to him. "Got that, Babe? Now get back out there and shag flies. Wind or not, you gotta practice if you plan to make the big leagues."

ABOUT THE AUTHOR

Bill Metzger served for three years in the United States Peace Corps, as a secondary education teacher trainer in Honduras, Central America. Upon his completion of service, Metzger returned to the United States, where he taught in public schools in Syracuse, Morris, and New York City, New York, and in Austin, Texas.

In addition to teaching during the subsequent fifteen years, Metzger served as a truancy prevention officer, social work assistant, and the director and hearing officer of the Suspension Alternative Program for the Syracuse City School District. In addition, Metzger coordinated a Breakfast Club attendance program, a teen single mothers support group, and a science achievement program for at-risk teens.

While teaching, Metzger worked for defense lawyers and judges in upstate New York court systems, translating for Spanish-only speaking defendants who were arrested and charged with drug trafficking.

Metzger currently lives in Buffalo, New York, where he writes and manages brewing newspapers, a brewpub, and a coffee house.

CPSIA information can be obtained at www.ICGtesting.com
Printed in the USA
BVOW04s0831070816

457915BV00001B/2/P